OUT COMES THE EVIL

Recent Titles by Stella Cameron from Severn House

The Alex Duggins series

FOLLY
OUT COMES THE EVIL

Other Titles

SECOND TO NONE
NO STRANGER
ALL SMILES
SHADOWS

OUT COMES THE EVIL

Stella Cameron

CRÈME de la CRIME

This first world hardcover edition published 2015
in Great Britain and 2015 in the USA by
Crème de la Crime, an imprint of
SEVERN HOUSE PUBLISHERS LTD of
19 Cedar Road, Sutton, Surrey, England, SM2 5DA.
Trade paperback edition first published 2016
in Great Britain and the USA by
SEVERN HOUSE PUBLISHERS LTD.

British Library Cataloguing in Publication Data

Cameron, Stella author.
  Out comes the evil. – (The Alex Duggins series)
  1. Cotswold Hills (England)–Fiction. 2. Murder–
  Investigation–Fiction. 3. Detective and mystery stories.
  I. Title II. Series
  813.5'4-dc23

ISBN-13: 978-1-78029-078-2 (cased)
ISBN-13: 978-1-78029-562-6 (trade paper)
ISBN-13: 978-1-78010-704-2 (e-book)

All Severn House titles are printed on acid-free paper.

Severn House Publishers support the Forest Stewardship Council™ [FSC™],
the leading international forest certification organisation.
All our titles that are printed on FSC certified paper carry the FSC logo.

Typeset by Palimpsest Book Production Ltd.,
Falkirk, Stirlingshire, Scotland.
Printed and bound in Great Britain by
TJ International, Padstow, Cornwall.

For Jerry

ACKNOWLEDGEMENTS

Phil and Lynn Lloyd-Worth: Many thanks for all the driving, walking, climbing and tolerance.

Linda Hankins, DVM: Extraordinary veterinary doctor and, above all else, animal lover. Thank you for your support and for sharing your knowledge of our beloved furry friends.

Matt Cameron: You have the best 'ear' and your enthusiasm and patience when I need a talented listener (and a gently calming influence) is priceless.

David Augustavo: Thank you for ensuring I didn't make really foolish mistakes!

Pam and David Tallboys: For looking after me so well at The Olive Branch in Broadway and for your kind answers to my many questions, my thanks.

And as always, my beautiful Cotswolds, their amazing people, and some of the best pubs in the land . . . I love you.

PROLOGUE

O ver-sexed slag? Pamela Gibbon was forty-three. She was a fit, attractive, sexual woman, and she enjoyed the company of men – one at a time – a few years younger. They enjoyed her, too – a lot. But she had overheard the snide, disgusting comments in Folly-on-Weir's village pub and if they were slamming her there, it wouldn't be the only place.

She had stood in the entrance to the public bar at the Black Dog just long enough to take in the sneering chuckles among a group of men and women she had considered, if not friends, at least friendly acquaintances. Being approachable shouldn't make her the butt of jokes.

For ten years she had lived among these people. She and her now dead husband bought their home, Cedric Chase, and lived there together until Charles died. Pamela had never thought of leaving. She loved the village and although she wasn't particularly gregarious, she was on nodding and smiling terms with most locals.

A flush washed her neck. She wouldn't have been at the pub tonight if she hadn't wanted an opportunity for another look at Hugh Rhys. Hugh, the new manager who the owner, Alex Duggins, had hired to fill a vacancy, had a raw vitality about him and Pamela enjoyed getting sucked into the circle of intelligent conversation he attracted. He also attracted Pamela in other ways, although she was more than well satisfied with Harry Stroud and expected to remain so, especially now. She enjoyed Harry, a lot, and had half-hoped she would find him at the Black Dog . . .

Damn them all. She'd do what she bloody well pleased, including meeting Harry Stroud in a broken tower at a ruined manor house, in the middle of the night, to do whatever made them laugh, and sweat, and shout out their pleasure. At least what was left of old Ebring Manor, the ragged stone outline of the fourteenth-century house, a badly damaged drum tower, part of a fortifying wall along the River Windrush, the shells of several cavernous rooms and an incongruous fireplace or two – at least it was too far out to draw local kids and too decimated to interest even intrepid tourists. And Ebring wasn't famous for anything in particular.

Within a couple of hours of turning away from the Black Dog, she had left home on the outskirts of Folly-on-Weir just before eleven and struck out through the back lanes leading to the neighboring village of Underhill. Silvering from a three-quarter moon was all she needed to find her way, but she did recoil from the sounds of birds flying up from hedgerows and animals slinking about their nightly business.

Perhaps she hadn't really intended to meet Harry tonight, not before she heard the jeers. Occasionally she liked to leave him waiting, make up an excuse when next she saw him, just to keep his interest bubbling. Not that she needed to, it just made her feel more desirable – and inventive – and it made Harry more ardent. But no, that wasn't what she had intended for this evening. It was time for them to have a more serious chat. Past time. Tonight she half-ran uphill to meet him. When she felt as she did now, it took too long to get there.

Initially she'd been annoyed that it was impossible to meet at his place. She lived alone but since it was important to Harry, the last thing she wanted was her housekeeper prying and spreading rumors – as if she hadn't heard proof that it was already happening.

There was always the danger that one of them would be seen – not in the ruins, but leaving the village on foot at all hours. But danger had come to heighten the excitement. But she didn't think that would matter for long.

She smiled in the chilled darkness, breathed in the scent of approaching spring, of earth still hard and cool, though she had seen the tips of the first daffodils trying to push bright green shoots into the light. The blooms would be delayed and small this year.

Even dampened by the late hour, the subtle fragrance of bluebells turned the night soft and sleepy. True spring would be very late.

The sky resembled a great, black velvet bowl swirled with specks of shattered crystal. It was a marvelous, mysterious night.

Crossing the road that ran toward Underhill, then into the hills above Folly-on-Weir took a little time. A driver who picked her up in the headlights might stop to see if she was OK. Awkward wouldn't cover that event. And she knew Harry didn't want his father, the major, to hear gossip about his love life. Major Stroud still expected his son to marry a 'suitable young gel.' Harry lived in his parents' house, the largest, most imposing one in the village.

Inheritance was a large issue in Harry's life, poor dear. Not that it had to be. She intended to help take the power out of Major and Mrs Stroud's hands.

A single vehicle came from the right and she leaped back into the cover of brush, and ducked down. If the driver of the car noticed her, he or she didn't believe their eyes and carried on – after a few seconds, or perhaps she only imagined the hesitation.

Her hours in the saddle kept her conditioned. Grateful for her strong rider's legs, she struck out at a jog. In the large flask she wore across her body under a tweed jacket, a good part of a bottle of Clos des Saveurs '76 Bas Armagnac bounced solidly against her. Harry had a weakness for fine cognac, one Pamela shared. And he knew his stuff. This would make him happy. She also carried a heavy green canvas bag, with the binoculars she wanted to return to Harry inside, and a box of the La Florentine Marrons Glaces Harry loved, especially when they lay together after sex. The little candied chestnuts from Italy were only one of the many delicacies he had a taste for.

Thick trees lined the rim of the hill in the direction she had to go. She quickened her pace. Harry's phone message had come in on her answer machine while she was on her way to the Black Dog. Thank God she hadn't missed it when she went home in a funk.

Once in the trees, she used her small flashlight and followed a familiar, if faint, track they had made for themselves with regular visits. A few more minutes and she broke into the clearing where what remained of Ebring Manor reflected the moonlight.

She switched off her torch and carried on. Every step of the way was familiar.

At the base of the tower she stopped, disappointed. Usually Harry greeted her there, but not tonight. Her heart speeded up. She hadn't got back to him, not that she always did. But he'd sounded as if he expected her. If he thought she wasn't coming he wouldn't be here either. Her breath shortened and tears of frustration prickled in her eyes. 'Harry?' she whispered up the spiral stone stairs.

The short tower acted like an echo chamber. Even a whisper slithered eerily upward.

Nothing.

Climbing carefully over broken stones and partially missing steps, she reached the top but didn't find him. It was the perfect night. They wouldn't need to huddle beneath a tarp to keep dry, although huddling with Harry was no hardship. Most of the roof had fallen away up here but they stored their supplies under what cover was left and rationalized that if it was ever found and taken, they would simply replace it. Pamela put down the bag with the heavy binoculars inside and waited, peering into the darkness from the broken walls of the tower.

She would soon get cold staying up here alone. This time she would have to be the one to wait at the foot of the stairs, looking for her lover. The tower trapped faint moonglow inside and darkness gathered beyond the open doorway. Outside, she leaned against the rough wall and filled her lungs with air that felt still.

A faint light came on – from the ground some twenty-five or so feet to her right. The light was a thin beam. There, then almost gone. There again, then all but gone again. Then it stayed on, shining upward through the circular grating that covered an ancient well. So many times she'd tried to persuade Harry to help her shift the heavy grill and climb down the rungs she could see driven into the wall inside. 'Those rungs have to lead to something,' she'd rationalized. He would never do it. She squeezed her eyes shut and heard how he insisted he couldn't risk her hurting herself. It was too dangerous.

Once again she looked. The feeble light was steady. She went closer – and choked back a scream. She slapped a hand over her mouth. The well was open. Another few steps and she could have fallen into the hole.

Someone had lifted the grill enough to swing it aside and let it rest mostly on the grass.

The light from below fizzled out.

Dropping to her knees, she crawled to the edge on all fours and trained her small torch downward, picking out the first few rusted metal rungs sunk into the stone sides of the well.

Harry! She grinned. He must have thought he could greet her with proof that her little obsession led nowhere interesting. He probably planned to leap out and shock her.

Tucking her torch away and leaving the bag behind, she swung a leg over the hole and felt around until she got it firmly on a metal bar. Quickly, keeping a firm hold on the rim where the grating usually rested, she concentrated on starting a stealthy descent. If he didn't realize she was coming down, when she got close he'd find out who was in for a shock!

The torch could only be used for brief periods since she needed both hands, but she shone it cautiously at her feet and saw how the rungs stretched into the blackness.

Harry must have seen her light by now. This wasn't feeling such a lark anymore.

Her skin turned damp and she felt sick, but she wasn't going back. One of the things Harry liked about her was her gutsy, if quiet, personality.

A couple more steps and she had to start hanging onto the rungs with her fingers, too. She stuffed the torch into a pocket and left it there.

Glass broke. It had to be glass although the sound was faint and brief.

A ping came. A pause, and another ping.

Something solid hit her right shoulder. 'Don't be stupid,' she cried out, flapping at her arm. Rapidly a cold object met the side of her face, slithered through her hair against her scalp and was gone. Flapping a hand at her head, she leaned against the wall. She turned on her light again, swung it upward, but saw only the opening above and a fuzzy halo blending into deep gloom.

Her muscles jerked and she shook, clutched the rungs, fighting for her breath. This was madness. She was getting out of here.

Her heart gradually stopped its painful beating in her throat and she put the torch away again – struck out, hand over hand, until her fingertips slid over the cold metal rim and into dirt and gravel.

Pamela felt tears wet on her cheeks. She coughed and released one hand to wipe at her eyes before grabbing hold again.

A clang, like a rusty bell, rang out above her.

With her mouth open to drag at what oxygen her short breaths could catch, she made to haul herself out.

Pain came without warning, seared her fingers, her hands, her arms. Her garbled, 'He-lp,' scarcely sounded around the vomit she couldn't control. The grate had dropped back in place, crushing her fingers beneath its horrendous weight.

For moments – she didn't know how long – her legs swung free. She couldn't think for the burning, mind-freezing pain. Drops hit her face and she tasted blood. Her own blood from her own hands.

'I'm down here.' It came as a gagging whisper and she concentrated every scrap of strength on raising her voice. 'Help me. I-I'm shut in the well.'

She heard the grill scrape, peered up through stinging eyes to see it moving aside again. A tiny slit appeared while someone, who grunted loudly, strained and lifted.

Her vision distorted – the edges of her consciousness blurred. Were her feet on the rungs again? Choking, she tried to move her crushed hands but there was no feeling.

'I can't hold on,' she screamed, feeling herself slide backward. 'Grab my wrists.' She screamed again.

Two strong, smooth hands pulled her bursting fingers free.

Rubber gloves, she thought, like a doctor.

He didn't have to push her, simply let go.

Pamela's head slammed into the stone walls as she fell.

With a mighty ringing, the grill smashed back into place, reverberated in waves all the way to her utter silence.

ONE

'The eye will have to come out.'

'Oh, no,' Alex said. 'There isn't any way to save it?'

'Too much damage. At least the right eye doesn't look bad. Some conjunctivitis but no discharge. You can see the dry crust on the cornea of the left eye and it's very swollen. There's no indication of sight. This needs to be dealt with now.'

She looked at her watch.

'Do you have to get back?'

'No. I'll stay while it's done.' She had no idea if the cat belonged to someone. 'I didn't see your assistant when I came in.'

'This isn't a clinic day,' Tony Harrison told Alex. 'Radhika doesn't come in until later. I'm just glad I was here.'

'I forgot.' She shrugged and said, 'Sorry.'

He held the cat she'd found in a rubbish bin in the yard at her pub, the Black Dog. The animal looked more dead than alive, its orange tabby fur matted, his ears torn and badly mended from fights, and his long-legged body hanging limp in Tony's arms.

'I'm going to get on with it. I'll let you know how he does.'

'I wonder who he belongs to,' Alex said. 'I haven't seen him before.'

Tony looked from the cat to Alex. He smiled a little, the corners of his mouth turned down, which she knew meant he was about to say something he didn't like. 'I don't think he belongs to anyone. If we pull him through we'll have to decide what to do next.'

'You can do his eye on your own?' Alex said, closer to tears than she would ever admit. 'Someone must have thrown him away.'

'Or he was looking for food,' Tony said, his dirty blond hair curling around his ears and jumbled everywhere else, the same as usual. Folly-on-Weir's only vet turned heads but not because he worried about details like frequent fashionable haircuts. 'I can manage on my own. It's not optimum but once he's under it's no sweat.'

'Under?'

'Anesthetized.'

She dumped her gilet and cardigan on a chair in the cottage clinic sitting room and started rolling up her sleeves. 'I can help. Just talk me through it.' She avoided looking at him. 'Come on, he doesn't look good.'

Without a word, he led the way to his combination examination and surgery room. He'd told her he was having a separate operating room designed but for now he made do.

'I won't ask if you're sure you're up to this but if you change your mind just tell me you're leaving.'

She snorted. 'Don't worry about me. I've always been bloodthirsty.'

Tony gave a short laugh, pulled out a heating pad and a towel from a drawer and set them on the steel table. He settled the cat on the table and plugged in the pad. 'Poor fellow,' Tony said when the cat didn't attempt to move.

'He seems out of it already,' she said, worried. 'Is he going to die?'

'Let's do this, nurse.' He gave an injection and the already lethargic animal relaxed in seconds. 'I'm going to intubate him and start some fluids in case he gets into any trouble and needs them. First, a little lidocaine spray to make it less painful for his throat and easier on all of us. Put your hand over the top of his head and grasp his upper jaw to hold it open . . . great. You're a natural.'

Through sliding a tube down the animal's throat, flushing out his eye with saline and trimming away fur and eyelashes, Tony didn't speak. Alex stroked the unconscious cat.

Tony looked up at her. 'Now we need to change the towels he's on for dry ones and get him positioned for the surgery. His head needs to be at this end. Can you do that while I set out a surgery pack and scrub up?'

'Yes, I can.' She was certain she could have done anything to help the cat and did as she'd been told.

'Then give your hands a good scrub.'

Alex did as he asked, grateful to be busy, too busy to give in to a jumpy tummy.

'Enucleation of the eye,' Tony said, glancing up at her over his mask, his dark-blue eyes darker than ever. But he was so matter-of-fact she knew this was where he was most comfortable, with his patients. 'This incision lets me get at the muscles. Hand me those scissors, please, the curved ones.'

She followed his instructions, aware that he gave her another glance as if gauging if she was about to pass out. 'It's interesting,' she said, although she felt a bit wobbly. 'I feel useful even if I'm not.' She laughed.

'You're wonderful, but we already know that.' There was no laughter in his eyes.

Alex returned her attention to the cat. She and Tony were great friends and could easily be more if the right things happened at the right moments.

'I clip all the muscle attachments to expose the globe and take out the eye,' he said. 'Not a moment too soon – it's leaking pus.'

Alex clenched her teeth and didn't look too closely.

'Clamping the stalk, including nerve and vessels. Two ligatures. Transecting the globe. Flush orbit with warmed saline.' Once again he looked at her before continuing. 'Adding some ampicillin – the orbit looks clean but infection is always the risk with something like this. That and bleeding. I'm trimming this small bit of tissue where the lashes were so the skin will grow together, and now I'll close.'

The lesson ended there. He stitched the wound and stood back an instant with his gloved hands held up. 'Good job, Nurse Duggins. I think I could use another assistant. I'm not sure how on-the-job training works but we'll figure it out.'

She stroked the cat's side again. 'You can't afford me,' she said. 'His breaths are short.'

'Regular,' he said. 'I know you must need to get back but thanks for the wonderful help. You are one capable woman.'

It was true they'd been through some nasty times together before and she hadn't swooned or crumpled. The thought made her smile. 'Harrison and Duggins. Emergency Situations, Ltd.'

This time his look was long enough to make her uncomfortable. They walked the fine line of trying to find their way to whatever they were meant to be to each other and it frequently became almost painful.

'Doesn't sound bad,' he said finally. 'Now, this fellow will be kept warm and watched for bleeding and infection. Radhika will be in before too long. She'll baby him.'

Alex nodded at that. 'Lucky you that she came along when she did.' Tony's former assistant had left to get married but Radhika, a knock-out gorgeous Hindu woman in her twenties, had moved into the village a few months earlier and had nursing skills that answered Tony's needs well.

In addition to being wonderful with the animals, Radhika was organized and managed the task Alex would have thought impossible, she ran Tony's practice smoothly. She was a friend of Vivian Seabrook who ran stables for the Derwinters, the big local landowners and self-appointed 'lords of the manor.' However, Radhika's reasons for settling in a small English village remained a mystery.

'Don't feel you have to stick around,' Tony said, taking a thin blanket from a warming drawer. 'I'll keep him beside me in the office until Radhika gets here.'

Already Alex was worrying about the cat's future. 'Should I put up signs to see if anyone's lost him?'

He reached out to ruffle her short, dark curls and she smiled. 'Ever the caretaker, Alex. Put something up at the Dog, if you like. The word will get out from there. All we have to do is tell Harriet and Mary Burke – they're as good as a megaphone.'

The elderly sisters owned Leaves of Comfort, the village tea and book shop, and kept their fingers on the pulse of local affairs from their reserved table at the Dog.

'You've got a point there,' Alex said. She bent over the scruffy, unconscious cat and kissed the top of his head through her mask before taking it off. 'OK, I'll get out of your way. If you feel like—'

'Tony, where are you?' a familiar male voice bellowed, cutting off the invitation Alex had almost issued for Tony to stop by for a pint and a pie at lunch time.

Tony's father, Doc James, the local GP, walked in. Even with his white hair and weathered network of life's lines on his angular face, there was no mistaking the resemblance between father and son.

Doc James went to give the cat a critical once-over. 'Poor fellow lost an eye? How's he doing?'

'We'll see in a few hours.'

'Looks like a punched-up fighter. How old?' He looked at Alex who shrugged.

'Alex found him in the rubbish,' Tony said. 'He's maybe a year. Eighteen months.'

Doc James took in the scene in the room, raised his brows, but made no comment.

'Police been here yet?'

Tony picked up the cat, the blanket wrapped around him, and

headed for the door. 'Why would the police come by? Did you give me as an alibi again?'

'No.' And Doc James didn't crack a smile. 'Were they at the Dog yet, Alex?'

'No.' She frowned at him as she followed Tony to his office. He had two kennels under the window and settled the still flaked-out cat in one. He turned on a small electric heater and pulled it to one side of the open door.

His dog, a big, sandy terrier named Katie wandered into the room, looked curiously into the open kennel and lay down almost inside, her head on her paws, her eyes watchfully worried.

'Katie's into patient care, too,' Tony said. 'What's up, Dad?'

'The police are searching the area. Constable Frye came to see me. He's no longer our dedicated plod but he made a point of coming in and talking to me. They're trying to get a timeline.'

Alex gave him her entire attention. A whisper of remembered awareness prickled up her spine. Tony's hand on her arm startled her. 'What?' she almost shouted.

'OK, OK, don't worry. We're in a different time now.'

He had felt her go on alert. 'Not a different place, though,' she said tightly.

'Prue Wally didn't notice anything was wrong until early this morning.' Doc James looked troubled. 'That's the problem when you deal with people who keep odd hours – or don't keep any particular hours at all. They're looking for Pamela Gibbon.' Prue was Pamela Gibbon's housekeeper.

The tiny stream that ran past the cottage where Tony held his clinic, one of a row of chocolate-box buildings, was suddenly too loud. So were the occasional quacks of ducks out there.

'She only goes into Cedric Chase in the afternoons so she didn't think anything about the house being empty the day before yesterday. Yesterday she noticed the mail was still on the hall table where she put it the day before and there was more mail on the floor inside the door.'

He shrugged. 'Doesn't have to mean anything. Some people are careless about that sort of thing. But they're going all over the village and searching any empty surrounding buildings, so I thought if they hadn't come yet, I'd warn you.'

'Dad, stop pussyfooting around. Just spit out what's on your mind.'

'You've both been through enough this year. You don't need more prodding and poking from the police. Frye said something about thinking they could need the Major Incident Team if things went badly.'

Alex froze inside. She swallowed and said, 'You mean Inspector O'Reilly?'

The man shrugged. 'If he's the one who draws the short straw, I suppose.'

'Did something happen to Prue as well?' Tony spoke slowly. 'Or are we only worried about Pam Gibbon?'

Doc James spread his hands and looked at the ceiling. 'How can one small place be cursed with this sort of thing? Prue's fine, shaken up but fine. It looks as if Pamela Gibbon has disappeared. There was nothing wrong with her before this as far as anyone knows. Alex's new manager said she was in the pub a few days ago, as . . .' He cleared his throat. 'Just as comfortable and friendly as she always is with the, er, men, he said. The police think she's been gone as long as two days – even three. Her car's in the garage and she hasn't been up to the Derwinter place to check her horse. Apparently she does that every day come hell or high water.'

'She could have taken off for a couple of days,' Alex said, but her heart beat hard. 'She doesn't have anything to tie her down.'

'Who knows anything about her,' Tony said. 'I never heard any mention of family and I don't think she and her husband had children.'

Doc James' mind was elsewhere. 'Pamela didn't call a taxi and so far no one says they took her to the station or saw her on the bus,' he said. 'She wouldn't get far on foot.'

'If they send in O'Reilly or someone like him,' Tony said, 'it'll be because they suspect foul play.'

Alex whispered, 'Murder.'

TWO

Hugh Rhys was one of those men women buzzed around like bees sucking up to lush roses in mid-summer.

There was nothing even vaguely feminine or rose-like about him. He was athletically built, tall, and he had magnetism . . . regular features, perfectly close-clipped dark hair and eyes just as dark that smiled, with or without help from a very sexy mouth. Hugh exuded an aura; it gave off his fearless view of life in waves. Even Alex sometimes looked at him and wondered what made a man like him happy to live in a small English village where he seemed to have few interests outside work – other than his outrageously gorgeous navy-blue-and-white Frazer Nash BMW 1937 convertible.

He nodded when she came through from the back of the pub and turned away from a larger than usual early-afternoon customer crowd. Liz Hadley who ran a struggling dress shop in nearby Broadway, but helped out at the Dog, flitted busily back and forth, keeping the customers happy.

'Smell that?' she said, passing Alex and rolling her eyes as if she'd pass out from bliss. 'The Cotswold Farmer's sausages and bacon. They're going over like mad. Simple Suppers is packaging them now. I think we should sell them if people want us to.'

Alex waggled her head. 'Always the entrepreneur, Liz. I think we'd get sent to Coventry by a few local businesses if we started retailing sausages, but they do smell good. I believe in getting along with people, though, especially when we do business with them.'

Smiling, Liz sailed on her way.

'You got out of here at the right time,' Hugh said, keeping his deep Scots voice low. His very Welsh name was something he'd never explained. 'You missed Constable Frye and another copper in here asking about Pamela Gibbon. They can't find her.'

'Doc James came to Tony's surgery and told us about it. Has Harry Stroud come in today? I've seen him in here talking with Pamela a few times.'

'Not today,' Hugh said. 'And if you listen to the general village talk, those two do more than talk in other places. Do you know a Detective Inspector O'Reilly?'

'Yes,' Alex said shortly. 'He's been in Folly-on-Weir before.'

'The plods said he might be back again.' He watched her too closely. When she didn't respond, he said, 'How's the wee cat? He looked half dead.'

··'Tony had to take that swollen eye out. It was already infected and useless.'

'Might be better if it died.'

She glanced at Hugh. 'If I ever have a bad eye infection, I'll stay out of your way. He's a lovely cat.'

Hugh grinned. 'If you say so. I'd say he's a rough and tumble bad laddie, that cat. But women go for bad boys, don't they?'

Alex had to smile back. She glanced around, checking on who was there, starting with the regulars by the bar. Harry's father, Major Stroud, was a fixture in the pub and she was relieved to see him, usual beer tankard in hand, sitting with Harriet and Mary Burke from the tea shop. Alex's dog, Bogie, black ears plastered to the sides of his head, managed to stay by the fire but as far from Major Stroud as possible. The dog was otherwise gray and a mix of terrier with possible long-ago connections to poodle. He was a faithful love.

An unlikely group, Alex realized. The major liked to stand at the bar where he enjoyed an audience of men when they would listen to him.

'He went straight over there,' Hugh said, as if he read her mind. 'Didn't have anything to say to his regular bunch.'

'I think it could be something to do with Pamela taking a hike,' Alex said. 'I hope she shows up, and fast.'

'Could be with Harry somewhere,' Hugh said. 'Haven't seen him in a couple of days. I bet that's what's making Stroud edgy. He's trying to fly the flag and be normal but he's not pulling it off.'

'They think Pamela's been gone as long as two or three days.'

'If she's been gone that long—'

'Exactly,' Alex said. 'It's too long for us not to start thinking the worst.'

Hugh leaned closer. 'As soon as this gets out – if she doesn't come back, that is – we'll have reporters all over us. Like as not the major will say something he'll wish he hadn't.'

'Please let her come back,' Alex said. 'I don't want to think about the alternatives.'

Harriet Burke's waving hand caught her attention. The wave turned into an urgent beckoning. Major Stroud and Mary Burke looked anxiously in her direction.

'Refills?' Alex said, hurrying over to them. 'A beef and onion pie would go well, too. I understand George's outdid themselves today. We also ordered some brilliant cakes from them just to see if we've got any sweet tooths in the house.'

'Has that O'Reilly man been in touch with you?' Mary said, ignoring the question. She gripped her walker with one hand and leaned forward to look at Alex through glasses as thick as a couple of closed portholes. 'You'd be the first to hear from him. We all know he's got a soft spot for you.'

The comment surprised Alex. She and Detective Inspector Dan O'Reilly had liked one another when he'd been working on a murder near the village only months ago – mostly liked – but this was the first suggestion she'd heard that there was anything more than that.

'Well?' Major Stroud prodded, his perfectly clipped gray mustache bristling. 'Have you?'

'No,' Alex said shortly. His demand annoyed her. 'Can I get you anything?'

Harriet Burke, her hair as white as her sister's but short and devoid of the sort of Spanish comb Mary favored wearing in her wiry chignon, held Alex's eyes and gave her a deliberate smile. Whatever that smile was supposed to mean didn't enlighten Alex.

The major's face had reddened. 'Would you tell us if you had?'

'What's the problem?' Alex said. 'Why not say what's really on your mind? And for the record, Major, I would have no reason to deny hearing from the inspector if I had.'

He snuffled into his mustache.

'Where's Harry?' Alex softened her voice and smiled. 'That's the problem with being a fixture anywhere. If you aren't there, you're missed.'

'I suppose you think you're subtle,' he snapped back. 'There are questions being asked about Harry and that woman. It's obvious. There's nothing between them. Never was anything but a conversation here and there. That's the end of it.'

'By *that woman* you mean, Pamela Gibbon, poor girl?' Mary asked innocently. 'Where can she be? You'd think someone would know. And she didn't take her car, isn't that what I heard?'

'I heard it, too,' Alex said rapidly, anxious to divert Major Stroud.

'Saw her just the other day,' Mary said. 'She's not a collector like you, Alex, but she does come into the shop for tea and she looks through any books that have just come in. She bought one or two.'

'Oh,' Alex said in mock horror. 'I hope you didn't forget to pull any children's volumes I might be looking for.' She collected hard-to-find children's books.

'Something about horses – no surprise there,' Mary said. 'And an old copy of a Kama Sutra book. She was thrilled with them.' Her expression never changed from one of pure innocence.

Alex swallowed and tried not to look at Major Stroud.

'Well,' Harriet said. 'You should have told me about that. I'm not so old I don't know what Kama Sutra is and neither are you, Mary, so take that silly look off your face.'

'Could have been a gift for Harry,' Mary said. 'They say he has broad interests.'

It was hard not to laugh. Mary had an evil sense of humor and both women, former teachers who had taught Alex as a small girl, were sharp enough to hurt sometimes.

'You're making something out of nothing,' the major sputtered. 'Harry's in the City for the day. He's got an important and busy job. Be back later. And he wouldn't want or need that book.' He turned slightly purple.

'I'm sure he wouldn't.' Harriet smiled. 'A man of the world like him. I expect he'll pop in at any moment. He's the speaker for that women's group tonight – over at the old Women's Institute place. I might even go myself now it looks as if it could be more interesting. What do the members call themselves? Are you going, Alex?'

She did some speedy thinking. 'TA. That's the name of it. They must know what it stands for. You'd have to ask one of them.'

'Vivian Seabrook knows all about it.'

'The woman who runs the stables and riding school up at Derwinters' place?' The major frowned. 'She looks like one of the horses. And Harry's going to talk about God knows what for her and that bunch of disgruntled females. He's probably going to explain why they'd have men in their lives if they knew their place.' His laugh came more from his nose than his mouth, a honking snort. 'Not that I'm sure Vivian wouldn't prefer to be a man herself.'

'Would you excuse us, please, Major?' Alex said pleasantly. The man was amazingly crass, stuck in some other century, but usually more amusing than annoying. 'Harriet and Mary have something to discuss with me. Tell Hugh I want you to sample one of the new meat pies.'

She waited while he stared at her, before adding, 'From the bakery. George's makes the best cakes and pies. Some of them are steak and ale. I know that's your favorite.' Hauling Bogie into her arms she managed to keep her face pointed at the floor until Major Stroud got up from his chair and his brown suede lace-up shoes moved away.

Mary said, 'Don't laugh, Harriet,' and managed to sound severe.

'He's an idiot,' Harriet said. 'How that wife of his stands him, I'll never know. And since I'm being honest, so is his son an idiot. What does TA stand for?'

Alex nuzzled Bogie's wet nose into her neck. 'I knew you'd ask. You'll have to ask Vivian.'

'She makes me nervous. Competent, horsey women always make me nervous.'

'Harriet! She's a strong woman, just like you. Be nice.' She sat down in the major's vacated chair. Bogie gave a huge, satisfied sigh when she moved him to her lap.

Alex studied the swags of dried hops looped along age-blackened beams. They'd started to get brittle and it would soon be time for new ones. The fire was always the heart of the place. Flames reflected in the bright surfaces of horse brasses and turned the elderly sisters' faces pink.

A Slade School of Art graduate, a successful graphic artist and then head of a department in her husband's, Mike Bailey-Jones', advertising firm until their divorce, she could never have imagined becoming the owner of a pub. She loved this place now.

The buzz in the bar covered for the silence that had fallen at the table by the fire. Harriet and Mary looked thoughtful, too, but Alex could feel them working toward a fresh barrage of questions and comments.

'How's that cat?' Mary asked suddenly.

Alex winced. 'Tony had to take the infected eye out but I think he'll do well with a lot of loving and patience.'

'Poor thing,' the sisters said in unison.

'I'm going to put up a notice to see if someone's interested in taking him. He's a survivor and you should have seen how brave he was for the surgery.'

Harriet and Mary gave each other a significant look. 'Does that mean you stayed with him?'

'It isn't a clinic day so Radhika wasn't coming in until later. Tony told me what to do so I could help – not that I did much but stroke the cat.'

'Smug' replaced 'significant' in the sisters' expressions and Harriet said, 'He trusts you to help him like that because he knows you're up to it.'

'I'm sure you're very fond of each other,' Mary added. 'I expect it's a bit difficult when you were friends as children.' She cleared her throat.

Alex didn't give either of them any encouragement to continue where they were heading . . . toward less than subtle suggestions about her getting together with Tony. Already, she spent some puzzling times trying to figure out where they were going, and if she should make a move if she wanted to. Frequently she felt as if he were watching her, waiting for some signal about what she felt for him. Or perhaps she just imagined what she hoped was true.

She caught a movement from the corner of her eye and turned around. Lily Duggins had come through an archway from the restaurant and inn wing of the Black Dog. Alex's mother ran that hectic part of the business with the ease of long practice. Lily had worked at the Dog since she was a single mum bringing up her little daughter.

She beckoned to Alex. There was no missing the likeness between mother and daughter. The silver strands in Lily's dark curls were becoming more numerous and she was statuesque beside Alex, but they both had the same green eyes the kids had called 'witchy' when Alex was in school.

'Excuse me a minute,' she said to the sisters. 'I'm being called.'

'What's up?' she asked when she reached her mum.

'Come through.' She led Alex into the empty restaurant. 'Obviously you've heard about Pamela Gibbon?'

'Yes. I'm scared for her.'

'I think I saw her,' Lily said, keeping her voice to a whisper. 'Three nights ago. I was on my way over from the cottage.' Lily lived at Corner Cottage, across Main Street from the Black Dog, one of a row of cottages that backed onto the village green.

Alex felt first hot, then cold. 'Why did you think you saw her? Where was she?'

'I'm afraid to raise hopes. She came from the Dog – the main entrance – but she didn't answer when I called out to her.'

'But you're sure it was her?'

'It was dark,' Lily said. 'She was hurrying away but she had to hear me.'

'She might not have, mum. If she had something on her mind and she was in a hurry. And you aren't completely sure it was her, are you?'

Lily shrugged. 'Do I tell the police or not?'

'Dammit,' Alex said through gritted teeth. 'Why doesn't it just go away? One murder attached to the village and even to this pub, was more than enough. We don't need another crime of some kind.

'Sorry,' Alex continued, 'I should only be thinking about Pamela and we don't know she hasn't decided to take off somewhere.'

Her mum frowned and tented her fingers against her chin, a familiar gesture when Lily Duggins was stressed. 'Pamela's always been a bit distant, at least with women, but she's a good sort and she likes living in Folly. If she hadn't she could easily have left after her husband died. She's made her life here.'

'True.' But racking up points against Pamela leaving on a whim, for a trip or something, didn't make Alex feel better. 'I just want her to turn up. I'm going to reach out to her more, try to help her believe people here care about her.'

Their eyes met. They both knew she was doing her best not to believe anything bad had happened to Pamela Gibbon.

Striding into the restaurant, his Barbour jacket flapping, trousers tucked into green Hunter boots, Tony looked perturbed and ruffled. He also looked wonderfully solid and reassuring. 'Lily,' he said, 'excuse me for interrupting but I'd like to borrow Alex if I may.'

Alex held her mother's arms. 'Don't do anything yet, OK? Wait till I get back from seeing how the cat's doing.'

Bogie shot ahead of them and the outer door closed. Tony stopped and squinted at the blue sky. 'This isn't about the cat. He's coming along well. Can you help me with a re-enactment or whatever they call it? Once it's dark tonight? I hope I'm wrong but I thought I saw a woman hiding by the road into the hills. It was three nights ago as far as I can place it. It was one of those snap decisions. If there was someone there, they obviously didn't want to be seen. So I drove on. Damn, I wish I'd followed my first instinct and stopped.'

THREE

Later that evening, Alex crouched where Tony had told her to wait, close to a clump of bushes beside the road. His headlights picked up her pale face as he drove on the other side. As he'd suggested, when he drew almost level, she ducked down and became invisible.

He made a U-turn and came to a stop on a stony grass verge just past Alex. She crunched rapidly to meet him when he jumped out of the Land Rover with Bogie close behind. 'Could you see me? Did it work?'

'Bloody hell, why didn't I stop.' Frustration overwhelmed him. Stuffing Bogie's lead into one pocket of his coat, he dropped his torch into another one and shoved his hands under his coat, on his hips. 'I saw you just fine.'

'And now you're blaming yourself because Pamela's missing? What sense does that make? You don't even know if it was her you saw – or if it was anyone. Tonight you knew where I was and you were looking. You were likely to see me.'

Rationalizations didn't untwist his gut. 'Thanks.'

Alex caught his arm in both of her hands. 'You do guilt too well, my friend. Too well. You're the most thoughtful man I've ever known. You made a decision and it was the right one for that moment.' She hugged him quickly, leaned on him.

A better man wouldn't be so pleased to hear how much she trusted him. And he wouldn't be giving a second thought to pressing an advantage even if he spent so much time thinking about just that, finding and pressing an advantage with Alex. They had work to do and fast if there was any hope of having an impact on what had happened to Pamela.

He rubbed her hands and kissed the top of her head lightly. 'I hope you're right about that.' Being careful not to push too soon or too hard with Alex had probably robbed him of a chance of something more with her. 'The most thoughtful man' she'd ever known wasn't the way he wanted her to think of him.

'Where would someone go from those bushes – in the dark like this? This is around the time you drove by before? It's not so late but you can't see much.'

When Alex moved away from him, he almost sighed. 'She – or whoever it was – was probably waiting to cross the road without being seen.'

'There's a bit of a beaten-down path leading up the hillside somewhere around here,' Alex said. She wore jeans, and a down gilet over a high-necked jumper and a cardigan, much as she had when she left him at his clinic that morning.

'Come on, and you stay close, Bogie.' At a rapid clip, she crossed the road and started searching, carefully, between more scrubby wild shrubs and bushes. Bogie snuffled along, his black ears perked up. A dog on a mission with his person.

Tony put away the keys to the Land Rover and followed.

The chilly breeze felt as if it would bring a shower, but the moon still slunk along a livid sky, silver behind thin veils of charcoal clouds.

'Alex.' He remembered bringing his dog Katie this way on a walk. 'I think there's a sort of path that goes all the way to—'

'To Ebring Manor?' she cut him off. 'What's left of it. Bogie and I have gone that way. Looks like he's found the trail again.'

'If this leads to anything useful, it'll be almost too easy,' he told her. 'Take my hand, we'll go faster.'

She laughed through gasps. 'In other words, I need help from someone stronger.'

'Yes. I'm supposed to be stronger. Anything wrong with that?'

She grabbed his hand and leaned into the hill. 'I'm not proud,' she said. 'I just find men and their egos funny sometimes. I wouldn't change places with you. This might be easier if we really knew our way.'

He paused to let them both catch breath. 'I'm starting to think this path is pretty well used.' His torch switched back and forth ahead of them. 'It looks trampled.'

An unexpected gust turned into wind and zipped through the almost bare trees, whipping the last scratchy skeletons of winter leaves into their faces. He glanced down at Alex, his torchlight picking out the gleam of her green eyes, and remembered how the kids had called them 'witchy.' She had put up with a lot from the children of narrow-minded parents, including whispers of *bastard.* He was glad he'd been around, and that he'd been older and bigger than the bully bunch.

He had always thought her beautiful, but unaffected. The feelings that went along with those reactions only intensified.

'Did I say Harry didn't show up for the women's meeting at the parish hall tonight?'

He paused. 'The hell you say. You didn't tell me. Has anyone seen him at all?'

'He called to say he had to stay in the city. At least he let them know he wasn't coming.'

Tony pushed a low branch out of their way. 'Whoever he spoke to would have asked if Pamela was with him. Not that he had to say one way or the other. We can hope she is.'

'This is a weird evening,' Alex said when they ploughed on. 'It's trying to be ominous. Or is that just in my head? I do love every season in this place. Too bad I had to leave it for a few years to find out how great it is.'

He looked toward her again, briefly, and squeezed her hand. They knew enough about one another not to rehash old demons, but they also understood that they still lived with those demons.

Bogie had shot ahead and was out of sight. With Alex, Tony broke out of the trees and looked ahead to where the outline of what had once been ancient Ebring Manor stood out, luminous and pallid on a large mound. The stubby drum tower and a few other pieces of the original buildings thrust sharply into the purple sky. The clouds looked like smoke from a smoldering fire now.

'What do we hope to find here?' Alex said. 'There isn't anyone else here that I can see.' She shivered forcefully and pulled her hand from his to wrap her arms around herself. 'There's no noise but I could swear everything is popping around me. It's all alive and I hate it.'

'Alex?'

Dark curls tossed forward around her pale face. 'Nothing,' she said.

'No, it's not nothing, what's the matter?'

She looked grim and cold, neither of which made particular sense. 'Leave it, Tony.'

Puzzled, he planted himself in front of her. 'I'm not going to leave it.'

'I've got a feeling.' She breathed out hard through her nose. 'I'd rather not give more ammunition for the stories about me being a bit spooky, but I do get . . . premonitions. Forget it. It's nothing, just a feeling, that's all.'

'Bogie's heading for the tower,' he said, glad of an excuse to switch topics. Delving into things she'd obviously rather not discuss wasn't a good thing. They respected one another's privacy – perhaps too much.

Stepping over the stones that made up the boundary of the building, they took off after Bogie. It wasn't an easy climb. Once inside the tower and halfway up a second flight of broken steps, the dog waited for them at the top. He ran away as soon as he saw them.

Tony was the first into the partially roofless top level. He shone his torch around the area, aiming first at the purple-tinged sky, then around the bare stone floor.

A bump moving under a rumpled tarpaulin gave Bogie's whereabouts away. The tarp and whatever it covered were pushed under what remained of the roof.

'Someone's been camping out up here,' Tony said, picking up a corner of the heavy waxed sheet. 'Or something.' He threw back the tarp, revealing a rolled-up quilt and what looked like a sleeping bag. It was two sleeping bags, zipped together, and there was a rolled up airbed.

'Looks well used but it's expensive stuff,' Alex said. 'Pillows in plastic bags. What's this? A down blanket. A box of cutlery. Plates. Glasses. All mod cons.' She shivered visibly.

'Someone walking on your grave again?' Tony said, and grimaced. 'That wasn't a bright thing to say.'

'I don't want to stay around here.' She pushed her hands inside the sleeves of her cardigan and shivered again. 'Bogie's gone back down. I don't want him running off.' She met Tony's eyes and he didn't recall her looking at him in quite that way before. Anxious, but searching, as if she were trying to read him at some deep level.

Wishful thinking. She was freaked out, looking for reassurance, and he didn't blame her.

'I shouldn't have brought you up here.'

'I'm a big girl. I bet that bag belongs under the tarp.' Capacious and made of green canvas, a bag leaned against a wall and Alex looked inside. She held it out for Tony to see and he lifted out the contents.

He produced a box of Italian glacé chestnuts, a sealed blue envelope, not addressed, that felt like a card, and a heavy, leather case. 'Crikey.' He had unclasped the lid. 'Zeiss binoculars – tip-top stuff.

Worth a bundle. No one would deliberately leave these here.' He snapped the lid shut and replaced the case in the bag.

'This isn't a kids' hangout,' Alex said quietly, picking her way to the top of the steps.

'It could belong to teenagers with imagination and major pocket money.'

Rather than answer him, Alex put a hand against one wall and started climbing down.

Tony put the bag with the rest of the supplies, swept the tarp back into place and went after her. Once outside they were met by a wind that stopped and started, unenthusiastic about its haphazard efforts.

'It *was* a mistake to bring you here,' he said, draping an arm around her shoulders. 'It's depressing and you don't need reminding of past . . .' He let his words trail off.

'Past horrors, is that what you were going to say?' Alex slipped a hand under his jacket and around his waist. He felt her hold on to his sweater.

Nose to the ground, Bogie snuffled back and forth, moving in and out of the torch beam, intent on some quest known only to him.

The ruins of the manor house, with its jagged reminders of lost walls, made a forlorn white sketch in the gloom.

'Let's get out of here,' Alex said. She called the dog but he continued to run aimless patterns on the ground with his black nose.

'Bogie,' Alex cried. 'Come, boy. Now.'

The answer she got was wild barking that trailed into a thin yowl. Alex found Bogie with her light. He stood near the grill-covered well, his neck stretched upward, barking in spurts that ended in almost soundless croaks.

Alex leaped forward but Tony caught her arm to stop her.

She looked back at him, her face stark, and jerked her arm away.

Tony ran toward the dog.

FOUR

The instant they closed on him, Bogie lay down, his head on his paws, dark eyes flicking from side to side.

He whimpered.

'Come on, boy,' Alex said gently, but her throat tightened sickeningly. Once before, on a snowy early morning she'd rather forget, Bogie had behaved like this. 'There's nothing here. You're being silly.'

There was nothing to see. Silence blanketed the whole deserted area and she noticed an ugly odor, as if sheep might have been grazing in the area.

'Would you mind staying here, Alex, and holding Bogie?' Tony kept a neutral expression on his face as if he weren't really telling her he was expecting something nasty and wanted to protect her.

Sometimes keeping the peace made things simpler. 'Come here, Bogie,' she said. And added, 'Now!' when he didn't move.

Slowly, bottom first, he raised himself from the ground. His head remained on his paws.

'I'll get him,' Tony said and moved in, saying gentle, mostly meaningless words all the way. He reached Bogie and scratched his head . . . then he stood still, staring at the clumps of pale grass and the rocks illuminated around the dog's feet.

Alex didn't wait another second. She ran to the spot and frowned at the debris.

'Oh, no,' she whispered when she saw what was different. 'My God, Tony, we've got to do something fast.'

'Sometimes I wish you didn't rush into the middle of everything,' he said. He clipped on Bogie's lead. 'You aren't trained for this type of thing.'

Alex crouched.

'Don't touch anything.'

'I know the drill,' she told him, glancing at the grill over the well. 'Could anyone be alive down there?'

'It's my job to find out. Your job is to get the police and anyone else who can deal with this.'

They stared at one another, both putting a hand over their noses and mouths. The stench that reached them grew stronger.

'The smell doesn't have to mean . . .' She broke off, pressing a fist to her thumping heart. 'It's vomit and other things, and if we mess with anything . . . Tony, it could be a crime scene. No one could do this to themselves. The police will go mad if we disturb anything.'

'And my conscience will go mad if I don't go down there,' he said, taking off his jacket and tossing it aside. 'Wish I had gloves.'

He was a very strong man and hauled the heavy grill aside without too much trouble. 'Don't let Bogie touch those,' he said as he lowered himself onto the ladder inside the well. Make some calls, please.' He even managed a little smile that looked more like a pain-induced grimace.

Watching him disappear into the hole, Alex made an emergency call and got the usual round of questions about what service she wanted and where she was calling from.

'I think someone's fallen into a well,' she said, gasping for non-existent fresh air. 'Up at the old Ebring Manor site. And it could be someone else put the grill back in place over them.' Thinking about that Alex added, 'Or someone messed with the grill and had an accident. They would have gone for help right away. But whoever it was left the severed tips of three fingers behind . . . how do I . . . I know because there are fingernails.'

FIVE

Alex sat on the ground, cradling Bogie in her lap. Having Tony down there where she couldn't see him was too much. Anything could happen to him. She heard him scuffling against the brick lining of the well.

Maybe it wasn't a well. But it was a deep hole in the ground and whoever lost the ends of their fingers to the kind of ghastly pain that made Alex shudder, could be at the bottom. She prayed it wasn't the case, that the police would check hospitals and find the person who mangled his or her fingers.

She hadn't looked down the shaft, hadn't wanted to. Tony's torch sent up a sickly, jiggling light that sometimes grew paler, as he had it pointed down, sometimes brighter when he palmed it to keep climbing.

The emergency dispatcher kept her on the phone but Alex had stopped trying to talk to him. She wanted to be sick and if she moved much she feared she'd faint. The breeze kept wafting an odor of animal dung.

'Tony?' she yelled when the waiting grew too long. 'Are you OK?'

'Yes,' came a short, hollow echo.

The wind blew in circles now, ladling up leaves and dancing them around as if this was a jolly celebration of the season.

Bogie leaned closer and licked her chin.

Shuffling sideways, Alex got close enough to lean over the edge of the hole. 'Are you at the bottom yet?' She kept her eyes averted from the mutilated fingertips.

'Yes.'

A distant siren sounded. 'I hear the police or someone coming. How can they be here so fast?' She was almost weak with relief at the sound of the sirens.

No reply came from below.

Tears stung Alex's eyes. 'Tony, is there someone down there?'

'Yes, Alex.' His echoing voice had an extra hollowness. 'I think it's Pamela Gibbon.'

Alex's mind didn't want to work. She glanced at the three black ends of fingers, nails jagged and caked with dried blood. 'No, no, no. Why?' What kind of hate made one human being do this to another. It couldn't be a mistake Pamela had made on her own.

'The sirens are getting closer,' she called out. 'There's nothing you can do . . .'

'Nothing, but try to find the bastard who did this.'

She squeezed her eyes shut. 'Come up. Please, Tony.'

His boots rang on the ladder rungs again, at the same time as the splitting sound of sirens and the scorching flash of red and blue lights arrived on the abandoned road a few hundred yards above the mansion ruins.

Figures running in her direction quickly took shape. She flashed her torch toward them. Detective Inspector Dan O'Reilly and Detective Sergeant Bill Lamb were easy to pick out. They were familiar and brought with them the kind of feelings Alex had hoped never to experience again. Uniformed officers fanned out behind them, making Alex feel trapped. Someone headed into the tower at a run and she wondered at the efficiency these people could show.

'That's O'Reilly and Lamb,' Tony said, making her jump. 'I hoped we'd never see them again. What do they do? Sit around in some dingy office in Gloucester waiting for a call about Folly-on-Weir?'

Before she could answer, Lamb steamed up with O'Reilly at his shoulder. The two men stopped short to survey the whole scene.

'Hugh told me Constable Frye said they might come to the village,' Alex said quietly.

The detective inspector had good ears. 'We got into the area a couple of hours ago,' he said. 'They needed help. Things didn't look good.'

Alex remained sitting, and holding Bogie. Had the police already expected to find Pamela dead? If so, why? Surely a village with a history of two murders only months earlier wasn't marked as a likely spot for more atrocities. Tony's head stuck out of the hole in the ground.

Both policemen put a hand over their noses.

'What happened?' O'Reilly said, sounding as Irish as Alex remembered.

'Do you know about a woman called Pamela Gibbon being missing?' Tony asked.

Lamb's face grew red. 'The Detective Chief Inspector asked you a fucking question,' he snapped.

Alex wondered if his last job around here had helped with O'Reilly's promotion.

'Bill, help Dr Harrison out of there,' O'Reilly said. He didn't look happy.

'Pamela Gibbon lives in Folly-on-Weir,' Alex said, stiff-lipped. 'She's been missing for several days. Tony and I came up here to have a look around and found bits of fingers there.' She pointed. 'Tony went down the shaft and found Pamela. She's dead.'

'We already know all about Pamela Gibbon going missing,' Lamb said, with no sign of a thaw in his manner. His sandy crew cut was just as it had been the last time she saw him. Thick and not a hair out of place. 'Why would we be here if it didn't look as if—'

'Come on out, Dr Harrison,' O'Reilly said, sounding pleasant enough, although the last time they'd all met, they'd been on Tony and Dan terms by the time it was all over.

Bill Lamb offered him a hand, which Tony ignored, vaulting out under his own steam. Bill turned to Dan O'Reilly. Alex couldn't see his face but imagined he was looking to his boss for instructions.

More vehicles arrived at the top of the acreage.

She recognized pale blue SOCO uniforms, rapidly being pulled on over other clothes. Scene of Crime types weren't her favorites. They went in for black humor that might help them but did nothing for her.

'Pathologist is on her way,' one man said, already completely suited, his head and feet covered and gloves in place. 'You want to go down and take a look?' he asked Dan O'Reilly.

'Not before Molly gets here. She hates it if she isn't first.'

'Bit late for that,' Bill said without looking at Tony.

Tony ignored him. 'There's not much room down there. You won't both be able to be with Pamela at the same time.'

'Don't worry about us,' Bill said. 'We work out our own logistics.'

Alex wondered why the detective sergeant was trying to bait Tony, not that it got any reaction from him.

'Tell your people to seal off everything,' the inspector told the SOCO team member. 'Hold off on tenting until Dr Lewis gets here and gives you the word. Plan on securing a large area. We could have a big crime scene.

'There's evidence right there beside the shaft opening. Bag it and say we want the area under lights. Until then, they snap on their wings and don't touch a thing, including the ground if they can get enough loft. You never know, we may have more fingers to come, among other things.'

'If I know Molly she won't be long, unless she's driving herself,' Bill said.

'She doesn't do that much anymore, and almost never at night.' O'Reilly planted his feet apart. Alex couldn't see his dark eyes but his wavy hair tossed in the wind. 'Our Molly is a whiz. Just can't find her way out of a paper bag.' His casual approach was something Alex liked, although she remembered well how tough he could be. 'Why don't we get preliminary statements from you and Tony?' he asked Alex.

What she really wanted was to get away from here and fast.

Spotlights were quickly put into place. They bathed everything in a sickly, blinding white that felt intrusive.

With Bill Lamb taking notes, Tony and Alex answered questions rapidly, those they could answer at all. She was aware of the silent row of police slowly covering the ground, their torches brilliant and each with a stick they occasionally used to move something aside. An officer had arrived with a dog.

'We came straight up here when we got to the village,' O'Reilly said. 'We'll need a lot more from you two. Want to toss in any ideas about who might have had a grudge against Pamela Gibbon?'

Alex and Tony looked at one another with matching frowns. 'Nope,' he said. 'This is . . . damned if I know.'

The sound of another engine got closer. Alex shuddered again, tried to calm herself. There was no need to fear the kind of hateful events that closed in around her the last time someone was murdered in Folly. Anyway, Pamela might have had an accident.

In your dreams.

Tony's hand, closing around hers, steadied her, and Alex didn't hesitate to lace her fingers with his.

A small, blond woman, already suited for business, strode toward them. When she got close enough, Dan O'Reilly said, 'Molly Lewis, this is Alex Duggins and Tony Harrison. They found the body.'

The woman, pretty and slim, but older than her initial impression suggested, snapped on her gloves and made for the open hole without more than a nod at Tony and Alex. She slid a light on a band over her head and settled it on her forehead, before disappearing down the ladder with sure, rapid movements.

'At the top of that drum tower, you'll find what looks like a bunch of supplies for people who plan to return, possibly regularly. It probably means nothing, but—'

'When did you intend to mention that?' Bill Lamb asked, his chin thrust forward.

Alex squeezed Tony's hand. 'You can be such an idiot, Bill Lamb,' she said. 'You think it's easy to get everything straight and in order on a night like this? I think I'm just going home. Hope you'll come with me, Tony. You people know where to find us.'

'Would that be at his place or yours?' Lamb said. 'Not that you're going anywhere until we say so.'

'Asshole,' Tony muttered, loudly enough for everyone to hear.

'I'll need to interview both of you,' Dan O'Reilly said. 'When we're finished here for tonight, where can I find each of you?'

'I'll be at the Black Dog,' Alex told him without hesitation.

'I might as well go there, too. Easier on everyone,' Tony said.

Lamb snickered.

'When did you say you thought the victim fell in here?' The pathologist, Molly something, popped her head just out of the shaft.

O'Reilly said, 'We're thinking as long as three days.'

'I thought that's what I heard,' the woman said, starting down again. 'Tell them to get the tent up. And we're going to need lights down here and some fast work. Poor thing could have been there a while. Looks like several blows to the head, but she may only have been dead hours.'

SIX

Tony stopped outside the Dog. He just stood still, arms crossed, staring at the ground. He hadn't spoken on the drive down to the village. A Mazda sports car had been parked, haphazard, across three parking spots. Alex didn't recognize the vehicle.

'Look at that,' Alex said, 'I don't have the energy to hunt down the owner tonight. Selfish creep.'

Tony remained quiet.

'Let's go in through the restaurant,' Alex said. 'I should have a word with my mum.'

'I don't feel like talking to anyone, Alex. Sorry.'

'You can't stay out here,' she said gently and touched his jaw. 'I can't make you think or do what I want you to, but none of this is your fault. And we don't know what happened up there or how.'

'We may never know what happened – or if her death was my fault. For all I know, she could have been saved if I'd stopped that night, or even looked for her earlier.' He drew her closer to the building. 'I do get it. I can't change what's happened but I would love to get rid of what I'm feeling right now.'

Alex nodded to a couple arriving at the restaurant and said, 'Good evening.'

Resting an elbow against the wall, Tony propped his head on his fist and waited until the door closed again – which gave Bogie an opportunity to whip inside. 'I think a brandy sounds good, how about you?' Alex said, ducking her head to see his face until he looked up. She gathered a handful of his coat and pressed her knuckles into his collarbone. 'We can do this, Tony. We've been through . . . horrible things.'

'There was so much blood. I knew she hadn't died instantly. There was glass – not much – a few sharp little pieces.'

Tears stung Alex's eyes. 'It's sick. I'm surprised you could see the glass amongst the junk that must be down there.'

Even with the tinted and dappled glow through stained-glass windows, Tony's eyes looked black, and empty. 'She'd hit the back of her head, hard – that's what the pathologist was talking about,

but she landed on her face. Bits of glass . . . there were some punc-
ture wounds in her face. Broken bones and who knows what other
damage they'll find at the post-mortem.'

She had to hold him and she did. Tucked her arms around his
neck and pulled his face down onto her shoulder. 'Tony, this wasn't
your fault. I've never met a man as decent as you are. I'm not
surprised you're beating yourself up, but I won't allow you not to
see that you're incredibly decent. Just believe what I say and let
me help you through this.'

He didn't say anything but neither did he lift his face from the
niche between her neck and shoulder.

Neither of them needed her to cry. 'Please come in with me. I
don't want you going off on your own. And we want to get the
questions out of the way as quickly as we can anyway. We need to
be here when the police come.'

'OK.' He straightened up, walked her to the door and pushed it
open for her. 'Thank you. I hope it doesn't scare you to hear it, but
you're the best friend I ever had – the best I ever hope to have.'

She smiled at him, holding back those wretched tears. 'That goes
for me, too.'

Tony held her tightly by her upper arms. 'Let's hope they come
quickly. But not till we've had that brandy.'

When they walked in, Lily was seating the latest patrons. She
saw Alex and Tony and she hurried over, her smile dissolving
instantly. The restaurant was almost full and the sounds of laughter,
conversation, clinking glass and dishes jarred Alex.

'Did you find out anything?' Lily asked.

Alex winced but Tony said, 'Yes, unfortunately,' in a flat voice.
'The Ebring Manor hill is crawling with plods, dogs and every
species of police you can think up. We should probably wait until
friends O'Reilly and Lamb finish with us before we say too much.'

'Oh, my God,' Lily said. She took a deep breath and blew it out
through pursed lips. 'Are they coming here? Tonight?'

'Yes.'

Lily bowed her head. 'Pamela is dead?'

'Yeah. You want to take off your gilet, Alex?' He held out a hand.

She gave him the gilet, aware that more than a few eyes were
trained in their direction and the noise level had faded.

Lily didn't raise her face. Tears ran down her cheeks.

'Hang in with us here, we'd like to sit in the bar with a brandy,'

Tony said, taking off his own coat. 'We've got to think our way through as much as we can.' The place glowed with good cheer and heat, body and fire heat.

Lily wiped her face and threaded a hand through one of each of their arms and turned them all away from the room. 'It's packed in there. Most standing so there's some tables. There's only one topic.' She sighed. 'And we've got reporters already.'

'That explains the lousy parking job,' Alex said. 'You know they sit around listening to emergency transmissions, don't you?'

Lily nodded. 'But they don't seem to know there's been a murder yet.'

'Let's hope we can keep it that way for a bit,' Tony said. 'When the detectives get here, could we use the snug? I don't want to be too isolated with those two.'

'I'll see to it,' Lily said. 'I should warn you that the women's group has been here for some time. When the speaker fell through they took over the up-room and pushed tables together. I'd stay away from them. They're laughing a lot but it's pretty intense.' The up-room was what locals called a one-step-up from the main level, an area beside the bar where people frequently chose to eat a pub meal. The trestle tables and high-backed banquets were popular.

'We need to be normal, Mum,' Alex said. She didn't feel normal. Her skin prickled and her muscles made small, involuntary twitches. 'Can I mention about you thinking you saw Pamela or do you want to wait for them to ask.'

'Tell them,' Lily said. 'I'd appreciate it even if they do ask again.'

'Your mum saw Pamela?' Tony put a hand at her back and walked her into the bar where the interest they raised was palpable.

'Thinks she did,' Alex said, sliding into one of two barrel chairs at an ancient little table tucked into a bay window. She waved at the sisters Burke who gave pleasant nods and studiously made sure they didn't appear to be watching Tony and Alex.

Tony didn't ask anymore about when and where Lily had seen Pamela Gibbon. 'I'll get those brandies. And some snacks. We haven't eaten for a long time.'

Watching Tony's loose-limbed walk and the way he swung his shoulders to thread through a crowd was always a pleasure. Just looking at him doing anything was a pleasure. Alex realized he really was the closest friend she'd ever had, but how long could they continue as they were?

That was as much up to her as to Tony.

Bogie had muscled in front of the fire where he was always comfortable to be with the sisters. He lay side-by-side with Katie and Alex frowned, wondering how she'd appeared at the Dog.

Picking out the two reporters didn't take much effort, one in a saggy gray raincoat, leaning on the bar, elbow-to-elbow with Kev Winslet from the Derwinter estate. Kev knew everything, even if he didn't really know a thing. And he loved a rapt audience. A female reporter with long dark hair had gone for the ruffled and ready-for-sex look. She had several men hanging on her every word.

In the up-room, banquets pushed together shielded the women sitting there but they didn't mute the volume.

A brandy in each hand, Tony returned. 'Hugh's putting together some bits he knows we'll like.' He smiled. 'That man was a find, one of a kind. His sidekick isn't so bad, either. A bit reserved but sharp.'

'And too good looking for his own good.' Alex grinned broadly and took a healthy swallow of her brandy. She coughed and thumped between her collar bones. 'I shouldn't say this but he's good for a certain type of business. The girls just stare. A name like Juste Vidal doesn't hurt. Adds to his mystery.'

Juste was a student at a divinity college in Cheltenham and managed to work at the pub three nights a week.

'Katie's here,' Alex said. 'I'm surprised she's not all over you.'

'Radhika must have brought her. She was going to look after her until I got back.'

'And the fire is more magnetic than you.' Alex smiled. 'Radhika's probably with the women's group. She doesn't drink, in fact I've never known her to come here before.'

'We're avoiding what's on our minds.' As if he'd channeled that the conversation had included him, Juste delivered two large plates of goodies to them and Alex sat back, waiting for him to leave.

Twenty-four years old, Juste looked at the world through steel-framed glasses that somehow managed to make his green eyes even more show-stopping. Reddish brown hair waved to the top of his collar around a sharply boned face. Alex could understand how he appealed to the female sex, especially if they liked to daydream stories about the man's life.

'Bite-sized pastry puffs filled with asparagus and camembert,' he said, his accent distinctly French, then cast up his eyes when he added, 'and steak and kidney pielets. Blinis with salmon and cream cheese. Baked eggs in corned beef cups. Enough to tickle your pallets.' He grinned, perfectly aware that these lovely little things had been whipped up in the main kitchen especially for the boss and her friend.

'Look at this,' Alex said, glancing at Juste walking away. 'And that man's voice could have the same effect on a woman as dark chocolate. He'll increase the congregation and the contributions in any church where he preaches.'

Tony nodded and slipped a baked egg into his mouth. 'Concentrate, hussy. We've likely got a murderer among us,' he said, chewing. 'Pamela lived here for ten years. What don't we know about her? There has to be something we could never even have guessed at. Something that caused this.'

With her elbows on the table, Alex held her snifter with both hands and concentrated on the taste and the fiery spread through her veins.

'Or could it have been an accident after all?'

'And after she was hanging from the rim of the shaft she moved the grill back into place herself?' Alex stared at him. 'She's . . . was possibly strong enough to move the grill, but you don't get your fingers cut off and not yell. That's supposing someone came along, saw the open grill, and moved it back into place. Pamela would have screamed and—'

'I'm sure she did. Nasty thought that she could have been heard and ignored while she took that fall. Or even when she was at the bottom of that shaft. It's all about motive, love. Let's see what kind of questions the police ask. We'll get a feeling for what they're thinking. What if she pulled the lid closed from below and didn't get her hand out of the way until too late.' He held a plate out to her until she took a pastry puff.

Shaking her head slowly, Alex said, 'I want to know exactly what her relationship was with Harry, and whether they were deeper in than we know. And more than that, who else was involved. There had to be someone – there is someone who knows why this happened.'

Katie loped over to Tony who gave her a good rub with both hands. 'All the gear in that tower must have been there for a reason. If it belonged to Pamela and someone she met up there, they didn't need it to play Monopoly.'

A gust of cold wind came in with the next customer. 'Holy hell,' Alex murmured. 'Take a glance behind you. I don't believe it, Tony.'

He did take a look, and sat very still, his hands still on Katie. 'That, I didn't expect.' He emphasized each word. 'Either he's stupid, or he's in the dark about everything, or this is bravado – chutzpah.'

Harry Stroud had walked in.

SEVEN

*E*very word spoken had to be considered first. There were enemies and potential enemies here. The rest made no difference – not now and not unless they pushed their noses where they didn't belong.

With care, the one who was finally going to pay a long overdue bill would quickly come under suspicion and there would be no need for anyone else to be touched by a necessary crime. But the past had already shown that there were those in Folly-on-Weir who saw themselves as the descendants of Sherlock Holmes combined with some ultimate angel of justice, and their passionate efforts could prove the harbinger of an unjust outcome – at least in this case. But that wouldn't be allowed to happen.

Everything had been meticulously worked out. Nothing had been rushed or done in an irrational rage, the kind of rage that inevitably led to disastrous mistakes.

Perhaps the past was now only a motive and a controlled memory of deep wrong which must serve to keep the mind sharp and directed. Was this the moment when justice would start its slow clawing out of darkness; was this the real beginning of the end of the story? Surely taking revenge and then walking away from chaos was the prize.

Yes, the ultimate prize and if any member of the Sherlock brigade got in the way . . . well, then . . .

'You're sure you should go over there?' Tony said. 'I'd rather you didn't if I can't come with you.'

'It's a women's club,' Alex told him with an amused little grin. 'Anyway, I'll have company. Look who's joining the party.' She stood and waved at Mary and Harriet who were getting to their feet. 'Let me know if the dynamic duo from Gloucester get here before we're finished. And make sure you get O'Reilly's rank right.'

He grinned and caught her hand. 'OK, but be careful. Could we have a brandy together when this evening is over? We never got to finish this one. I'd like to take you to my place, if you'll come.'

It was late and his invitation didn't sound like one of their casual get-togethers.

'Thank you,' she said. 'We need some relaxed time.' Although she felt anything but relaxed.

'Yes.' Tony's smile was pleased but intense. 'Here come the ladies.'

'Do you know who's up there?' Alex asked the Burke sisters when they joined her.

Harriet kept her voice down while they all smiled around. 'I don't know if I missed anyone. Winifred George from the bakery is there.'

'Sibyl Davis, the interim vicar's wife,' Mary added quickly. 'And Heather Derwinter, if you can believe that.'

Alex could believe that their local self-appointed lady of the manor wasn't likely to miss a chance to hear women from Folly discussing . . . whatever it was these people discussed. Svelte, pretty, with an enviable body, young Mrs Derwinter considered her opinion important in all things.

'Valery Perkins from the wool shop,' Harriet cut in. 'And her grandmother who's supposedly deaf as a post. Fay Winslet – that lug of a husband of hers, Kev, he's in the bar. Vivian Seabrook, of course. I don't like her, although Heather seems to. I suppose they have horses in common. They'd be bound to go in for animals – they don't talk back.'

With Harriet keeping up with her, Bogie bustling ahead to see what was going on, and Mary making good enough time with her walker, Alex threaded her way to the up-room, arriving on the other side of the banquet barricade before Harry had talked himself into a seat. From his reception, she wondered if he would be staying long. He stood to one side of the tables looking sheepish.

'Life in the city is like this,' he said in a pleading tone. 'The only thing you can count on is someone throwing a spanner in the works and messing up other people's plans. Quite a schmo we had today, I can tell you, although I can't really tell you. I could not get away any earlier.'

Carafes of house wine, red and white stood on the table and each woman, except for Fay Winslet and Radhika, nursed a glass. Radhika and Fay had coffee. Bowls of popcorn were mostly empty.

Waves greeted Alex, Mary and Harriet. Bogie snuffled at Radhika's glorious orange and lime green silk skirt and she hauled him onto her lap.

'Argh,' Alex said. 'Don't let him slobber on that. It's so beautiful.'

'Bogie does not *slobber*,' Radhika said in her mellifluous voice. 'He is a most well behaved fellow.'

In addition to Radhika, the sisters had missed Charlotte Restrick, wife of the permanent vicar of St Aldwyn's who was recovering from a serious accident. Sibyl Davis sat next to Charlotte.

Several of the women shifted to make room for the newcomers, but there still wasn't enough room so they captured some chairs from the bar and set them at each end of the tables. Three chairs.

Alex wanted to be sure Harry didn't leave, and offered him her seat while she squished in beside Fay Winslet, small, fair, with tiny bones and pointy features that made her brown eyes look huge. It was a mystery to them all that she had married big, mouthy Kev Winslet, the Derwinters' gamekeeper, but he treated his wife with something close to reverence and used a soft voice with her that brought some people close to guffawing.

Harry slid into the spare chair and busily pulled a notebook from the inner pocket of his jacket.

'I really thought Pamela would come,' Vivian Seabrook said. She cast anxious blue eyes toward the door and looked worried. 'Has anyone heard from her? I've been told all the rubbish about her taking off yesterday, or whatever, but that just wouldn't be like her. Hasn't she contacted someone?' A tall, rangy woman, Vivian was a dark blond and good looking. A dramatic, sharp-featured face with eyebrows several shades darker than her hair made sure she didn't go anywhere without drawing a lot of interest. Tonight she seemed close to tears. Her right cheek was bruised and scraped and she sat awkwardly.

'What happened to you?' Alex asked her.

Vivian showed more deep, fresh scratches on her wrists and palms. 'Bloody mare kicked a door into me. Knocked me on my arse among other things. My back's a mess. But I've had worse done to me.' She sniffed and felt her cheek. 'Back to Pamela.'

Harry rested his elbows on the table and scrubbed at his face. He seemed tense, upset even.

'Has anyone called her?' Fay Winslet said, her voice anxious and high.

'She knew when the meeting was,' Vivian said through the tissue she held to her nose. 'I keep hearing gossip about her going missing but I don't believe it. Why would she leave?'

'Let's calm down,' Winifred George said. 'She's still grieving. Perhaps she isn't ready for this sort of thing.'

'It's been eons since her husband died,' Vivian snapped. 'She's over it.'

'I believe she loved Charles a great deal,' Harriet said. 'Despite the difference in their ages. We can't put a one-size-fits-all on emotions. What about other relatives? Anyone know about that?'

'Never heard her mention any,' Harry said. He covered his mouth as if he wished he hadn't spoken.

'Mrs Stroud isn't here either.' Vivian looked at Harry as if that must be his fault. 'This would have been her first visit to our club. She doesn't seem to go anywhere in the village but she promised she'd come.'

He gave a humorless laugh and said, 'Probably heard I'd be talking and decided to knit instead.'

'Your mother's a wonderful knitter.' Valery Perkins from the wool shop wagged a finger at him. 'Now there's someone we should get to give us a demonstration. She could give a whole class.'

Pulling her shoulder-length blond hair back and slipping on a band to make a ponytail, Heather Derwinter said, 'What are we discussing this evening, Harry?'

'How are men adjusting to women's equality?' Vivian said in clear, ringing tones. Tears stood in her eyes but she spoke with no sign of being upset.

Harry turned pages in his notebook. 'That's not what I was told. I prepared some insights into women managing their money. Certainly a very suitable subject.'

'Undoubtedly,' Vivian said. 'But when you didn't come on time we had to improvise. The new topic seems appropriate and you can certainly be appropriate on this, Harry.'

Color rose over his already ruddy cheeks. 'Really. Why?' Harry's dark hair curled quite close to his head and he had distinctly arched eyebrows. His looks were appealing in an English gentlemanly way – a man of the upper country class – but more muscular and fit looking than many. He was slim, his belly flat beneath his finely tailored striped shirt. Grey eyes failed to be arresting, despite thick, curly lashes.

'Why would I be *appropriate* to discuss equality?' he pressed.

'You are a man, Mr Stroud.' Radhika didn't crack a smile but everyone else sniggered.

'Wouldn't you say the financial world belongs primarily to men?' Heather said, lightly enough to more or less mask an argumentative trend. 'You're in finance.'

'So are many women.'

'But the balance is . . . well, that's not the point. Women can no longer be considered less intellectually capable than men, don't you think?'

Alex watched the exchange between Heather and Harry, which didn't go anywhere, and wondered if Heather saw herself as an intellectual.

'I don't think we can do this now,' Radhika said. She pulled a small, lace-edged handkerchief from her purse and held it to the bridge of her nose. 'We should be helping search for Pamela. Making telephone calls. Asking questions.'

'When Radhika first came here, Pamela took her in until she could find a place,' Mrs George said. 'I agree, we should do something useful.'

Alex kept watching Harry who shuffled his notebook back and forth between his hands. Could they assume he had nothing to do with what happened to Pamela? Would he just walk in here as if nothing had happened – if he had been responsible for her death?

Credible actors weren't that rare, she supposed. Most of his healthy color had drained away and he kept his gaze on the table.

'We could call everyone in the village to find out if she's been seen in the last day or two.' Radhika turned to Harry. 'Could I use your notebook, please?'

'She was gone three days,' Alex said and instantly wished she'd never come to sit with these people.

'How do you know?' Harry leaned forward, stared at her. 'Does that mean she's back now?' He swallowed loudly.

'Why didn't you tell us at once?' Vivian took her wine glass in a shaky hand and swallowed deeply. 'You can see how upset we all are. What's the matter with you?' Her voice rose enough to produce another lull in conversation among the bar patrons. 'Where is she?'

Alex closed her eyes. 'I shouldn't have come. Bad judgment on my part. I knew the police wouldn't want me blabbing before they question anyone.'

'Have they found her?' Harry stood up, his body rigid. 'Tell me now.'

'Pamela's dead.'

EIGHT

Conversation in the bar remained subdued but Tony could tell this was because the clientele could hear what was happening in the up-room.

Alex was under siege.

Quickly, he found Lily and gave her instructions before making a rapid path through the bar. Harry Stroud bumped into him on the way to the door. The man looked ghastly.

When Tony reached the area where the group sat, Alex was wide-eyed and silent. Several of the other women were crying openly.

'We're being called,' he said, sidestepping to get to her. 'We'd better not keep the police waiting.'

'The *police?*' Radhika cried. 'What happened to Pamela?'

Tony took Alex's elbow as she rose and felt a tremor running through her. Bogie promptly jumped from Radhika's lap and followed.

'There you are,' Lily said when they reached her in front of the snug. 'Should I bring some coffee?'

'I don't know,' Alex muttered.

Tony smiled at Lily and said, 'We'll give a call if we need anything.'

He barely stopped himself from taking a backward step when he saw O'Reilly and Lamb. They must just have arrived and were tossing their coats and hats aside.

'Let's get on with it,' Bill Lamb said. 'We've got rooms here tonight and the sooner I get to mine, the better.'

'Sit down, please,' Dan O'Reilly told Alex. 'You've had a time of it. Let me buy you a drink.'

Alex's indecision showed and it looked as if she would refuse, then thought better of it. 'A glass of Sauvignon Blanc would be lovely,' she said and when Dan looked questioningly at Tony he added, 'I'll have a half of Old Sodbury Mild, please.'

Dan went to the small, frosted glass window that opened into the bar to place their order.

When they were settled with their drinks – both Bill and Dan had beer – Dan leaned back in his chair and stared at the table where he made damp circles with the bottom of his glass.

'What are you thinking?' Tony asked. 'How difficult was it to get Pamela out?'

Alex made a small sound but it was quickly muffled when she drank some wine.

'You are the one with all the questions,' Bill said after a gulp of beer, his eyes skewering Tony.

'Reasonable enough,' Dan said. 'It was a problem but we've got some gifted people. You'd understand we wanted to move the body – or rearrange it – as little as possible, but photography wasn't as easy as we'd like. When this gets out we'll have to make sure people stay away from the crime scene, and it's a big one.'

Tony thought of the two reporters in the other bar but saw no reason to mention them. The detectives must be accustomed to the media crawling all over their patch.

Dan O'Reilly leaned back in his chair. 'Now I want to go over everything that happened as far as you two were concerned, and anything else you think may be useful.'

'Anything you know at all, in other words,' Bill said, but there was nothing antagonistic about the way he asked.

It seemed to take a long time to sketch in all the details of going to see if Tony might have seen a face in the bushes and what happened afterward.

Dan and Bill didn't interrupt once.

'It's going to haunt me forever that I didn't stop that night, regardless of what I did or didn't see, just to make sure,' Tony said.

'Who knows why we make split decisions,' Alex said, and her earnest belief in him showed. It gave him strength. 'My mother thinks she saw Pamela hurrying away from the pub that same night. Mum called out. Whoever it was didn't answer but my mum still feels it was Pamela Gibbon. Mum thinks she's somehow responsible for what happened. How can she be? How can *you* be, Tony?'

'Your mum thought she saw her?' Dan said, making a note.

'Yes.' Alex didn't seem bothered by making the announcement but both Dan and Bill made another entry in their notebooks.

'What did you think of the gear in the tower?' Dan said. He began to work a paper bag out of his trouser pocket. 'Did you think it was cheap?'

He felt around in the bag and produced a sticky sherbet lemon which he popped into a cheek. The rest of them declined his offer of a sweet.

'It's expensive stuff,' Alex said. 'We could probably track it all down to Broadway or Bourton-on-the-Water, or Burford. You can get all that stuff in Burford. Some high-quality products available there – or Chipping Campden.'

'So, not cheap tack a teenager might come up with,' Bill said.

'If the teenager had money – or borrowed the stuff from home, it could be.' Dan moved his sweet from one cheek to the other. Bogie had sidled up to sit beside him and watch his face with a look that meant he was trying to remember if this was friend or foe. Dan ruffled the dog's head.

'Tell me who was up there at the tête-à-tête when we came in?' Dan said. 'Sounded a bit subdued.'

'That's because I just got myself into a stupid corner and told them Pamela was dead,' Alex said. She crossed her legs, and her arms, and rested her chin on her chest. 'I walked right into it.'

'That's unfortunate.' She got the full, uncanny effect of Bill Lamb's innocent, pale-blue stare. 'Did you tell them the location of the body, or—'

'Doesn't matter,' Dan interrupted. 'Time to stir the pot anyway. Did you get anything that might be useful? From their reactions?'

'I didn't say anything other than Pamela's dead. They were all upset. Several of them cried. Harry looked devastated.'

'He walked out,' Tony said. 'Looked like hell.'

'I didn't see anything but shock and sadness,' Alex said.

Dan took a long draft of his beer. 'To be honest, Alex, I have to think of you as a potentially hostile witness. I think you'd be very reluctant to point the finger at anyone in Folly without a lot of evidence. Not that I'm saying I suspect Harry Stroud.'

'I can't believe this is happening again, in this little place. Do you think there's a connection?'

Dan settled his eyes on Alex. He smiled and replied, 'I don't know – yet. But it's definitely something to consider when there is another apparent murder in a place as small as Folly-on-Weir. We have to look for a connection between the last crime and this one.'

Bill studied his glass, took a swig and set it down. 'We felt there were holes in what happened last winter. It all tied up too neatly. But we'd be fools not to look for connections.'

'Connections?' Tony wanted to take the man by the throat. 'Alex nearly died. We were all lucky to get out of that mess alive. And what do you mean by holes? Why would you wait to mention any of this?'

Bill stared at Dan who surprised Tony by avoiding everyone's eyes. 'Let's see how things boil down this time.'

'Are you looking for Pamela's relatives?' Tony asked. 'I don't think I've heard anyone mention them.'

Letting out an irritated sigh, Bill said, 'You don't think looking for relatives is the first thing we do?'

'Of course.'

'They're on that in Gloucester,' Dan said. 'Did you move anything when you went down after the victim?'

'Probably her collar,' Tony said. 'Checking for a pulse. From all the blood I knew she'd taken a while to die but I doubt she moved much. I didn't see any blood on the lowest rungs in the wall. If she'd reached for them, there would have been. There had to be broken bones and probably internal injuries. With any luck, she was unconscious.'

'Post-mortem should tell us all that,' Dan said. 'They're backed up but they'll get to it as soon as they can.'

'Did you see the glass? Some of it was in her face.'

'Reckon we can just go home and leave this case to the good doctor, boss.' Bill looked pleased with himself.

Alex half-stood up. 'Why are you so nasty? It infuriates me when you talk to Tony that way. I thought we got over all that.'

An unexpected shade of rose pink spread over the detective sergeant's cheekbones but he didn't attempt to mollify either of them.

'We know about the glass,' Dan said. He gave Bill a warning glance. 'What did it look like to you, Tony?'

'It was pretty thin. Looked as if it just about exploded. Couldn't have been a big piece to start with – at least, I don't think so. The torch would have been a good size, though – businesslike. I didn't really take a lot of time studying the stuff.'

Someone tapped on the door and Dan called, 'Come in.'

A man, probably in his mid-forties, of average height and thin stepped through the door and closed it. He looked around the four faces staring at him.

'This is a private meeting,' Bill said.

'Someone called me.' He ran a hand over straight brown hair combed straight back. He appeared perfectly comfortable. 'I only live in Cheltenham, so I came right over. I must say I'm impressed with how efficient you people are. You give the public new faith in our police force. Not that I can suppose the officer didn't hit it lucky when she found me. That policewoman on the phone said you were staying here so I thought I'd see if you were still up and about. Detective Chief Inspector O'Reilly and Detective Sergeant Lamb?'

The two detectives grunted.

'I'm Jay Gibbon, Charles Gibbon's son by his first marriage – his only child. Pamela Gibbon was my stepmother.' He crossed himself when he said her name.

NINE

Wind buffeted Tony's Land Rover on the way up the hill to the area at the top where both he and Alex had houses, in a shallow, bowl-shaped valley known as the Dimple. Light rain on the windscreen made the wipers squeal.

'They could hardly wait to get us out of there,' Alex said, laughing a little. 'I don't think Dan cares that much. He sees us as on the side of right, but Bill seems to want to brand us as Potential Enemy Number One.'

Tony pulled a chamois from the cubby and wiped condensation from the inside of the windscreen. 'Don't be fooled. Neither of them wanted us there after Jay Gibbon arrived. Strange none of us knew he even existed. Did you think it was funny for him to rush over like that when he obviously had no bond with Pamela? That's a rhetorical question, I could be wrong but don't you think the man could be sniffing around in case there was a provision for him after Pamela's death?'

'We'll have to wait and see how things line up. Maybe we should ask a few questions about Pamela's relationship with her stepson – who looks older than she did.' She twisted toward him in her seat. 'If there is something significant for him in the will – either left over from Charles Gibbon's estate, or directly from Pamela's will, if she made one. You know what that could mean.'

'True.' Tony glanced at her. 'Sounds like a case for Duggins and Harrison.' He laughed. 'We should probably stay out of it or we'll have our detectives on our backs.'

Settling her head back, Alex considered what had happened so far. 'I know I should be tougher, but this scared me. It feels as if there are things moving where I can't see them. It's hard to explain. I don't think this is going to turn out to be anything simple. Do you?'

He took his time answering. 'Uh uh. I don't, but like you, I have no idea why. We could step back and just answer the questions they're bound to ask.'

'Surely we could. We're going to do that – more or less. I won't suggest we overstep the bounds – not too much, anyway – but this all came our way and we can't pretend we don't have a responsibility to help if we can.'

Tony didn't say anything and when she glanced at him she was surprised to see him grinning. 'What? What's funny?'

'Nothing except I think I read you very well. You'd have shocked me if you'd said anything else. But there's a lot here that could be very dangerous. This is murder. I want it to be the only murder in this case.'

Alex drove her clenched hands into her middle. 'Me too.'

'Then we have to be careful. And I don't want you scared, love. I'll make sure you're OK.'

Oddly, all he had to do was say he was in charge and she felt better – which amused her. 'We'll look out for each other,' she said. 'That's fair.' Women's equality being sabotaged from the inside? Not at all. She was an independent person who happened to enjoy the notion of a big, strong, take-charge bloke . . . occasionally.

They passed the entrance to Lime Tree Lodge, its tall gateposts topped by griffons. Alex had bought the big, plain house when she'd first returned to Folly-on-Weir after her divorce. The grounds had been the most attractive feature but she'd done a lot to make the inside of the house charming.

When she first came back to Folly-on-Weir she also bought Corner Cottage for her mother who had always loved the place. They remained happy with their choices.

'Are you sure it's not too late for me—'

'Absolutely sure,' Tony cut in. 'And you promised. I know you don't break promises.'

She didn't, but . . . 'Tomorrow could be a really difficult day for both of us.'

The Land Rover slowed a little. 'Would you prefer to go home, Alex? I don't want to think I forced you to come with me.'

Alex knew how she felt and why. 'I'm coming with you and you're not forcing me. I think it's about time we worked out a few things about ourselves – or us, I suppose, the two of us. I want to be with you. It just seems funny somehow and I'm a chicken about uncertain situations.'

He settled back to a regular speed and didn't say anything for several moments. 'I think we should have . . . sheesh, we've taken a hell of a long time to give ourselves a chance to see if we're ever going to be more than friends. Not that I'm complaining,' he finished in a hurry. 'And you're anything but a chicken, about anything.'

She leaned across to rest her head on his shoulder. 'I'm not complaining either. But who wants to pass up a chance for – cripes, I don't know where I'm going with this. I'd better shut up. Let's just get home and warm up. You wouldn't think it was almost spring.'

'Sounds good to me, especially the things you say that include both of us. If you don't fall asleep on me, I'd like us to discuss us.'

Alex straightened in her seat again. 'We're both gun-shy, Tony. And why wouldn't we be? What we have is good. I don't want to lose it and . . . I don't know what to say. Except I'd hate to think of losing your friendship.'

'I don't think you could. Not if we make a pact to be friends whatever happens. Let's face it, we've got some pretty strong stuff that binds us together.'

He was right about that but she didn't say so. 'Your house doesn't have a name.' They turned in at the entrance to the most beautiful gardens in the area as far as Alex was concerned. 'Ever thought of coming up with something brilliant?'

'No.' He drove down the driveway and swept around in front of the very large building. 'I still wonder why I bought such a big place. I know I love the grounds but they are a pain to maintain and I can only find time to do just so much myself.'

'I love the gardens,' Alex said. Then she closed her mouth and held her hands tightly together in her lap.

Tony turned off the engine, removed the key and started opening the door. 'You OK?' He leaned in to see her face and put one hand over hers. 'If I didn't know you better, I'd think you were scared of something.'

'This is so calculated,' she muttered. 'We're going to see if . . . if we would be good lovers.' She slapped a hand over her mouth and felt as if she'd cry.

Tony put a hand around her jaw and turned her face toward him. 'I don't know where we're going. I honestly don't. But we won't know until we give the idea a whirl. Could we just get inside with the dogs and follow our instincts?' He held up his other hand. 'I promise not to be pushy. Yes, this is strange, but at least we seem to be able to face it head on. We'll know what comes next and if you walk in and want to go home, I'll take you home.'

Pushing open her door, Alex climbed out into steady rain. She pulled up the hood on her jacket and went to the back of the vehicle. These days Katie and Bogie were happy lying together on a rug.

Tony opened the rear door and the two animals jumped out. They made a rapid run for the front door. Alex glanced at Tony, felt goosebumps rising all over her skin and followed the dogs.

'What do you think I should call the house?' Reaching past her, Tony unlocked the doors and let Katie and Bogie burst inside. He touched the back of Alex's neck and she went after them. 'Honeysuckle Haven? Lots of honeysuckle around here. Lonely Lodge? I'm the only one who comes here, unless I can trick you into coming with me.'

'My Place?' Alex suggested.

'Not quite what I have in mind.' He held her coat until she slipped her arms from the sleeves.

There wasn't an easy answer to that.

She couldn't imagine how this night couldn't turn into either an embarrassing one-night stand or a painful destruction of a great friendship – both spelled a change she didn't want to make.

'Listen to that rain,' Tony said, taking off his own coat. 'The seasons are going backward. We could have a fire, would you like that?'

The dogs had taken off upstairs, where Alex had never been. She liked the cozy room where Tony kept a fire laid. 'I'd love it. And don't forget the brandy.'

The cranberry colored room that had been converted from a breakfast into a sitting room was Alex's favorite place of what she'd seen in the house. She loved the soft old Chinese rug and dark, striped wingback chairs. Waist-high wainscoting was a deeper shade of cranberry than the walls.

Tony put a match to the fire and went into the kitchen.

Alex sat in one of the chairs that felt like a cocoon made exactly to fit her, and kicked off her shoes. Then she wondered if she should put them back on.

'Brandy for Duggins and Harrison,' Tony said, returning to give her a cut crystal glass. 'How's the fire doing?'

Logs crackled and flames curled up the chimney already. 'You're a master fire builder.'

Tony smiled, the firelight doing good work with the distinct bones in his face. He worked each shoe off and left them where they lay. 'Right,' he said and dropped to sit on the carpet, cross-legged, with his back propped against her chair. 'O'Reilly and Lamb didn't say they wanted us again. Did they forget, or do they really not intend to repeat the grilling?'

Alex didn't want to keep thinking about Pamela's death. She reminded herself that this was the wrong time to either laugh hysterically, or cry. 'We'll find out. Probably tomorrow. I think there will be more questions, especially for you.'

'Because of the little pieces of glass? You're probably right. They looked clean. Not like they'd been down there for long to get covered with dirt and dust.' Tony sniffed at his brandy and took a drink. 'All right, huh?'

'Very all right.' Heat from the first sip of a brandy was one of her favorite things.

'Someone planned out what was done to Pamela. The police have a lot of clues to check out and it won't hurt having this stepson to occupy them for a while.'

'You sound as if you don't want them bothering us.'

'I don't, love. I want them to stay far away. I'm a man who prefers to follow what interests me without interference.'

'I like this brandy.' Feeling jumpy, she drank again. 'Where do those four-legged kids of ours go when they sneak off upstairs?'

Tony coughed and shifted to rest his head against her thigh. 'To bed. At least that's what I assume. They probably like mine – it's got the best mattress. I bet they're flaked out on my comforter hoping we don't disturb them too soon.'

There was no point pretending she didn't know how she was reacting. Even to the sensation of his head against her leg. So where and how did they go from here? 'Being comfortable with someone you trust is appealing,' she said. Now that was subtle.

'Mmm.'

He put his glass on the hearth and settled back against her.

To Alex his breathing sounded regular – like a man drifting asleep. If he wasn't already asleep.

Damn him! She wasn't going to sleep. The brandy was good and she swallowed some more. Would it be so bad to drift off like this, comfortable, confident in the rightness of just being together?

Tears welled in her eyes and she clamped her eyes shut. Women were always silly. They wanted things tidy, put away in drawers, settled.

His head grew heavier and her tears went away. This was good.

Tomorrow all hell would break loose again and it would be back to murder and the horrors attached to it. For now, being together and relaxed should be enough.

Alex touched his head.

Tony didn't move.

She ran her fingers through his hair, stroked it, and bent to place a cautious kiss on the windswept curls. He smelled of pine and cedar and the outdoors. Under her lips, his hair was alive.

Alex smiled against his temple, kissed him there and bent over to cradle him more comfortably.

Dark blue eyes snapped wide open, as if he had been lying in wait. She felt more than saw his smile. And she felt his arm snake up around her neck, his other arm take her weight as he swung her around him until she landed on the rug, resting against his knees, his face inches from hers.

And then not even air separated their mouths.

TEN

The dogs capered and dashed around one another like puppies. They hadn't been pleased when Tony moved them from his to another bedroom after they had settled in for a long nap, but neither had they done anything to disturb a memorable night afterward.

Squinting against the rain, he trudged across the empty, wet field next to his house, looking up at his bedroom window as he went. Why would he expect to see anything? If he'd had any hopes of seeing Alex there waving at him, he was an ass. OK, so he was an ass.

The Land Rover was still in the driveway and she wouldn't leave on foot or without Bogie. That was a hopeful sign. Not that Alex was the type to run from a potentially awkward encounter.

He could play the night's scenes over and over in his head with no effort. He'd been doing that since Katie woke him up by licking the foot he'd carelessly left trailing from beneath the covers. In truth a good deal of both Alex and his own naked bodies trailed from the twisted sheets but he'd covered her carefully before leaving with the dogs before eight.

Covering her was a shame. She looked as lovely as he'd expected, just as she was – and if the dogs hadn't been nipping at him, he would probably have woken Alex and started saying a lot of things he might regret later.

Or he might not . . . regret anything at all that he might say . . .

The rain hadn't stopped. In fact it grew ever heavier. Katie and Bogie galloped for the back door where Tony had dropped a couple of large towels in the porch as they left.

Both dogs panted and flipped this way and that as he did his best to dry them off. When they started a wild shaking of fur, he covered his face.

For once he'd remembered to lock the door as he went out. The sounds and warmth that met him in the kitchen let him know that rather than trying to leave, Alex was making breakfast.

Breathing wasn't so easy.

'Were they good dogs?' she asked as if this was part of a daily ritual. 'Hang up your things and have coffee.'

He didn't usually have difficulty coming up with an answer. This wasn't a usual time. He shed his coat, took a towel to his wet hair and rubbed hard, and hopped back and forth taking off his boots.

Alex flitted about the kitchen as if she had used it many times, rather than this being her first venture into his culinary quarters. Coffee bubbled, mugs with hot water inside to warm them sat beside the carafe and she beat eggs in a bowl. 'Do you take cream?'

'I think you know I do,' he said, raking his hair away from his face. 'Just like you.'

She tossed out water from the mugs, poured coffee and added cream. 'Mmm. Smells wonderful. I'm making scrambled eggs. You don't have any bacon but I couldn't resist the Cotswold Farmers sausages – unless you'd rather have something else.'

He'd rather have her, but it probably wasn't a wise move to say so. 'That'll be great but you don't have to cook for me. I'm used to doing it myself. I could cook for you.'

'Shut up and sit down, dopey. I like to feel domesticated now and then. Something bothered me while you were gone. Do you believe the police could have found Jay Gibbon so quickly? He said they called him.'

'They could have.'

'But it would have happened so fast. I don't know, but I'd like to find out if he was the one who called in, not the other way around. And if so, how did he know about Pamela's death? It wasn't in any papers yet, was it? How could it be? Hugh would have said if the reporters at the Dog got anything useful from Kev Winslet. I'm not suggesting they'd say no to a juicy piece of information but Kev couldn't have known the police were looking for relatives, not for sure.'

'I don't know. It could have been on TV or the radio.'

Alex said, 'I'm sure we would have heard about it by now, but not last night when supposedly no one knew anything. I'd like to ask the dynamic duo about that.'

'Let's keep it to ourselves and see how it works out.'

'You really do mean Duggins and Harrison are on the job, don't you? That surprises me.' She gave him his coffee and went back to beating the eggs. She dropped bread into the toaster and rolled fat sausages in a pan. 'I've been thinking of trying to construct our own chart. You know, a wheel or something on a big piece of paper. We could add to it as we come up with more things.'

'Like a story wheel,' he said.

She nodded, yes. 'Do you like mustard with your sausages? You've got Coleman's. Or brown sauce – there's HP, and some catsup.'

'Just Coleman's, thanks.'

'Marmalade with your toast?'

'No thanks. Let's not talk about all that stuff now,' he said, feeling a little heat in his neck. 'So, how do you think it worked. Were we good?'

'What?' She was pink and not from cooking.

'You said we were going to find out whether or not we were good lovers. When we were on our way here you said that. So, what do you think?'

'I think you're amazing.'

'Thank you.'

She barely stopped herself from pouring the eggs on the stove rather than into the pan. The sausages spat madly and the toast, still half-cooked, flew out of the toaster.

He did feel both sheepish and a bit of a smart mouth. 'I should have told you about the toaster. You have to hold the button down with one hand, then keep the other over the top so the bread doesn't fly away. You were amazing, too, Alex. I didn't want it to stop – ever. Well, breaks to catch your breath are necessary, but . . .'

Staring at him over her shoulder, Alex's eyes warned him to stop talking.

'Sorry,' he muttered. 'I'm rusty at . . . just a bit rusty.'

'To clarify, I think it's amazing for you to bring up a careless comment I made hours ago. I was embarrassed and confused.' The toast went back in the toaster, she risked taking a hand away to stir the eggs and gave the sausages a quick turn.

'Is that why you're still babbling about anything but the obvious? Oh, God! Sorry.'

Keeping one finger on the toaster button, she gave the eggs another good stir and took the sausages off the heat. At least she didn't bang things when she was mad – or worse yet, throw something.

He thought she was seething. Of course she was seething.

What an idiot he was. 'Look, love, I'm messing everything up. Being with you was wonderful.'

Clattering of dishes and utensils filled up what would be silence – except for the battering rain on the windows. Both dogs had slunk out of the kitchen. They didn't need banging pots to sense tension.

Alex piled toast on a plate, put it on the table with some butter, served the rest of the food and walked around the table. She put her own dish down next to Tony's place but continued to hold his in her right hand. 'It's good to know I'm not the only one who feels as if she's just skydived and wonders if the shoot will open.'

The plate settled in front of him and Alex kissed him lightly on the forehead.

'Wait,' he said when she started to sit down. He got up, wrapped her tightly enough in his arms to make her gasp for breath, and kissed her, hard, long and with a sensation he was tipping over an edge he must back away from, at least for now. And he paused before kissing her again.

They both pushed away, but reluctantly, and sat down.

'Eat,' Alex said in a voice that cracked. 'I'm glad. That's all I want to say for now.'

'But—'

'I've got an idea.'

'Beginner's luck.' He couldn't seem to stop his inane comebacks.

She ignored him. 'If anyone will be picking up chatter on the rumor mill it'll be Harriet and Mary. I'd like to go and see them after you drop me off. I think they've got some books for me to look at anyway.'

'This is good,' Tony said. He had become used to fending for himself. 'Funny how much better food tastes when it's cooked for you.'

'Right. And if it's well cooked it doesn't hurt.'

'I should say so! That's what I meant really. I'd like to come with you to Leaves of Comfort, if you don't mind. Radhika will be in by now. I'll call and make sure there aren't any emergencies. She's doing the office stuff today and I'm not due up at the Derwinters until late this afternoon. If your scruffy fur boy's having any problems, I'll have to go check him out.'

Leaves of Comfort was the Burke's tea and book shop. The name infuriated Harriet.

Alex passed Tony her phone. 'Check on him now, please. And he's not scruffy. You'll see, he'll be beautiful.'

'You have to find him a home.' His own phone was in his pocket but he decided against pulling it out.

Her scowl was unnerving. 'I know that. You don't have to keep on about it. I'll get those posters up around Folly.'

A fresh burst of wind and rain thrashed a branch against the windows. They both glanced around. 'This is one mean year for weather,' he said and dialed his clinic number.

'Radhika still sounds upset,' he said after he ended the call. 'She didn't mention Pamela but I think she'd been crying again. All clear at the clinic. Tomorrow is a clinic day and it'll be busy. And our patient is doing very well. He's nosing around the cottage – a bit wobbly still, but mending fast. He's eaten, probably more than he should, and doesn't seem interested in trying to get outside. Soon he can go home.'

'Poor boy, all he wants is someone to love him and a safe, warm home where he'll get fed.'

'Like Lime Tree Lodge?' he said with a grin.

'No! Of course not. I can't manage another animal but I will find someone for him.'

Her phone rang and he handed it over. She looked at the read out and raised her eyebrows. 'Good morning, Harriet and Mary,' Alex said as if both women were on the phone. 'Um, no, it isn't good afternoon yet. And it won't be today. What can I do for you?'

She put a hand over the mouthpiece and said, 'Speak of the devil.'

'Yes, Harriet, my car is still at the Black Dog, but how do you know that?' Her brow furrowed but she looked amused and took a moment for a mouthful of what had to be cold coffee. Tony got up to reheat the pot.

'Of course not,' Alex said. 'I wouldn't dream of asking you for names but you can tell me later. I'm, er, Tony and I are coming to see you if that's all right.'

A long pause followed. 'Really? People do like to gossip, don't they? Looking forward to seeing you. Bye.'

'I'll top you up with some hot coffee,' Tony said, filling her mug. 'What's got you looking so thoughtful?'

'Mostly trying to figure out how I feel about being the object of . . . um, speculation, will do. My Land Rover was at the Dog all night but I wasn't. You and I were seen leaving together. The gossip mongers have been very busy.'

'I don't know about you,' Tony said, pouring more coffee for himself, 'but I'm not going to their place to be grilled about our private business.'

'They may aim a few smug and knowing smiles in our direction, but evidently it's Vivian Seabrook they want to talk about. Word is that she hasn't been seen or heard from in Folly since last night after she left the Dog. She's not at home and she didn't show up at the Derwinters for work. They said this is the first time she's missed a day.'

ELEVEN

Behind two royal blue front doors, one originally the entrance to a single row cottage on Pond Street, the other to the cottage next door, the Burke sisters' Leaves of Comfort waited, warm, fragrant and ready to serve the best afternoon teas for miles around. Or it would be in a couple of hours.

Tony opened the car door for Alex and she hopped out. They'd dropped the two dogs at Corner Cottage with Lily. Prepared for questions, Alex had been grateful when her mum took the animals in with nothing more than a smile and a 'See you later. We'll probably be across the road.' She meant she would take the dogs to the pub when she went to work.

What could possibly make a woman feel more tightly strung than she already did, Alex wondered. The past couple of days came and went from her mind in vivid bursts. And mixed up feelings followed in their wake.

'Alex?'

She started and said, 'Yes?' He must have said something she didn't hear. 'I was miles away.'

'I saw that. We're being watched. Which means they're waiting for us. Are you certain we're not in for a grilling ourselves?'

'That's the routine,' Alex said, waving at Harriet in the window of their upstairs sitting room. 'But no, I'm not sure they aren't just popping to find out something about us. We're old enough to manage that without having nervous breakdowns.'

The window opened a crack. 'Door's open. Come on up. Tea ready when you are. Battenberg and Eccles freshly delivered. And some of your Bourbon biscuits, Tony.'

'Thank you,' Alex and Tony called back together.

'Bag of books at the bottom of the stairs. Take them or leave them. Up to you.' Harriet snickered as she shut the window again.

'That had better be as snide as it gets,' Tony said, although he couldn't suppress a grin.

Inside, the two cottages had been knocked into one. The small kitchen was only intended for making hot tea and coffee and heating pies or occasionally soup. A great array of cakes and pastries was delivered fresh from George's Bakery each day.

Decorated with a crocheted antimacassar that dipped to many points, a shelf ran around the walls to hold books, mostly used, hand-knitted items, teapots complete with cozies used as occasional bookends, knitted animals and dolls, and myriad small china or glass ornaments. Every table was different, antique and for sale, as were the tablecloths made by local needle workers. The place did a brisk business every day from three to six although appointments could be made to view items on sale at other times.

'What's keeping you,' Mary called down. 'Oliver's getting impatient.'

Their rangy tabby cat didn't give a fig for anyone but the sisters. 'Coming,' Alex said and picked up the promised bag of books before climbing the stairs with Tony behind her.

As usual, Mary sat in an armchair facing the window. All of the overstuffed furniture, mostly in shades of deep pink or red, was covered with slightly faded velvet. The couch sagged in each of its three possible seats. A fire brightened the room.

'Sit down,' Mary said. 'Tea's on its way.' She was looking the wrong way to see her younger sister roll her eyes while carrying a teapot in one hand and dangling a tiered cake plate by its top ring with the other.

Harriet set her burdens on a much polished tea trolley and started pouring milk into the bottoms of cups. 'This is as pleasant as our meeting is likely to get,' she said, ignoring the cat, Oliver, who had appeared from deep in the fireplace nook when he heard the approach of potential nibbles.

Alex looked at Tony who shook his head, she presumed because he thought it best to let Harriet continue without prompting.

Tea was passed around, cakes and biscuits selected for tiny plates to balance precariously on the knee.

'Now,' Mary said. 'How much do you know?'

'About what?' Tony was quick to respond.

Let him think he was in charge. She knew how to pick her battles.

'We've got a murderer on the loose again.'

'We certainly do.' Oliver had arrived to swish around Tony's legs. Despite much tutting, he gave the cat a crumb.

'Now Vivian Seabrook's gone.' Harriet lined up tiny morsels of Eccles cake along the side of her plate. No mystery about who those were intended for.

'Who came up with this brilliant deduction?' Alex said. Her stomach had already knotted despite skepticism at the announcement.

Mary took off her thick glasses and polished them with a lace-edged handkerchief. 'We think it's starting all over again. We even wonder if there's some connection to the other murders.'

'Not possible.' Tony finished his cake and picked up a biscuit. He faced them all. 'If anyone goes off in that direction it'll only muddy the waters.'

'That's what I said.' Harriet didn't look at her sister. 'I said the only disturbing thing – apart from the obvious – is that here we are again with people dropping like flies around Folly.'

'One person.' Alex put her teacup and uneaten cake aside. 'So why do you think Vivian's missing?'

'She isn't around here, that's all.' Mary raised her shoulders in a decidedly huffy way.

'What's being done to find her?'

'Well,' Mary said. 'That's the other thing. Winifred . . . someone said the police won't take any interest at all. They're ignoring the whole thing.'

Sighing hugely, Harriet went to the window and looked toward St Aldwyn's Church. 'They aren't ignoring it. They're trying to keep their movements a secret.

They probably have Vivian themselves. There's a rumor she was seen in the back of one of those horrid police cars being driven out of Folly.'

'She could have been arrested,' Mary added with gusto.

'Why didn't you say that first?' Tony's words hung for a long time.

TWELVE

They had taken over the snug at the Black Dog again, although since they couldn't kid themselves they were off duty, and it was too late for lunch, Dan O'Reilly and Bill Lamb made do with coffee.

'I could kill a beer,' Bill said. 'How long d'you think it'll be before someone thinks up an excuse to come in here?'

'Any time now, we can hope.' Dan had let the two resident dogs in from their spot by the bar fire. 'I'd rather be out there but we've got more privacy here. If someone wants to talk to us, they'll be more likely to approach us in here. Anyway, anything's better than that parky parish hall. I'd hoped never to see the inside of the place again. I keep expecting rain to come through the roof. Can't even get any peace from the local plods. In and out and arguing about who's on break.'

'If it wasn't cold and wet all over the country, I'd say this place was cursed with foul weather.' Picking up his mug, Bill drank his cooling coffee morosely. 'You don't think we're looking at any connection to the bother earlier in the winter, do you?'

They had closed the hatch to the bar but Dan still glanced at it. Bogie had managed to maneuver himself onto the detective's lap but that suited Dan. If he ever had a home he could really call a home, with a garden – and someone there to share things with again – he'd have a dog.

'I'm not ruling anything out, but I'd be lying if I didn't admit the old saying that lightning doesn't strike twice, is starting to ring hollow. I hope Tony Harrison gets our message soon. I'd like to see him show up. I do have some questions for him.'

'Bloody hell, I could *kill* a beer.'

With a sigh, Dan said, 'You already told me that.'

'Yeah, sorry. Do you think Vivian Seabrook could have done it?'

'No, not really,' Dan said, 'but we had reason enough to take her in and she could shake someone else loose.'

'Like Harry Stroud?'

'Careful what you say. Seems safe enough in here, but you can't be sure.'

Bill pushed his coffee aside. 'If there's any question, I'm off duty boss, right?'

Dan shrugged and Bill went to raise the stained-glass hatch and get himself a pint of Double Donn. He raised a brow at his guv'nor who shook his head.

When Bill returned, he said, 'Did we miss something the first time around? Were Tony and Alex deeper in than we thought – I don't mean they did the killings, we know all about that, but could they have known more than we ever realized. They have a way of showing up at crime sites.'

What he couldn't say, Dan thought, was that he liked, more than liked, Alex Duggins too much to even consider she'd been involved in a crime. 'Nope. Reckon not. But I don't think we can afford to forget the story about Tony Harrison and his wife. I checked with the Aussies. They don't have any more definite information about the wife's death than they did last time.'

Bill looked pensive, which was unusual.

'What is it?' Dan said.

'This is one of those times when I wish we were more of a mind to use a shrink. How would a man pull off the death of his wife and come back here smelling like a rose? How would he convince everyone he was innocent?'

'He was found innocent in Australia, Bill. I don't think we can believe what happened there is salient to what's happening here. This time God knows what the motive is – but we'll find it. And it's going to be different from the first time around. That was all about hiding another crime, an old one.'

'How do you know this isn't the same?'

'Think about it.' He skewered his sergeant with a stare. 'As far as we know the dead woman doesn't have any significant history in the area. She's an incomer. Know what that makes me think?'

A long quaff of his beer and Bill narrowed his eyes in question.

'This one's going to be tougher,' Dan said. 'No obvious local drama going on. Finding the events that led to this killing will take patience and sharp ears. I've got a feeling this killer thinks he's got us by the short hairs.'

Bill grunted and shrugged. 'He probably does – or she. We haven't got anywhere. The house-to-house seems to be taking forever considering there aren't that many houses. Let's hope everyone doesn't stick together and not tell us if they know something.'

'I can't see them trying to hide this.' Bill's beer was starting to look good to him and he didn't even like the stuff much. 'You can be pretty sure the tea and biscuits at every house are responsible for a lot of the time the PCs are taking.'

He glanced up from his cold coffee to see Tony Harrison looking at him around the door. 'You called?' Tony said. 'We heard you were here. Hope you don't mind us interrupting your meeting. It's all over Folly that you've got Vivian Seabrook under arrest. Does that mean she's a suspect?'

'Either get in here or get out,' Bill said. 'Every busybody in the place is trying to pick up bits of gossip. Gossip can ruin an investigation.'

Tony stood back to let Alex in. Pale and obviously anxious, she slipped into the snug and sat down. Bogie promptly abandoned Dan's lap for hers and she snuggled him close. Dan studied her and saw all the signs of extreme tension, not that he was surprised.

'Ms Seabrook is helping us—'

'Helping you with your investigations,' Tony finished for Bill who shied a beer mat across the little room at him.

'Right,' Dan said. 'We hoped you'd get our message. Although Alex doesn't really need to be here for what we'd like to talk about.'

'I want to stay with Tony.' Her voice was firm now, and the way she looked at the vet suggested she'd have to be thrown out if they wanted to talk to Tony alone.

Tony said nothing but Dan sighed.

'I was there the whole time,' she added. 'I might remember some little thing he forgets. It's hard to remember everything when you've been in such a horrible situation. I'm getting a Bitter Lemon, what will the rest of you have?'

Her take-charge manner made Dan smile. The woman had chutzpah, even under pressure. 'Sit where you are,' he said. 'I'll get it. What'll it be, Tony?'

'What have you got, Bill?' That kind of cheerful approach didn't make it easy for Bill to be churlish. 'Double Donn and it's good,' he said.

'A half for me,' Tony said, settling himself in another chair. His dog stood with her head on his knee and adoring brown eyes watching his face.

'What made you decide to take Vivian in?'

Bill could deal with that, Dan decided.

'That's privileged information. I doubt you'd be pleased if we discussed your business with anyone who asked.'

'You can't blame me for trying.'

'I frickin' well can,' Bill sputtered on a swallow of his beer. 'We had this problem with you two before. You don't see yourselves as Joe Public. You're special. Well, you can forget that. We'll do the questioning.'

Tony's pleasant smile only deepened Bill's frown.

Dan delivered the drinks, including a fresh coffee for himself. 'Why didn't you stop if you thought you saw someone crouching beside the road at night? Didn't it occur to you that whoever it was might have been in trouble?'

'I think it would be more useful to find out if that was Pamela rather than asking for a bunch of hypothetical answers.' Tony didn't sound as relaxed as he looked.

In the following silence, voices reached them from the bar. As it got a bit later, more customers were arriving. Lily Duggins must be guarding the snug door to keep anyone from wandering in.

'What you think,' Dan said to Tony, 'may be true, but I'll have your hypothetical answers just the same. And do your best to make them useful.'

Alex responded to a tap on the hatch window and took two plates of sandwiches from Hugh. 'Thought you might all have a use for these,' he said and closed the window again.

'Thank you,' Dan said. They might have to go back to the parish hall. This could get a bit too cozy. He winced at the thought of the draughty old hall with its sputtering radiators reeking of cooked dust.

'Cheese and tomato,' Bill said, having taken a huge bite of a sandwich. 'My favorite food.'

'I should have stopped,' Tony said. 'Of course I should. But instead of trying to signal me, the person crouched lower. I thought he or she was hiding and I didn't want to interfere. I was wrong. That was a bad call.'

'You might have saved a life if you had stopped.' It was Bill's way to call a spade a shovel and he went for the kill every time. He chomped steadily through his sandwich.

'There's no reason to suggest that,' Alex said. 'It isn't fair.'

'Is there any way to find out who it was?' Tony said. He looked knackered.

Another rap, this one on the door, brought a sigh from him. 'Come in,' he said and the pathologist, Molly Lewis, joined them. Her greetings were brief and she sat at the table, put a briefcase on the floor.

'I've got some interesting bits,' she said, reaching into her brief-case and passing a sheet of paper to Dan. 'This falls into your bailiwick.'

'Should we leave?' Tony said, starting to rise.

'Mm, no,' Dan told him, realizing he was famished and reaching for a sandwich himself. 'Who knows if you can help us with this?'

Alex took a sandwich. They all took it in turns to spread some pickle relish inside the bread, including Molly.

'Now can we concentrate?' Dan said. 'So the glass wasn't there very long?'

'No.' Molly slid photographs from her briefcase and glanced at Tony and Alex, then, with question, at Dan. 'And it was from a small piece in the first place.'

'Tony's going to have to help us out with this,' he said. 'At least he's going to have to give us some honest answers. Let's see those.'

The stark pictures left nothing to the imagination. Pamela Gibbon's deeply discolored face had a number of short, mostly curved cuts. Caked blood remained, although in all but two photos, the glass had been removed.

He passed the photos around and didn't feel good about Alex's intake of breath. But what he needed were some leads, and treading lightly on people's feelings wouldn't get him those. And she'd insisted on staying although he had given her an opportunity to leave.

'What do these tell us, doctor?' Tony asked Molly. 'The wounds bled so Pamela wasn't dead when she landed on the glass?'

'We got an early break,' Molly said in her dry, Oxford accent. 'The glass is from a flashlight. Must have broken before she fell.'

'Pamela's flashlight?' Alex said. 'She dropped it?'

Dan held up a hand. 'Molly, what about fingerprints? Any on the glass?'

She shook her head. 'But plenty on the rungs of the ladder. All Pamela Gibbon's and Tony Harrison's, apart from some old smudges.'

'Tony went down to see if he could help,' Alex said at once.

'But I couldn't.' Tony drained his glass and went to get another beer, a pint this time. Back in his chair, he leaned forward, resting his forearms on the table. 'You know why I was down there and it had nothing to do with how Pamela died. If you're going in that direction, you're wasting good time.'

Dr Lewis look a plastic evidence bag out and put it on the table. 'That was in the victim's pocket.'

They all leaned closer to see a steel encased torch. The lens was still intact.

'So the glass was from another torch,' Bill said. 'Was it there?'

Molly shook her head. 'No. And it makes sense to assume that someone went down and retrieved it.'

'So where are their fingerprints?' Alex said. *Damn her loose lips.*

THIRTEEN

At ten the following morning, after spending the night with her mother at Corner Cottage, Alex walked over to Tony's surgery and found he was already seeing patients.

Radhika put her in a tiny sitting room behind the area where owners waited with their pets.

'This is a horrible time,' Alex said.

'Yes.' Radhika didn't smile. 'I can't be gone more than minutes. When I hear Tony coming out, I'll have to get back. I'll let him know you're here. Tell me what's going on. You talked to the police at the Dog yesterday. Did they tell you anything?'

Nothing was missed by the sharp-eyed people in Folly. 'I did talk to them.' Every word spoken, every move was as clear as if she watched it all over again on a screen. 'Pamela died because she fell down that shaft and smashed her head.' The photos were something she would never forget.

'I heard the grate was back over the top.'

'Radhika, I shouldn't talk about it. I was told to be quiet.'

The beautiful woman inclined her head in acceptance but her eyes were deeply sad.

'You can't repeat anything I say,' Alex said. 'The grate was back over the hole. I don't know for certain what that means but I can guess. So can you. They don't seem to have any real leads although they're starting to push at Tony which infuriates me. He couldn't possibly have had anything to do with it but they're pushing him because they don't know what else to do.'

'It's wrong,' Radhika said. 'So wrong. Also, they took Vivian into a police station. Why did they do that?'

'I honestly don't know. I hope we'll find out today. They can't keep her for long without charging her. That's the kind of stuff I don't really understand.'

'I don't know what to think. How can we know who did this? Vivian could not have done it? Such foolishness. They were fine friends. Vivian is kind.'

Alex shook her head. She just didn't know.

'That's Dr T coming out,' Radhika said and hurried from the room.

Only minutes passed before Tony came in and shut the door behind him.

'You look awful,' she said. 'Didn't you sleep?'

He shook his head, no.

'Why didn't you call me? We could have talked.'

'I didn't want to wake you up.' He looked away. 'But I wanted you with me. I should have made more of asking you to come.'

'We were both tired,' Alex said. She went to take his arm and get him to sit down but he pulled her against him and just stood there, holding her tight, his chin on top of her head. She kissed his neck.

'I can't get it out of my head, Alex. Bill Lamb said I might have saved a life if I'd stopped and I might have. I might have stopped her from going through the fear and the pain – and there was a lot of both.'

'I know. If it was Pamela by the road, and she didn't want to be seen because she was meeting someone . . .'

'We don't know she *was* on her way to meet someone.'

'Darn it, Tony.' She moved away from him. 'You didn't kill Pamela Gibbon. And if she was the one hiding in the bushes then she didn't want to be found.'

He sat down abruptly and dropped his hands between his knees.

'You said we could work as a team. I've accepted the offer so pull yourself together. Bill Lamb hates you. Don't ask me why. He doesn't think much of me either. So what? You and I know what happened the night we went up there and now we're going to work on finding out who did that ghastly thing and why. The motive has to be brought out. But if you walk around looking as if you're guilty of something, it won't help us much, will it?'

Smacking his hands down on the arms of the chintz chair, Tony pushed to his feet. He took her by the back of the neck and kissed her – hard. 'You're in charge, Ms Duggins, but only until I can look at this with a clear head.' He narrowed his eyes. 'And that's going to happen fast. I've got every right to ask how many sets of my fingerprints they found. By my count it would have to show I went down and up that ladder at least twice. When . . . to get back the torch they now say is missing, and then when I went down while we were up there together. I only went down once. And there's no reason why I would kill Pamela.'

'Great. Your patients are making a racket in there.'

Tony grinned at her. 'See you later.' He stopped on the way to the door and turned back. 'I forgot I had some early visitors. Harriet came over in a taxi.'

'What's wrong with Oliver?'

'They came to adopt—' he frowned and took an index card from the pocket of his white coat – 'Maxwell Aloysius Brady. Otherwise known as the scruffy, one-eyed orange cat you helped me put back together.'

How could she object? She'd already insisted she couldn't take another pet. Her eyes stung but she concentrated on the backs of her hands. 'I hope Oliver isn't too put out.'

'We'll see,' Tony said, his hand on the door. 'Any ideas on what we do next?'

'Yes, I'll tell you about it later. You'd better get going.'

'You're not planning to do something without telling me first, are you?'

'That's something else we should discuss later, Tony. I try not to do anything stupid, but I don't ask permission for whatever I decide to do.'

FOURTEEN

The Vines, home to the Stroud family for three generations, stood in large grounds at the edge of Folly-on-Weir. A short approach from the main road took visitors to iron front gates that rose in a curve between mellow, honey-colored stone gateposts. Those passing on the road to or from Underhill, the small village just over a ridge that kept it's less than splendid buildings out of sight of Folly, could see only the chimneys and multi-angled stone roofs of the Stroud mansion.

Once the afternoon crowd at the Black Dog had dwindled and she'd taken care of overseeing some additional orders put in by the kitchen, walking seemed the best means for Alex to get to The Vines. That way she might get in with little fuss through a small, green pedestrian door set in the wall between one gatepost and an immaculately clipped hedge. Green iron fencing topped with unfriendly-looking spikes surrounded the entire expanse of the estate.

If she had driven she would have had to use the intercom and ask if she could pass the gates. That idea didn't daunt her, but the possibility of being turned away by a disembodied voice certainly did.

As a small girl she had peeked through those gates, but she'd never been invited inside, not even when she and Harry were on friendly terms as teenagers.

The walk from the Dog had done her good. She'd shaken off the unsettling feelings her encounter with Tony had left behind. Yes, she'd been overly snippy, but some things needed to be understood, the sooner the better.

Through the wide open door beside the gates, Alex could see a large landscaper's lorry, its tailgate down and a riding lawn mower already loaded. Two men stacked overflowing rubbish bins and tools aboard. They nodded when they saw her.

Gravel crunched like exploding glass as she walked to the front door. This was a beautiful house made of yellow Cotswold stone that had only improved from years of wear in the often harsh weather.

This was why Harry went out of his way to please his parents. With an older brother who had followed in the major's footsteps and become an army officer, Harry couldn't afford to tick off his parents, not if he wanted a share of all this when the older generation popped their clogs.

She climbed well-worn front steps and stood, staring at the door and wavering about going ahead with her hasty plan. If he knew what she was doing, Tony would be furious, but it was better for her to do this alone, not that she was too hopeful of finding Harry at home. The silver Maserati wasn't around and its owner might be in London, but the major was at the Dog and that might mean there would be a chance to talk to Mrs Stroud alone. Alex didn't know the woman and rarely saw her unless she was driving through Folly in an indigo-colored Morgan Plus Four with a mohair roof, a large hat shielding her face. The vehicle didn't fit the woman who seemed a quiet soul and might not be as prickly as the rest of her family, which could be useful.

Alex gave one clanging rap with an overlarge but plain brass knocker. Immediately she stepped a respectful distance away from the front door. She might have grown up the daughter of a single mother who lived in a dowdy but immaculate Underhill cottage, but Lily had been a stickler for good manners.

Sonorous barks met her knock. It took minutes longer for the door to be opened by a blond and permed woman with an apron over her brown jumper and skirt. Gladys something from Underhill. Alex recognized her. She came into the Black Dog with her husband. Gladys Lymer, that was it, and her husband was Frank.

An elderly golden Lab fussed forward to sniff Alex and she rubbed his velvety head.

The two women smiled at one another. 'Hello, Alex,' Gladys said. 'What a surprise.' She grimaced at the sound of the lorry engine roaring to life and waited for it to drive away. The gates swung closed again.

'Yes. I've never been here before.' It took her years to realize why Harry never invited her home. 'I was hoping to talk to Harry, or one of his parents.' Poor bastard children of questionable means wouldn't have been welcomed by his family.

'Come in.' Gladys waved her inside. 'Harry lives in the back wing but I know he's out. Mrs Stroud's in the conservatory. She'll be glad of the company. A visitor is a rare thing. Come on, Batman. Let's find your mum.'

'Batman?' Alex said. 'Is there a Superman, too?'

'Don't tempt me,' Gladys chuckled. 'The major remembers his

army days fondly. I'm thinking he had a batman then, too. I expect he wishes he still did, but this old fellow has to do.'

'Quite a house,' Alex said, following Gladys with Batman at her side. Doors stood open to rooms furnished with antiques, and these appeared to be the real thing. Soft old rugs in muted colors broke up acres of grey slate-tiled floors. The latter rang under the heels of Alex's shoes.

The deeper they went into the house, the more overpowering a slightly sick sensation became. Her brow felt cold and slick. She should have thought this through more. Her idea had been to surprise Harry, although she had known she was more likely to talk to Mrs Stroud – or no one at all. She had thought she knew what to say, what to ask, but now she wasn't so sure.

And the flip of her stomach meant she had not quite got over being *persona non grata* when she was a child.

'Through here,' Gladys said, leading the way into a smaller conservatory than Alex had expected. She doubted it could be more stunning, regardless of size. A misting system kept the air moist and smelling of peat and fertilizers and floral fragrance. There was plenty of color where hothouse blooms thrived happily among ferns and plants Alex didn't recognize.

'You've got a visitor, Mrs S,' Gladys announced. 'Alex Duggins from the Black Dog.'

An unexpectedly strong voice said, 'Good heavens. A visitor, you say?' Just like that.

Alex cringed. She should have thought to remind Gladys to let Mrs Stroud know Alex was asking to see her, before bringing her back. 'Good afternoon,' she said, following the voice to shelves where peat seed pots were packed tightly together. 'It's beautiful out here. Forgive me for dropping in unannounced. I was hoping to have a word with Harry.'

Of medium height, slim in a wiry way, Mrs Stroud straightened up and faced her. Brown curly hair, cut short, suited her oval face well enough. Her eyes were hazel and sharp, made more arresting by shadow and a liberal coat of mascara. She also wore bright red lipstick which was all puzzling since Alex had only seen the woman in the street, and at a distance, but she had no recollection of noticing heavy make-up.

'I didn't think you were a friend of Harry's,' she said. 'He's not in but he lives upstairs over there. Above the garages. We kept horses there, too, when the boys were young.' With the point of a trowel aimed upward through the glass dome of the conservatory, she indicated a wing that looked as if it might be older than the rest of the house.

At a little past four, the light was already going out of the day. The wind lashed through tall trees. Alex wanted to leave.

'How silly of me,' she said. Her mouth and throat were dry. 'We've known each other since we were children. Folly is a small place so I doubt there are many strangers. But I should have expected him to be in the City at this time.'

'He isn't. I'm Venetia, by the way. Would you like tea?'

'No, thank you.'

'In that case you can take Bat off and get him fed, then go on home,' Venetia told Gladys. 'We'll be quite happy out here.'

As soon as Gladys had left, Venetia peeled off gardening gloves, revealing well-manicured hands, and threw them and a trowel on a bench. 'Did the police send you?' she said without looking at Alex. 'If they did, speak up and tell me why.' This time she stared into Alex's face.

If the unflinching stare was meant to intimidate, it did its job. A watery sensation assailed Alex's legs. 'Why would you think the police sent me? They don't have civilians run errands for them, do they?'

'You're pretty close with the detectives, aren't you? That's what I heard. Do you think Harry had anything to do with that woman's death? He didn't, you know, even if they have sent Vivian Seabrook home.'

'I didn't know Vivian was back, or not back, come to that. And I'm not close with any detectives.'

'That's not what the major said.'

The major? Now she thought about it, Alex didn't remember hearing if the man even had a first name.

'Doesn't matter. Harry had an appointment in Bourton-on-the-Water. From what he said he should be back soon.'

'What sort of meeting?' Alex said without thinking. She really ought to go.

Venetia gave another stare.

'I'm taking up your time. I should have called first.'

'I have all the time in the world. You got plenty of money from your marriage. Why did you come back here and buy a pub of all things? I should have thought you'd want to forget how it was when you grew up in Underhill. You could go anywhere you like now, there are lots of places where no one would know you.'

Alex wondered how quickly she could get out of the house. 'I'm doing what I like. Living where I really like living, too. And I still paint.'

'Are you any good at it?'

This was all wrong. 'Sometimes. Like most artists. You're really involved with your plants and your garden. They're beautiful.'

'What d'you want with Harry?'

This was a corner of her own making, Alex thought. 'I . . . I think it's really unfair that people have made unfounded assumptions about him and I want to tell him so. I was out walking and decided to stop on a whim.' That seemed quite brilliant and might pull some useful nugget out.

Venetia took in a loud breath through her nose. 'We're talking twaddle,' she announced, tipping back her head and giving a full-throated laugh. 'Filling in the spaces. But then, we're strangers, aren't we? Harry never brings women here. Sometimes I wonder if he's gay, but then, he doesn't bring men here, either.'

'I think I should go,' Alex said.

'Everyone thinks I don't know anything that goes on. Funny really. I probably know more than most of you put together. I'm used to research so I like ferreting things out. I took a first at Oxford, you know. I read anthropology.'

'Congratulations.'

'Yes, well, I do know what you're up to. Never mind, I owe it to Harry to make sure he gets to talk with you. It would be wrong for me not to make sure that happens. You can wait for him in his flat – he just has the upper floor. Not that it isn't as big as most houses. Come along.'

Alex didn't want to 'come along' anywhere with Venetia Stroud.

'Did you know our other son is in the army?' Venetia said with a fond smile. She took off the smock she wore over an elegant gray dress and jacket and pulled black pumps from beneath a bench. With her rubber gardening shoes kicked off and in their place the black shoes with several inch heels, she was suddenly much taller than Alex. An elegant woman with presence who seemed to have shed the first impression she had given Alex like a snake shed its skin. 'Older than Harry, of course. But not much. Stuart is a major already and doing frightfully well. We have high hopes for his progress.'

'I had heard Harry has an older brother although I never met him. How nice.'

'Are you interested in Harry?' Venetia looked her up and down. Alex smiled politely. 'I like Harry. He was always nice to me.'

'That's not what I asked.'

'It's the best I can do.'

'Right.' Venetia took Alex's elbow in strong fingers and guided her out of the conservatory, back into the hall where she released her arm so suddenly that Alex stumbled and caught herself against the wall.

'Sorry about that.' Venetia held Alex's arm through a number of corridors and finally up a flight of stairs to the second story. A billiard room felt out of place in the open area at the top of the stairs. Venetia continued to propel Alex ahead of her to a green baize door that opened into a short corridor.

'This is Harry,' Venetia said, her fingers growing even tighter. 'Plenty of privacy and he is a private man.'

A dark wooden door faced them at the end of the corridor and Harry's mother had no compunction about letting herself in. She closed the door behind them.

'Really, Venetia, I'd rather come back another day. I'll call Harry and make an appointment.' Only she had no intention of coming back. Next time she'd arrange to meet him on neutral ground – if there was a next time.

'Rubbish. He can't be much longer. Come into his little library – his favorite room. You'll be comfortable there.'

Harry's fifties modern décor was a shock after the rest of the house. They passed a kitchen that was any chef's dream. Walls had been removed to allow for an open plan look where smooth upholstery and chrome legs abounded. A glass dining table reflected a hanging light fixture that swooped and resembled a flight of bronze birds.

Red, gray, black and lime green were undoubtedly the work of interior designers.

'This is it,' Venetia said, indicating a book-lined room beyond a ceiling-high door.

To the left, a stairwell led down to a front door with panels of glass on either side where slender contemporary nudes reminiscent of Erte figures stood tall but hung their heads, the better for their sleek, sharp bobs to slide forward and hide their faces.

'Sherry?' Venetia asked, already pouring a glass when Alex followed her into the library. 'So nice and comforting as a day draws in. Sit down. That thing that looks like a green hand is actually very comfortable to sit in. I do have to get on. Going up to Town. Ballet – I do love it.'

As soon as she was sure this woman had left, Alex would get out as fast as she could. She gave Venetia a bright smile. 'You're very kind, thank you.' She sat in the green hand chair and accepted the glass of sherry.

Venetia fluttered her hands in a completely out of character manner. 'Everything's tickety-boo, then?'

Alex didn't think she'd ever actually heard someone use the arcane phrase, other than in a period production. 'Absolutely fine,' she said and watched the woman click away over black marble tiles.

When she heard the door to the rest of the house close, she put down the glass and covered her face with her hands. This was bizarre, creepy, frightening. When her breathing slowed, she went to a window overlooking the paved area in front of this wing. The windows were of an oddly wavy glass that distorted everything. She tucked herself against a wall to one side, listened, and occasionally took a careful look out. Venetia Stroud had said the garages were below Harry's flat so she'd have to come this way.

What if she was being picked up?

Alex cracked a window open. She would hear the big gates if they opened. Wouldn't she?

Why not ask Tony to come for her? Venetia wouldn't think anything of it if she was still here when he arrived. It would be perfectly normal. She reached for her phone in a back jeans' pocket.

Not there.

She ran her hands over the green hand chair and looked underneath. Nothing. Where could she have dropped it? Surely she would have felt it happen – except that her mind had been all over the place.

There was no phone in the library, or in the kitchen or large living area. Not hers, or one belonging to Harry.

Her heart bumped when she saw what she'd missed on a kitchen counter, more or less hidden by a chrome basket of brightly painted wooden eggs. A mobile. She hurried to snatch it up and turn the thing over and punch the first button she saw. Where was the key pad?

Greensleeves . . . The first notes of the ballad, played on a piano, spilled out.

Alex stared at it and had to lower her head against sudden faintness. It wasn't a mobile but one of those small recorders some people used. She hit rewind, turned off and slid it close to the egg basket once more.

She had another, disjointed thought. Vivian and Pamela had been really close. It was Vivian they needed to talk to and find out what she knew about Pamela's life. The two of them rode together and had a lot in common. Surely Vivian would know what Pamela had been up to lately, and with whom.

Later, Alex told herself. She had to stay focused. Another look from a window showed no movement and she heard nothing.

She could just walk out. Probably down the stairs to Harry's front door here would be easiest so she didn't have to find her way through the house. But she wished she weren't alone.

Beyond the library were several more doors. He must have a phone in his bedroom. The first door led to a white bathroom with both shower and bath, and an atmosphere of never having been used. Windows in the next room were covered with white wood shutters on the inside. The room contained only a good deal of luggage, tidily stored in matching sets, and a number of wooden crates that were still nailed shut.

Across the hall two more doors were locked. She turned from them at once, panic closing her throat, and went to another set of floor to ceiling double doors. This must be Harry's bedroom.

The handles wouldn't budge.

Alex backed away, turned and ran to the front door, almost tripping on the stairs. Bolts top and bottom were easy to slide open. Her heartbeat throbbed in her ears but she took a deep breath and tried to open the door. It wouldn't budge. Rattling and pulling made no difference.

The deadbolt! It opened and she tried again, but looking at the door higher up she saw evidence of another deadbolt, this one with no visible means of opening from the inside. Who installed something like that except on a storeroom?

This wasn't her way out.

She didn't want to see Harry, or be questioned by him.

Back up she went, running, her leather soles were slick on the marble but she ran anyway. She should have come this way first.

The door they'd come in by was padded with buttoned silver material on the inside.

And it was locked from the outside.

FIFTEEN

The wind snatched what was left of withered leaves and dead twigs among the new tree growth and turned them into projectiles. Tony tugged up the collar on his coat, put his hands in his pockets and hunched his shoulders.

Walking from his house on the far edge of the Dimple, as they called a wide oval dip where several houses nestled on large, heavily treed lots, down the hill and across the green into Folly gave him good thinking time. Katie stayed by his side. She wasn't a stormy weather lover. He would check on the Burke sisters' new inmate then go to the Dog. Alex would give him a lift home. It didn't matter which home . . .

He had to circle the pond to come to the gap between cottages and the road in front of the Black Dog.

Going straight in to find Alex was tempting, but Maxwell Aloysius Brady needed his wound checked.

Katie headed for the pub.

Tony whistled her back and put on her lead. He did take a look down the side of the building and his spirits lifted at the sight of a light glinting off the windscreen of Alex's Land Rover.

'C'mon, girl, let's get business over . . . before we deal with more business, or whatever.' To Katie's delight, he broke into a run. He knew every crack and dip in the pavement and didn't worry about the encroaching darkness.

When he turned in at the path in front of Leaves of Comfort, he couldn't miss the silhouettes of Harriet and Mary sitting at a table close to the tea-shop window. He had telephoned ahead but afraid to shock them, he still called out. Harriet's hearing was excellent and she got up immediately to let him in.

'Sorry I'm so late,' he told her. 'Should I leave Katie tied up out here?'

'Bring her in. Oliver's shut in upstairs and we should see how Maxwell behaves around dogs.'

'He's already met Katie. She's a fair nurse when she wants to be.' He went in, took off his coat and accepted the mug of coffee Mary held up to him. 'Thanks. Where's the new boy?'

'Here,' Mary said, pointing at her lap.

He hadn't noticed the battered orange cat tucked into a woolen, child-sized quilt, his good eye tightly closed.

'Nap time,' Mary said. 'He's been asleep most of the day, but I think he's settling in already.'

Harriet snorted. 'How do we know when he's asleep most of the time?'

'Oliver's given him a good look over. He's not impressed but there's been no hissing yet, either. We'll get them sorted out.'

'May I have a look?' Tony pulled a chair close to Mary's and she lifted Maxwell into his arms.

'The wound's healing nicely,' he said, pleased there was no sign of infection. He'd brought his stethoscope in his pocket and listened to the animal's heart and lungs. 'Everything sounds good. He's bound to be exhausted. Did he find the litter box on his own?'

Approaching fussily, Katie gave the cat a good sniff. Apparently satisfied, she slid to the floor under Tony's chair.

'No problem with the litter box,' Harriet said. 'And he's eating for England. We don't believe in letting our cats outside so he'll have to get used to that.'

While Tony stroked fur that might be silky once it was clean, Maxwell opened his one golden eye to peer at him, yawned wide enough to show a full complement of very good teeth and crawled back to Mary who promptly wrapped him up in his bright wool blanket again.

'I want him to continue his antibiotics for a few more days,' Tony said and put a bottle on the table. 'He did have a shot but these are pills. Give them to him in bits of soft food. I'll call back again in a couple of days unless you decide I should come sooner.'

'Does Alex know we've got him?' Harriet looked worried. 'I wondered if we should have told her what we were going to do.'

'Tell the truth and shame the devil,' Mary said, smiling fondly at her sister. 'We were afraid Alex wouldn't think we were up to looking after two cats so we nipped over to your surgery nice and early.'

'She's glad you've taken him in.' It was a slight fabrication but in a good cause.

The only lights on downstairs were two sconces behind the kitchen display cases. Tony gulped his coffee, thinking how peaceful the place was. He had hoped Folly would stay unspoiled for a very long time. Vicious killings weren't what he'd had in mind.

'Can I ask you something personal?' Mary said, a gentle, gnarled old hand repeatedly smoothing Maxwell's head. 'We never said anything before and it must have been well more than five years since you came back from Australia. Did you and Penny get a divorce? We've been sad about it because we know how much in love you were. Oh, dear . . .' She bowed her head. 'I've overstepped the mark.'

It overwhelmed Tony to hear the questions that hadn't been asked directly in all this time. Not by anyone outside his family. He rested his elbows on the table and rubbed his forefingers between his eyebrows. After he got back to Folly, the locals had not needed to ask if something had gone wrong with his marriage, that or they kept schtum out of respect for his dad, the general practitioner they had trusted for so many years.

'Don't be angry,' Harriet said tentatively. 'Alex has had a bad time. We think it was a lot worse than we know. And we think she . . . well, we think she might care for you . . . a lot.'

Smiling probably wasn't the appropriate reaction but he smiled anyway, glancing from one old lady to the other. Best not to tell them he reciprocated Alex's feelings – if they were right about hers, that was. 'Penny drowned in a diving accident. We had a boat. She loved to go out there alone and read on the deck. That day she went diving alone and those aren't safe waters without a partner. I don't like talking about it.'

Mary took off her thick glasses to wipe tears away with a lace handkerchief. 'Poor young things. That's terrible.'

'We were probably moving toward a divorce anyway, but . . . God, it was horrible. I wanted her to move on and be happy. Alex knows about it, and Lily, and my dad, of course.'

'We won't be talking about it.' Harriet poured more coffee before he could stop her. 'I'm glad you and Alex found each other again. You know . . . no, that's enough said. But if you ever want to talk about losing someone, we're here.'

'Yes,' Mary said. 'But that's all a long way in the past for us. Have you seen Vivian Seabrook yet?'

Harriet looked uncomfortable. 'She was brought back to the parish hall in a police car early in the afternoon. Wasn't a few minutes before she walked past here. She looked tired, and angry. I called the Dog to warn Alex she might be coming that way to make some sort of trouble but Alex was out on an errand. The police came back around asking more questions, too. Why would they think we'd have more to say if they gave us a second chance? They must think we've got another life we don't usually talk about.'

Processing the pieces of what they were saying didn't add up to a comforting picture. 'I'm going over to Alex now,' he said. 'She seems like a rock, as if nothing would shake her. But I see the cracks sometimes. What happened to her before . . . she lost too much and she's still coming to terms with it. I don't want anyone upsetting her. I'm not going to let anyone upset her.'

'Doc James and your mother raised a good boy, Tony Harrison.' Harriet waited for him to put on his jacket and pull slumbering Katie from beneath the chair. 'Get yourself over there and look after Alex.'

Tony set off from Leaves of Comfort with Katie pulling enthusiastically at the lead. She wiggled from nose to tail. 'In a hurry to get in the warm?' Tony said. Katie always expected to go to the pub and she often got her wish.

Driven by the wind, a tall Goldenrod bush slapped stalks into his face. He moved to the outside of the pavement, away from the cottage gardens. March had certainly blustered in. Dark and heavy, low clouds pushed down acrid chimney smoke that stung his eyes.

'I want to talk to you,' a woman said from behind him.

Swinging around, he was literally face-to-face with Vivian Seabrook. Even in near darkness she was easy to recognize and the moon had risen behind the clouds to add a little silver to the scene.

'Of course,' he said. 'Right here?'

'This is a good place. We're not likely to be interrupted. I've been waiting for you. You came up to where we were all sitting at the Dog the other night. Alex was already there. Did she tell you what we'd been talking about?'

He frowned at her. 'I think if you've got questions for Alex, you should ask her.'

'Simple question, dammit.' She took deep breaths. 'And I'm asking you, not her. She follows you like a puppy. Stands to reason she tells you everything. What did Alex say about me afterward? Someone made a suggestion to the police that got me hauled off like a common criminal. I'm not amused, Tony, and I want to know who did that. They'd have had to twist something to put the plods on me.'

'Alex wouldn't do a thing like that.'

'An Irish Hunter – Pamela Gibbon's as a matter of fact – kicked the outside door to her stall into me. Sent me flying and I got grazes on my wrists, among other places. Someone blew that up into how I could have been injured killing Pamela rather than a horse doing something to me – which is too bloody stupid to imagine – and I got whisked off. I've been through everyone who was there and the only one who's cozy with the detectives is Alex. I'm not making anything of them being comfortable together – not my business – but what would you think if you were me?'

'Did O'Reilly and Lamb talk about the injuries?'

'Of course they bloody did. I just said so.'

'Anyone there could have made a comment to them. How many people have you told? And Alex isn't cozy with O'Reilly and Lamb. Alex is polite to everyone.'

'I was hoping you'd tell me what I need to know but you're obviously going to cover for her. I'm going over to the Dog myself. Almost went earlier but I needed some sleep after what I've been put through. I phoned Mr and Mrs Derwinter to explain and they aren't too happy with her, I can tell you. Pamela and I were best friends. We were very close. She was one of the reasons I came here.'

Furious, Tony set off again and Vivian strode beside him. 'I'm not covering for Alex,' he said. 'She hasn't done anything. I'd appreciate it if you'd let me arrange for you to meet in private. If you're still sure that's what you want to push for.'

'I make my own decisions.'

Katie stayed as far ahead as the lead would reach all the way to the Black Dog. When they got there, Tony opened the door and let the lead go. Katie disappeared into the bar.

Keeping his voice low, Tony asked, 'Why would Alex do that to you, Vivian? Why would she try to hurt you?'

'I don't think you know why, Tony, and you won't like it when you find out. But I'd rather not be the one to tell you.'

'Stop playing games. What have you got against Alex? What has she ever done to you?'

'I've got my sources, too,' Vivian said. 'And I won't be repeating what I've been told to you, Tony. But I will say that people in glass houses shouldn't throw stones. It's not original but it fits. I'm not coming in now. I need to think some more. You can tell Alex I expect an explanation.'

'Tell her yourself—'

'What were you doing up at the manor last night? Really doing? We've only got your word for the reason you were there.'

Tony ignored her and went toward the door.

The pub was blessedly warm. Vivian had hurried away before he got inside and he walked into the bar with a sense of dread. The woman wanted someone to blame for her misfortune and had singled Alex out as a troublemaker. Vivian obviously had the tenacity to hang on to her theory – until it could be disproved.

As he would have expected, the bar was crammed and the babble had reached a deafening pitch. Tony's dad stood at the bar with his back to him and Tony threaded a path in his direction, nodding to people as he went. Katie had already reached her target, the fire.

'Hey Tony,' Kev Winslet, the Derwinters' gamekeeper said, pushing his florid face into Tony's. 'Another right balls up, eh? What are they thinking? Not very likely to have two separate deadly crimes in a little place like this, is it?'

Kev smelled like a brewery. 'What do you mean?' Tony said.

'They're connected, aren't they? Didn't the police say it's too much of a coincidence yet? I must say I'm surprised they've latched on to Vivian so quickly, though. She's a piece of work. I always knew there was something not right with her, but murder?'

'Vivian's been released,' Tony said. 'She's back home.' That's all he intended to say.

'Alex went to the Tits and Ass meeting—'

'You'd better not let any of the women hear you say that.'

Kev guffawed. 'What's it stand for, then? TA. They think they're being clever. What did Alex let on about it? I heard some of 'em cried when they heard about Pamela.' He stopped grinning. 'She was all right, Pamela. She didn't have much to hold onto except money and they say that won't keep you warm at night. Some were too hard on her.'

Including you.

Lily came through from the empty restaurant and raised a hand to attract Tony's attention.

He said, 'Excuse me,' to Winslet and caught up with Lily beside his dad. Polishing a glass, Hugh went to them and waited for their order.

'Hello, Lily, Dad,' Tony said. 'Heard anything useful?'

They both shook their heads. Lily looked miserable. 'I know what happened to Pamela is all we should be worrying about, but you'd have to have ice water in your veins not to feel threatened. I don't think Vivian could have done it, do you?'

'She didn't,' Tony said. 'And she's back home. Apparently someone gave the police bad information about her.' He wasn't about to mention that Vivian had tried to blame Alex.

'What will you have?' Hugh said and Tony noticed for the first time how strained the man looked.

'Lily?' Tony said.

'Nothing for me.'

'I'm fine,' his dad said.

'Lagavulin, neat,' Tony said. 'Feels like a Scotch night.'

'Do you know what Alex would like?' Hugh asked.

Tony looked around. 'Where is she?'

'Lady's loo?' Hugh said, sounding puzzled. 'Where did she say she was going? She came in with you, didn't she?'

'No.' He didn't have to search around to know he wouldn't find her there.

Hugh slid the Scotch across the bar.

Tony felt disoriented. 'Alex isn't here? Where did she go?'

'She said she had errands but that was hours ago. You called looking for her and I assumed the two of you had met up.'

Tony took out his mobile and called Lime Tree Lodge, although it didn't make sense for her to be up there with her vehicle behind the pub. She wouldn't be likely to go for long walks in the dark, not with the possibility of a murderer running around the area. There was no answer on the phone and he didn't leave a message. Next he tried her mobile. She didn't pick up and it didn't go to messages. 'Lily. You haven't seen her either?'

'She'd already left when I came in.' She pressed her lips into a tight line. 'Did she take Bogie? No, of course she didn't, he's in the restaurant.'

'Let's calm down,' Doc James said. 'We'll run through her movements, or what we know of them. Hugh, she must have taken her car.'

'No, it's still in the yard.'

Tony punched in Alex's mobile and home numbers again, waited for the answer machine to come on each time and rubbed a hand over his face. He slid from his chair and hurried to the restaurant. Lying down, head on paws, Bogie swiveled his eyes to see him. The dog didn't get up or show signs of wanting to go out. But he whimpered softly.

SIXTEEN

With her arms tightly crossed, Alex paced back and forth. She couldn't believe she'd been locked in.

No, she was locked in, but it didn't have to have happened deliberately. The flat grew dimmer. Darkness had well and truly fallen outside. She took a deep breath. 'Pull yourself together.' One by one, she switched on lights. If nothing else, someone might notice Harry's place was lit up like a Tesco's. She found herself hoping the major would come home but he was probably dug in at the Dog until closing.

Unless there was a phone behind one of the locked doors she had to think Harry did what so many did now and lived with just a mobile.

The sound of a key turning in the lock on the padded door jolted through her and she spun to watch it swing open. She dropped her hands to her sides, and deliberately relaxed her face. Fear had power, especially if you let it show.

Harry came in looking sleekly professional in a gray pinstripe suit, white collar, a gray and blue silk tie. 'Hello, Alex,' he almost sang out, and cheerfully. 'I went in to see Mama but she'd left a note to say she was going out and you were here.'

'Yes.' She breathed through her mouth.

He looked back at the door and frowned. 'How did you get in?'

'Your mother brought me through that door. She must have locked it without thinking when she left me here.'

'But you tried it? You wanted to get out?' His face settled into a hurt expression. 'You wanted to leave before I got back?'

These people were no less odd than she'd decided already. 'No! I just wanted to call the Dog and let them know I'd be later than I expected, but I must have dropped my phone somewhere. Your mother insisted I wait for you.'

'Black and white phone?' he said and when she nodded, added, 'There's one like that on a table in the front hall.'

'Good,' she said. So why hadn't Venetia, and supposedly she'd been the only one left in the main part of the house, why hadn't she brought it back to her – unless she had deliberately knocked her off balance and taken the phone then? The housekeeper wouldn't have just put it on a table before leaving. 'I looked for your phone but apparently you don't believe in them.'

He laughed almost under his breath. 'Got the good old mobile.' He patted an inside pocket in his jacket. 'But there's one in my bedroom. I'd have forgiven you for taking a look. No skeletons in my cupboards.'

Muscles tightened in her jaw but she didn't tell him she'd already tried and found all his doors locked.

'I'm . . . well, I couldn't have hoped to find you here but I'm glad,' Harry said. 'How super. Come and sit with me. It's time we got to know each other again – it's been years since we had a real talk.'

He held her arm just above the elbow, tighter than necessary she thought, and walked her into the library – Venetia style. 'Bless that mother of mine. I see she poured you something.' He lifted the sherry glass and his nose wrinkled. 'God, she lives in the dark ages. Ladies still only drink sherry on such occasions, just because she does.'

'It was sweet of her,' Alex said, thinking there was not much about Venetia Stroud that was 'sweet.'

'But you like a good cognac. I remember that. There's something about a woman with a nose for my favorite poison. Sit. I'll find something special for you.'

She started to protest, but it was to his back. She sank to sit on the nearest chair.

He stood and placed an extraordinary scalloped bottle on his bar trolley. 'Cuvée is the best I can do,' he said with something close to a giggle. And he splashed generous pours of deep gold liquor into two glasses.

Alex had to stop herself from gaping and rather hoped he'd decanted something less expensive into a Camus bottle.

She took the glass with raised eyebrows, sniffed the contents, swirled and sniffed again before tasting. No expert, she still knew when she was drinking something exquisite. 'My goodness,' she said, clearing her throat. 'Velvet and fire. Wonderful. I've never tasted anything like it.' That was true but there was too much in the glass and she wanted to leave as soon as possible. She toyed with making up something banal to get her out of there.

'There are very few women who should have nothing but the best, Alex. I've always known you were one of them. If Bailey-Jones hadn't beaten me to the punch . . . well, he did, but he's not in the picture now.'

Aghast, Alex felt her cheeks color and let her eyes wander over small pieces of modern art she didn't know or care about. A glass-fronted bookcase was filled with what she wouldn't be surprised to find were valuable first editions.

'You have some beautiful things, Harry.'

'I've embarrassed you.' He sat on the floor beside her, one knee raised and his glass balanced on top. 'You were always a shy little thing. But you've overcome so much from the past to make a life for yourself.'

He was patronizing her and she hated it. Did he really think this was a visit intended to spark some sort of liaison between them? She drank again, being careful to take very little. 'As I told your mother earlier, I enjoy living and working here in Folly,' she said evenly. 'That's why I came back. I never thought I'd overcome such a lot – apart from a divorce, and I'm fine about that. Or was it something else you thought I'd overcome?' Like humble beginnings.

He patted her thigh, let his hand rest there and stared earnestly into her eyes. 'Word spreads. You've dealt with more than any woman should have to bear and come through with your head high, thank God.'

'Thanks.' What was she supposed to say to that?

Harry removed his hand from her leg. 'Alex, you've thrown yourself into life again and you've made some huge decisions. Buying the Dog was a gutsy move. You haven't given yourself time to rest and balance yourself.'

Balance herself?

'I don't want to upset you,' he said, 'but the girl I knew when we were kids wouldn't want to cause trouble for other people. Not if she was herself.'

'Stop right there, Harry. What are you suggesting?'

'Shh. Don't excite yourself. I'm a good friend, remember. Look, I've got a wonderful idea. Why don't you stay here with me, at least for a while, and give yourself a chance to think through what's happened and what it's done to you.'

His handsome face, the concern that looked genuine, almost made her think she'd misunderstood, but when she returned his stare, he blinked rapidly and his eyes slid away for an instant.

'You've got to be joking,' she told him. 'I've got a full and satisfying life. In the past few months I've had some sickening experiences, but I'm just fine, thanks.'

'Why are you here?' he snapped, the sympathetic smile wiped away. 'What are you trying to do? Do you have any idea what you put Vivian Seabrook through? What has she ever done to you?'

Alex gaped.

'Nothing to say? I'm not surprised. You should be mortified and if I have my way you'll get your head on straight and stop causing trouble for decent, innocent people.'

She gathered herself. 'This is mad. All of it. When did you and Vivian become buddies? I haven't done anything to either of you.' But she had strong suspicions about Harry and she'd been a fool to come here alone. 'I'm sorry I've interrupted your evening but I need to get back to work.'

'I've done this all wrong.' He worked off his jacket and threw it on the green chair, pulled off his tie and tossed it on top. 'Let's settle down and talk sensibly. I lost my temper and I shouldn't have. Pamela and I were friends – that's no secret, but we were a convenience to each other, nothing more. She was older than me.'

'So what? If you were older than her, she'd still be dead.' And if Pamela had been older than him, it couldn't have been by much.

'You're not helping me out here. Losing Pamela is a blow, but I've got to think about myself now. Having you and Tony Harrison spreading rumors about me is dangerous. I don't deserve that, Alex.' He stood and looked down at her. 'That detective thinks the sun shines out of your arse – after the last mess, he believes anything you say. For some reason they decided you were a heroine. But that was something different. It was all about Folly and old issues. This is obviously a random killing by a maniac.'

'I want to go, Harry. You sound unhinged.' And she knew her mistake as soon as the words were out of her mouth. She went on quickly. 'I don't blame you for being so upset. She was a close friend and now she's been snuffed out. Just like that.'

The silence that followed unsettled her more than his accusations and weird suggestions.

'Don't waste that cognac,' he said, beginning to pace. He swallowed some of his own, then some more. 'You don't have your car here.'

'I walked. It's not far. I came on a whim because I haven't had a chance for a private word with you since this all started.'

'And you've decided I'm a murderer,' he shouted, chopping the side of his hand onto her shoulder for emphasis.

Rubbing aching bone, Alex stood and tried to move away. He opened his fist and held her where she was.

'That hurt,' she told him. 'You're not sober. Let me go. Now.'

'I don't think so,' Harry said. 'Perhaps I'll get those detectives over here and have you tell them what you believe about me. And while you're at it you can apologize for maligning Vivian just because you don't like her. You can tell them you took what she said about the horse and twisted it. Obviously they've already figured out she told the truth but you can back her up. That's the only way I can see for you to show how sorry you are.'

'Tripe,' she snapped. 'I don't know what you're up to and I don't want to know.'

Taking her by the shoulders, he shook her hard. 'Don't lie to me, you little bitch. You never did know your place and you don't now. Money doesn't buy class and don't you forget it.'

He was pathetic, but he scared her. Alex kept her voice even and controlled. 'You aren't yourself, Harry. You were never a spiteful kid like so many of them were.' She had nothing to lose by pushing her original excuse for being here. 'Venetia asked me why I came and I told her. I think it's unfair that some people are putting about some absurd innuendoes about you and I wanted you to know that.'

So much time ticked by that she started to panic inwardly.

'You've always been one of the good ones,' he said in a low voice and pulled her against him, wrapping her in his arms. 'I'm sorry, Alex. This has been a bloody hard time for me and nothing seems to be getting any better. I was too hasty about you and I should have known better. You were a little love as a kid and you still are. Forgive me?'

He held her away just enough to look into her face. Quickly, she nodded, keeping her face at a difficult angle in case he tried to kiss her. She couldn't help shuddering.

'Are you cold, sweetheart?' He rubbed her back and she felt light-headed.

'I did this to you and I'm sorry. I've been out of my mind with worry about what's gone on and why. I'm going to look out for you, Alex, just like I did when we were kids.'

'Thank you.' He horrified her. 'I'm fine now. What I need is another walk in the fresh air. But you've been wonderful, Harry, and I won't forget it.' And she never would.

'It's dark,' he told her. 'Let me drive you.'

'It's not that late and I'm a night person. I enjoy it. They'll expect me back at the Dog. Bye, Harry, and thanks for everything.'

He managed to look incredibly sad but held the door to the house open for her. 'If you insist. Don't forget your phone on the hall table.'

'I won't,' she said and set off through the dim house, grateful for her excellent sense of direction.

'I'll be watching you, dear Alex.' Harry's voice started her running.

Several times she paused to think about the direction she took. She'd been preoccupied by Venetia when she came up and now a corridor or set of steps didn't seem familiar. Alex pushed on.

If she got out safely she would never, ever, put herself in such a position again. She had a fleeting recollection of a previous occasion when she'd made such a promise. She had better have learned her lesson this time – if she got out in one piece.

Her heart hammered in her throat.

She arrived at another landing and realized the stairs to the main floor lay ahead. Swallowing sobs of relief, she rushed downward, holding the banister, taking two steps at a time.

And caught a heel in the carpet. She crashed down the last three stairs to the slate tiles in the hall.

SEVENTEEN

More than anything, Tony wanted to call the police, or at least O'Reilly. They'd been through tough times together. Under all the detective tough, Dan was human and should feel the same desperation Tony felt.

Not for twenty-four hours, his father had insisted despite Lily's pleading and Tony's wavering.

If he didn't find her or hear from her within the hour, he was going to O'Reilly and damn the twenty-four-hour rule for missing persons. A hell of a lot could happen in that time. Life only took an instant to snuff out.

Driving to the ruined manor in Alex's vehicle took all the guts he had and then some. The thought of checking that shaft again turned his hands white-knuckled on the wheel. And if Alex . . . A shape caught his eye and he jumped, but it was only the sharp outline of the folly the town was named after coming into view. High on the hill behind the Dimple, Tinley Tower, or the Tooth as locals called it, was a grim sight. Fallen away in parts, it poked ragged points into a sky suddenly bloodstained purple. As children, they'd all spent a lot of time playing in and around the once fanciful folly, whole only in engravings today.

He hadn't thought that signs of a crime scene would still be there, but the tapes flapped with a light still illuminating the top of the shaft. The truth was he wasn't thinking clearly about much tonight. Of course it was still a crime scene. A TV van was parked, nose in, and he could see figures in the front seat with binoculars trained on the scene. Even at a distance he could make out a copper lounging in a chair and activity around the base of the drum tower. SOCO was working around the clock, Tony supposed, his heart lifting just enough in relief to urge him into making a U-turn and driving back to the main hill road where he turned left toward Underhill. He didn't want to disturb the policemen with questions that were bound to raise eyebrows, but he was glad to see the men there since they would keep anyone with evil intent away.

Abruptly, nausea doubled him over the steering wheel. He pulled to the side of the road for a moment, just to settle down. If he could take in a complete breath it would help.

After checking Alex's room at The Dog kept primarily for weather emergencies when it was safer not to drive into the hills, Lily had gone to Corner Cottage to make sure she wasn't there. She wasn't.

Tony had driven a circle, physically checking Lime Tree Lodge to which he had a key. Tony even went to his own house before carrying on.

Where would he go next?

The cottages of Underhill lay ahead.

Lights showed, dim through lace-curtained windows. A bulb kept on all night above a shop window picked up the words: 'Millers' Groceries and Sundries,' which meant they carried a little of everything. The people here were decent and hard working. Too bad there were those in Folly who needed someone to look down on.

Through the village and up a rise, he went. 'Alex, where are you, dammit.' If he were honest with himself he'd admit she was too impulsive. Well, she was, but what could she have done to put herself in an awkward – a dangerous – position? And his gut told him that's what she had done. When she left him earlier, she had made sure he got the message that she was an independent woman.

He hadn't a clue where she might have gone.

On the last run down toward Folly itself he felt the unmistakable spear of helplessness. Sweat broke on his forehead and between his shoulder blades. She had some sort of sixth sense. Nothing definite like seeing apparitions, but premonitions. He wished to hell he'd get some guidance and he didn't care where it came from.

Past the few large homes on the downward run, he went, and speeded up as the rest of Folly came into sight.

Something moved.

On the left side of the road. He was almost upon it and slammed on the brakes. A figure, limping and holding onto walls and plants turned to back against a tree and his headlights picked up her face.

'Alex,' he yelled and stopped hard enough to slew the back wheels. Throwing open his door, he shouted, 'Alex' again as he ran to grab and lift her up. 'My God, where have you been? Why are you limping? We're all out of our minds worrying about you.'

EIGHTEEN

Her ankle throbbed but she didn't complain. She had already decided never to mention that Harry punched her shoulder or that it was bruised. Tony seemed furious with her. No, he *was* furious with her. There had been an instant after he'd ignored her protests and lifted her into her car when she thought he would shake her. Instead he pushed her trembling hands out of the way and fastened her seat belt before slamming the door on her.

'I'm sorry,' she said when he joined her and straightened the Land Rover at the side of the road. 'I've worried you. I was going to call as soon as I was sure I was safely away.'

He crossed his hands on the wheel and rested his forehead on top. 'You couldn't walk and talk or . . . Alex, I don't understand. Call your mother now. Tell her you're with me and you're safe. She'll spread the word.'

Hardly able to hold her phone still, she did as he told her and listened to Lily cry – she didn't remember hearing her cry. Lily said she had people to reassure and she'd see Alex in the morning when they'd all slept.

Tony turned the key in the ignition. 'Why are you limping?'

She found a tissue in her pocket and blew her nose. 'I didn't know what would happen. Nothing could have prepared me.' He didn't say anything. 'I fell down some steps.'

He steered onto the road and accelerated. Alex dared to look sideways at him in the dash light. His hair was wild and even now his face bore lines of anxiety . . . and anger.

'Where should I take you? My wheels are at my place so I had to bring yours up from Folly.'

She fought back tears, tears of self-pity and tears of longing for him to smile at her and understand what she would have to tell him.

'I haven't been home for a couple of nights – it'll be cold at my house, and, and I don't want to go there. I want to be with you,' she finished in a rush. 'Mum will take Bogie home with her.'

'Alex—'

'I would have called you hours ago,' she broke in. 'Take me to your house, please. Light a fire and just listen to me. You're going to be mad – even madder with me – but then you'll understand why I did what I did and why I couldn't call sooner. When I was finally out of there and trying to walk to Folly, I was too scared to think straight. I just wanted you there.'

The look he gave her brought more tears.

'You're important to me, don't you understand?' he said. 'I'm mad because I'm still frightened out of my skull. I feel like a parent whose child ran into the street.' He paused, glancing at her frequently, and frowning while they drove straight through Folly. 'Where did you have to get away from? Where have you been?'

'I got locked in the Strouds' house. It was horrible, Tony. They're not right. If they aren't mad, they're close. Something is very, very wrong there.'

He drove too fast but she didn't care. Hunched over the wheel, he shot up into the hills, past her house and on until he turned in at his own gates.

'The *Strouds'* house,' he muttered, leaping out when he had screeched to a stop at the front door. 'The *Strouds'* house? Till this time of night? You fell down steps. Damn it all, Alex, *you* sound unhinged.'

He got out, slammed his door and went to the back to let Katie out of a kennel. Alex opened her door and swung out her legs. When she slid to the ground she couldn't avoid a sharp intake of breath. Sharp pain racked her shoulder and arm. She longed to take off her shoe but feared she would never get it on again if her foot and ankle were as swollen as she expected.

Katie arrived to sniff at her and Tony put an arm around her waist, all but carrying her into the house. He didn't speak, but his rigid body gave off waves of frustration.

In his sitting room next to the kitchen he took off her jacket. 'This isn't warm enough for this kind of weather, is it?' he said but she didn't think he wanted an answer.

With pillows slapped at one end of the couch, she was propped, fairly gently, with a big afghan stretched over her. He pulled the blanket back enough to look at her feet. 'What did you fall on? A pile of rocks? I want my dad to look at this but we'll manage till morning.'

Alex looked up at his tight face and he looked back, his blue eyes black with intensity. She was grateful he hadn't noticed how she favored her left arm.

'This will hurt,' he said, starting to slip the shoe from her injured foot. She pushed her fists into the couch cushion and bent forward, hissing against the pain. The shoe was off and his cold fingers prodded her ankle – as carefully as possible, she supposed although it hurt like hell.

Her shoulder ached with each tiny move.

Damn, Harry Stroud!

Alex felt tears squeeze free but swallowed and didn't make a sound. 'Do not move from there,' Tony said, all flat efficiency. 'If we're lucky, the ankle's badly sprained and there's nothing broken, but a sprain can be about as much trouble as a break.'

He took off her other shoe and turned the blanket down again. Alex didn't complain that the weight of the wool was too much.

Finally he took off his coat and lit the fire. Katie came to sit beside her and rest her head on the edge of the couch. The big dog's eyes watched her mournfully.

'I'm going to strap that,' Tony said, 'and pack some ice around it. Then you'll go through whatever foolishness you got into – step by step.'

Alex pressed her lips together. Telling him to back off wouldn't achieve anything positive, not from a position of weakness.

He went into the kitchen and things banged out there. Within minutes he returned with a steaming mug in one hand and a large plastic box in the other. 'Horlicks,' he said. 'You like it, right? It'll settle you or so they've always said.'

She nodded although she hadn't tasted the milky, malty drink in years. He put down the box, moved a small table beside her and put the mug down. 'That might feel good in your hands. Comforting.'

From the box he produced a wide elastic bandage and began at her instep, winding quickly and efficiently until she had a tidy, herringboned effort wrapped well past her ankle.

'Thank you, Tony,' she said.

He clipped the bandage in place and didn't answer. Once the box was closed, he set it aside and pulled an armchair close to the couch where he could look straight at her. He sat down, forearms on thighs, his fingers laced between his knees.

Alex remembered the Horlicks, already cooled, and took several swallows.

And Tony remained silent and watchful.

'I made a mistake,' she said when she couldn't stand the waiting anymore. 'But that doesn't mean you were right and I was wrong when I told you I make my own decisions. This turned out badly, but my motivation was good. It doesn't seem like anyone's got a clue what happened to Pamela and I feel . . . we found her and that makes me feel responsible. The dead can't help themselves and this needs to get sorted out fast, for her and because unless we find a motive, we'll always be expecting another unnatural death.'

'The police are on the case, Alex. Let them do their job.'

'And what have they accomplished so far?'

'They've only been here a couple of days. And we can't know exactly what they've found out.'

'What happened to it being OK for us to do our own gentle poking around?'

'You scared the hell out of me, that's what happened. I thought I'd lost you once before, remember?'

She remembered, but she wasn't buying it that she had to be wrapped in cotton wool.

'Why did you go to the Strouds'? What happened there?'

He was going to blow his top a few more times before she finished explaining.

'I walked up there this afternoon and asked to see Harry.'

'You, what? My God.'

'He wasn't in but his mother was. Venetia Stroud. She was the one who locked me in his flat – if you can call it that. It's the whole top wing over the garages at the back. Garages that are big enough to have stables incorporated when Harry and his brother were younger.

'If she was questioned about everything from today she'd deny it, and although Harry knows the truth, he'd back up his mother.'

He pulled his chair closer and never took his eyes from her face. 'Why did you go there? What did you expect to gain?'

She reached to set down her mug and winced. Even moving the right arm pulled the left. 'I wasn't completely sure but—'

'Your arm hurts.'

'It's nothing.'

Tony took hold of her left elbow and hand and straightened the arm. Alex kept her face impassive. He took the arm gently to the side, horizontal to her body, brought it back and slowly lifted it into the perpendicular extension. She moaned, couldn't help it, and supported her own upper arm. Tony carefully put her arm down and pulled her shirt away from her shoulder.

She looked away, hoping there was nothing to see. All she needed now was some sort of altercation between Tony and Harry.

'Your shoulder's got a large, single bruise.' He felt around. 'There's a hematoma from the look of it, and your shoulder is swollen. What happened?'

'It probably happened when I slipped downstairs.'

His stare made it impossible for her to look back.

'Did you turn upside down and land head first?'

'Just leave it, Tony? Stop pestering me.'

He got up, went to the kitchen and returned with several ice bags and some cloths. The one he strapped to her shoulder with a towel underneath was miserable. The others he packed around her ankle.

'I don't want to be accused of pestering you again so just give me chapter and verse, from the beginning until I found you beside the road.'

Crying uncontrollably might stop him for a minute or two, but then he'd start in again. 'Do you have brandy?'

Wordlessly he got her some but didn't bring a glass for himself.

The dulling warmth felt delicious . . . for a few seconds. 'I walked up there and asked to see Harry. He was out. I talked to Venetia Stroud who's a piece of work. She asked off-the-wall questions, accused me of being a meddler, asked me if I had designs on Harry, reminded me what an unworthy friend I'd be for him and generally told me off in a beastly snide way. When I told her I thought Harry was being treated badly she turned into sugar and spice and half pushed me upstairs to his flat. I think that's when I dropped my phone. I discovered it was gone after she left me there and if Harry has a phone up there it's locked in his bedroom.'

'This is unbelievable.' With his elbows on his knees, Tony massaged his forehead. 'We don't know who the murderer is, but there is one, Alex, and you choose this time to play amateur sleuth – on your own. Go on.'

'Eventually Harry came back and I got out.' She clamped her teeth together and willed Tony to stop digging, at least for now.

Tony stood up. He was still very close and she had to strain her neck to see his face.

'Why are you covering for Harry?'

'What?' She crossed her arms and sucked in another painful breath. 'I'm not covering for Harry. I made every mistake in the book today and I've paid for it. I'm still paying for it.'

When he continued to glower at her she had a rush of self-pity. 'The next person I'm going to track down for a private talk is Vivian

Seabrook. She was Pamela's closest friend here and I think she knows more than she's admitted to so far. I'm going to pursue this in a logical and sane manner.'

'Really? How sensible you sound. Now I'd appreciate your giving me a detailed description of exactly what happened after Harry got there. You were gone far too long for what you've said to cover it.'

Katie whimpered softly and Alex went to scratch her head – pain shot from her shoulder and into her chest. 'Could I have more brandy, please?'

Without a word, he did as she asked and sat down again, silently waiting.

All the fear and desperation she'd felt in Harry's flat crowded in and Alex felt tears slide down her cheeks. She didn't try to wipe them away but she did start talking.

She left almost nothing out, including Harry's suggestion that she go to stay with him. 'He sounded crazy,' she said at that point. 'He had accused me of victimizing Vivian. He said I made up some story about her and told the police. In the end I was really scared. I thought he would hurt me.' And he had.

'What made him let you go?' Tony's voice was flat with anger. 'I need to know everything because I'm going over for a little discussion.'

Taking a gulp of breath, Alex said, 'No, you're not. This is bigger than what happened to me today. We'll work it out together like we promised,' and her tone climbed the scale with every word.

'How did you get away?'

Lifting her chin, she snapped out to him, 'When I thought he was going to do something to me, I told him it wasn't fair he was being suspected. I said I just wanted him to know that. He said I'd always been one of the nice kids and I still am. And he's going to be watching me, whatever that means. Maybe he means, he'll be protective or something.'

'I'll kill him,' Tony said.

'Don't say that.'

'Fine, I'll scare him out of Folly and he'll never come back.'

'Testosterone,' she muttered, swinging her feet to the ground and struggling to stand. 'Get over it. We need to keep all avenues open to see what we can find.'

'Sit down—'

Her skin turned icy and prickly, her stomach turned over.

The lights faded out. Faintly she heard, 'Alex!'

NINETEEN

Whatever they had shot her full of had done a good job of putting her out. A mild sedative, they'd said. He smiled. The hospital had Dr Harrison of Folly-on-Weir on file but they hadn't checked the first name and discovered he was Tony, the DVM, not James, the MD!

Tony paced back and forth around the bed, watching Alex's sleeping face. A two-hour snooze was long enough. It was late evening by now, but the hospital staff shouldn't let her sleep through the night without checking on her.

He was a damned idiot not to have taken more notice of the shoulder. *Bruised and swollen, big deal, that ankle might be sprained.* So he'd missed the scapula fracture.

'I'm a fool!'

'Why?'

He stopped pacing and stared at her. She must have asked the question without opening her eyes, but her lids rose slowly as if they were being held down.

'You're waking up. Finally.'

'You noticed.'

He sucked back a grin. 'You will do just fine, my satin-tongued one. If you are concussed, which the people around here think you could be, it hasn't dimmed your rapier wit. How do you feel?' He sat on the bedside chair. 'Sorry. You bring out the worst in me . . . and the best. You've got a hairline fracture on that left clavicle. I'm sorry, Alex, I was too focused on the ankle and didn't look long enough at the shoulder. I was too tied up with my own shock and my reaction and that was unforgivable.'

'S'not. I'd be mad at you, too.'

Could you hold someone to a comment they made while partially drugged? 'The good news is there's no other fracture, just a sprain.' He'd let her find out for herself how much of a nuisance a sprain could be.

'I want to leave. Don't like hospitals.' She raised her head a couple of inches to look around. 'Yes, this is a hospital. Thought so. Get me out.'

'I want to take you away from here, too. Someone will be round to check you soon enough. Unless they've come up with something else, we'll go. I want to know something, Alex. Did Harry do anything to you . . . like give that shoulder a good whack?'

She blinked several times. 'No.'

That wasn't a ringing denial. 'You didn't say anything about your shoulder until I saw it was hurting.'

Her green eyes stared into his and seemed well focused now. 'It was all pretty emotional. You were angry and you had a right to be. I should have got myself together and called as soon as I was out of that house. Then I was nervous. Just a mess, Tony. Hang in here with me. We've got enough trouble without making more.'

He would lay odds that she was holding something back but he couldn't figure out why.

'Knock knock.' Hugh from the Black Dog poked his head into the room. He smiled at Alex. 'You're verra lucky. At least you aren't in one of those damn wards, Alex. What's going on with you?'

'Cracked clavicle and sprained ankle,' Tony said. The man was a bit too good looking, gave off too much male self-assurance for comfort. 'How did you know we were here?'

And what was his story anyway. He looked like someone who already had the world at his feet and didn't need to manage a pub in an English backwater. He looked relaxed and confident – and concerned about Alex.

'Are you doing all right, Alex?' Hugh asked, frowning. 'What happened to you . . . ah, no, I shouldn't press you on that, not tonight. And I better be quick before they chuck me out of here. I had to use my Scottish charm to be allowed to visit you at all.'

'You didn't tell Lily,' Alex said, using her right hand to push herself up. 'It would be better if she saw me back in Folly—'

'No, I didn't tell her.' He looked around the plain room. 'At least it's a bit quiet in here at night, hm?'

'Yes,' Tony replied for Alex. 'You didn't say how you knew to come.'

'A reporter told me – at the Dog.'

Tony saw Alex gape.

Hugh held up a hand. 'I know, who would expect someone like that to know? Apparently the media have people listening in on emergency broadcasts of any kind. That's how he knew to come to the Dog in the first place. The call about Alex came in while he was trying to be subtle but grilling me about what's happened in Folly – to Pamela.'

'He just came in and started asking questions?' Alex said. 'Did he think you'd know everything and tell him every detail for some reason?'

Tony rubbed the back of her neck. 'It's their job, love. They get paid for digging out stories and if they have to be obnoxious I suppose it's part of what they're paid for.'

The trust with which she looked at him did some interesting things to a heart he used to think was partly frozen. 'We don't want anymore open poking around than we can help. These people get in the way.'

A glance at Hugh showed his curiosity at Alex's remarks.

He cleared his throat and moved to the bottom of the bed. 'That's why I came as soon as we had our reporter tucked up in one of the rooms at the inn. He said some things I think you'd like to know, even if only to file away.'

Their reputation as self-appointed sleuths on their winter adventures had obviously reached Hugh, which, naturally, they would.

'Excuse me,' Alex said. 'I need to use the lavatory.'

'I'll call a nurse,' Hugh said.

'That's not necessary. All I need is a hand to the door. I'll be fine – I've got to be if I want to get out of here by morning.' Carefully, she moved the sheet aside and swung her legs over the side of the bed.

Tony stood behind her and firmly tied her gown shut. He got her safely to her destination and she gave him a bright smile – with raised eyebrows – as she shut the door.

'You two are pretty close,' Hugh said, amusement in his eyes and a quirky smile in place.

'Is there anything you'd like to say that might upset her?' Tony said, ignoring the personal remark.

'I don't think so. It's all about Pamela and what could be a heap of scuttlebutt – I don't know what to think.'

The toilet flushed and water ran in a sink as Alex must be doing her best to wash her hands. She opened the door, hopping, and grasped Tony's arm. 'I could go home. Really, I feel great. Sore in places but OK. Can I get out now, do you think?' She looked as if she expected him to spirit her away. 'You know the longer you're in a hospital the more likely you are to get some deadly bug.'

He laughed. With an arm under her elbow, supporting her by the wrist, he guided her back to the bed, pulled up the pillows and made her lean against them while he replaced the sheet. 'I promise we'll probably be away from here just as soon as someone with the right papers and a pen comes to kick you out.'

The corners of her mouth turned down. 'What do you know, Hugh?'

'This is weird,' he said and walked to the window to look out at a night sky. 'The reporter – his name is Patrick Guest from a Gloucester paper – waited for the bar to empty out. The major and Leonard Derwinter were tucked on a window seat with their heads together, but that was all.'

'Not Heather Derwinter, though?' Alex said. 'She doesn't have enough to do. It makes her nosy.'

'Not Heather,' Hugh said. 'And they couldn't hear what we were saying. Guest was all sweetness and light, but he was trying to ask questions without giving anything away. I don't think he's too good at assessing others. I was the barman and probably a bit thick. He wanted to know if Pamela had boyfriends.'

'Where would that come from?' Tony said. 'She's . . . she was a widow and I don't see how he'd pick up anything from emergency radios that would lead him in that direction.'

'I said I didn't know.'

'Good for you,' Alex said approvingly. 'Nosy parker. He's adding two and two—'

'And coming up with four,' Tony said. 'But she wasn't running around with lots of people. Not as far as I know.'

Alex's secret smile made him bring his face level with hers. 'What's that for?'

A shrug didn't feel so good and she sucked in a breath before telling him, 'You're not the man people go to with so-called Folly facts, or dreamed up rubbish, Tony. I don't think Pamela had *lots of* men in her life, but she liked their company and she was very . . . feminine. But what business is that of anyone else?'

'If someone she was seeing killed her, it's the business of quite a few,' Hugh said. 'This Guest chappie never took his eyes off my face when he said he'd a tip that Pamela Gibbon could have been pregnant when she died.'

TWENTY

The paper was thin, faintly watermarked with shadows of small flowers, and smelled of rosewater. It slipped easily from the matching envelope pushed through the letterbox in the middle of the night.

My friend, *the letter began.*

Dread made it hard to read, dread and fury.

The little fool. She must learn never to speak or write again. Teaching that lesson would be a pleasure.

The letter went on:

> I loved Pamela as much as you did (those words were paralyzing), in my way, and I know how sharp must be your pain, how dark your despair. My own heart is broken. When I wake I think it's been a dream and she will be there if I call her. I have rung her home phone but now they've even taken her message away. Did they want to scrub it all clean as if she were never with us?
>
> It is so hard to lose Pamela. There will never be another like her. I expect every distant rider to be her. Then the horse grows closer with a stranger on its back and I run away to cry.
>
> You know I will always be here when you want a friend. You can share your feelings with me whenever and wherever you please. Perhaps we can help unravel this most dreadful crime against a sweet one.
>
> Never hesitate to come to me.

The paper crumpled and burned easily in the fireplace.

Damn her. She wouldn't have long to wait for that visit.

TWENTY-ONE

When Alex walked into the bar, the sight of O'Reilly and Lamb sitting in the grey light of early morning made her want to order them out, to tell them a woman was entitled to some privacy, particularly when she'd had such a horrible time.

'How did you get in here?' She flipped on lights, including the fairy lights strung along the roofline outside. They made her feel better.

'We're staying here,' Lamb said, but softly enough as he took in a crutch, a surgical boot, one arm in a sling. She couldn't manage the crutch very well anyway. Two had been impossible with her shoulder injury, but it had been this or a wheelchair and that wasn't happening.

'Turn that coffee pot on,' Alex said. 'It's all ready. There are some of yesterday's pastries but they won't be too bad.' She was starving.

Lamb followed her orders and she caught the sparkle in Dan O'Reilly's eyes. Nice of him to find this amusing.

'Sit down,' he told her, holding a chair out for her at the Burke sisters' table. 'We'll get the fire going.'

'Hugh will be right in once he's parked. He'll do that.' She didn't say Tony was also parking, having dropped her at the door. Let them all deal with their dislike of each other. What would be annoying would be the arrival of the reporter. She hoped he was a late sleeper.

Alex sat down.

'You've had an accident,' Dan said. 'What happened?'

'You can see what happened,' she said but didn't feel proud of snapping.

'Yes, but how? You've come from a hospital, haven't you?'

'I fell and yes, I had to go to the hospital. I've got a cracked clavicle and a sprained ankle. Doesn't feel very good but I'll manage.'

He sat with his chair turned so he could see her. 'Of course it doesn't feel good. I'm sorry.'

His unblinking regard made her uncomfortable. She looked at her watch. 'Five thirty. I'm going to need some relief staff today. We start serving breakfast for guests at seven.'

'That's just us and it doesn't matter. So forget that.'

She didn't mention Patrick Guest from the Gloucester newspaper.

Tony came into the bar with Hugh. She almost grinned at the irritation on Tony's face, then saw a mirrored expression from Dan and covered the lower half of her face until the bubble in her throat came under control. If she wasn't careful she'd get hysterical and ruin her reputation!

Bill Lamb came with coffee and a plate of pastries that turned her stomach.

'She takes cream,' Tony said and the look Bill gave him should have felled most people.

Tony had the grace to get the cream himself, and manage to bring two more mugs of coffee. He went back for another two and gave one to Hugh.

'I could eat cardboard,' Bill said, sinking his teeth into an iced bun that required some tugging with the teeth to release a bite.

Hugh got the fire going, stood and smacked his palms together.

'Isn't this cozy,' Tony said, sitting beside Alex. 'We should do it more often.'

Dan grinned at him and turned his attention to Hugh who was on his mobile, calling extra staff to come in early.

'Must have been some fall,' Dan said and he wasn't visibly amused anymore. 'Down some stairs, perhaps?'

'Yes.' This was a subject that must be downplayed, difficult as that might me. 'Missed the edge of a step and bam, I was surprised to haul myself up and not be dead.'

The company laughed.

'But you didn't do it here,' Dan said. 'I'd have heard. I'm right near the stairs.'

'At my house,' Tony said without looking at Alex.

She was grateful but she also caught the satisfaction with which Tony delivered his bail out. He liked laying claim to her – OK, she rather liked it, too.

Hugh's stare was something she felt. He frowned and she realized Lily must have told him she'd heard from Alex after she was injured and before she arrived at Tony's house. She gave Hugh a hard look and he nodded slightly.

'What do any of you know about Jay Gibbon? Did he visit Pamela? Did you all know him?' Dan asked.

'Never saw him before he came in here that night,' Alex said and the others agreed. 'Which doesn't mean he didn't visit Pamela, or that she might not have gone to see him. Is he her next of kin, Dan?'

'We're still working on that.'

He might as well have said, *And I wouldn't tell you anyway.* Alex kept her attention on the flames now curling over the blackened chimney breast.

'Surely Pamela had family somewhere,' Hugh said.

Bill's expression left no doubt that he didn't welcome another civilian sticking his spoon into the official pot.

'Eventually we'll be able to talk about it,' Dan said. 'We're going to be working in the lovely parish hall again. Too bad spring can't make up its mind. That place is parky. And we'll have to beg the heavens to keep its rain away from the holes in the roof.'

Bill gave a derisive snort.

'All part of the job, though,' Hugh said. 'We should be able to look after you better, though. I'll look into some portable heaters – and buckets.' His smile was definitely a bone crusher although the two detectives weren't enamored. 'We'll also make sure you get plenty of coffee and fresh snacks. Just call if you need anything we don't think of.'

'Thank you,' Dan said. 'We'll provide a donations pot.'

Alex barely stopped herself from saying she'd provide a bill. 'Have you been hearing the rumors running around?'

'What rumors? About what?'

Tony leaned toward Dan and asked in a stage whisper, 'Pamela Gibbon, *was* she pregnant when she died?'

The fire got a vigorous poking from Hugh.

The detectives' faces closed, but not before they gave each other an irritated glance.

'Where did you hear that?' Bill took the lead this time.

'Nowhere in particular.' Tony drank more coffee. 'But it's likely to gather steam if we can't snuff it out.'

'You know where you heard it,' Dan said flatly. 'But I'll know all about that soon enough. And you'd better keep your mouths shut, and shut up any other gossipmongers because that is just gossip. The post-mortem report isn't in. They've been backed up with work.'

Alex's often too creative mind saw a flash image of rows and rows of white-draped bodies on gurneys. She collected herself. 'How many murders have there been in the area . . . in the last few days?'

Dan shook his head, raised one brow and said, 'Did you know Jay Gibbon is staying in Pamela's house? Moved in last night.'

Confused glances followed – and silence.

'He didn't want to stay here any longer, not with Bill and me in residence. There didn't seem to be any reason why he shouldn't be at Cedric Chase, not since he was the stepson and the solicitor had no difficulty with it. He has a very complete inventory of the house contents. Believe it or not, it was Harry Stroud's idea. That man never holds back from joining a conversation.'

Swallowing with difficulty, Alex tried to interpret reactions around the table. Mostly they were blank except for Bill Lamb who was also studying faces with his unusual guileless blue eyes.

'I'm surprised you're finished with the house,' Tony said finally and wandered off to refill his coffee.

'We've taken away what we need,' Dan said. 'The housekeeper had been going in and out since Mrs Gibbon left. There was already a lot disturbed, and we feel confident we've done a very good job.'

'Why would he stay here at all?' Hugh said.

He got a sideways flick of the eyes from Dan that suggested he'd forgotten the other man was there. 'Think about it. You'll come up with some reasons.'

Alex was uncomfortable and growing short-tempered. 'I've got work to do,' she said. 'I'll be in the kitchen.'

'No you won't,' Tony said mildly. 'You could have a concussion.'

'I rounded up plenty of help.' Hugh took the carafe Tony had been holding and added to Alex's and his own mug. 'They'll start arriving soon.'

His phone ringing had Tony patting pockets in various parts of his clothing until he located the mobile. He answered and grew very still.

'Yes, Reverend,' he said after a few seconds. 'I'm on my way. No, no, never second guess a decision like that.'

TWENTY-TWO

O'Reilly studied Alex with interest. As soon as Tony had more or less sprinted from the building, she shifted in her chair as if she wanted to be anywhere but in her own bar. When she caught his eye she gave him an unconvincing little smile. 'Mystery after mystery.' The dismissive lightness didn't come off.

'Hugh, could you help me upstairs? I need to lie down. Dan, sorry to burden you, but when staff starts coming in, please explain I'm wiped out and I said to carry on. They all know what they need to do.'

Bill waited long enough for Hugh and Alex to be out of sight and leaned close to Dan. 'We need to see where Harrison's gone.'

'We will. Stand by to follow when Hugh leaves. Ms Duggins is probably phoning Harrison as we speak. Hugh will go to help out with whatever's going on.' Flames in the fire flickered lower and he automatically got up to place more logs in the grate. He turned and closed his eyes, listening. 'Is that a vehicle coming this way?'

Bill went to kneel on one side of a window seat, behind a curtain, and took a cautious look. 'Not sure if it's coming here, but it's a powerful engine.'

'See if we can get Harrison's position from his mobile.'

'You've got it.' Bill paused, flattened to the wall with the curtain held open a fraction. 'Big, burgundy Mercedes. That's Doc James' car. He's driving around the back of the pub.'

'They don't get medals for subtlety,' Dan said.

Bill was already talking to the station urgently about Tony's whereabouts.

The Reverend Ivor Davis ran into the middle of the narrow road where he'd been waiting for Tony. 'Please hurry. I shouldn't have left but I was afraid you wouldn't find me.'

Ivor Davis stood six and a half feet tall and was built like a discus thrower, all long, lean muscle – with the upper body of a rower. Under one arm, a ginger long-haired dachshund flopped in a sack-of-potatoes position.

'This way.' Around the next leftward bend in the road, the vicar took off up a lane anyone could be forgiven for missing. Larches had grown so thick and tall they all but camouflaged the overgrown little path.

Ivor had said it was some sort of medical emergency and Tony had already asked his father to stand by.

He had a sudden revelation. 'We're coming in at the back,' he said. 'Radhika rents a little place up here.'

'Yes,' Ivor said. 'Keep with me.' He reached a point where they could see a one-story, gray stone cottage not much bigger than a small barn.

'Come on.' Ivor veered from the small road that came in from a lane at the far side of the property and which people would use to go to the cottage, and crashed through a waist-high tangle of woodland shrubs and weeds. The pungent scent of dog's mercury blooms assaulted the nose.

'Tell me something,' Tony shouted, his gut in knots.

'Over there.' Ivor pointed.

At first Tony didn't know what he was pointing at, then he saw a little heap among the weeds at the base of a tree. As he dashed closer, there were pieces of bright silk poking out beneath a black coat draped on top.

'Good God.' He reached what he knew was Radhika in a couple of strides and dropped down beside her. The silk scarf had dropped from her hair which lay in great twisted lengths. 'Radhika?' He felt her neck, found a pulse and dropped his chin onto his chest for a moment of relief.

'I think she's been beaten,' Ivor said, coming to crouch beside Tony. He put the dog down and pulled back the collar of his own black raincoat. 'She wouldn't speak at first. Then she said she only wanted you. She said no one else but you.'

Tony placed another call and his dad answered with the sound of his powerful car engine in the background. With one hand, he continued moving hair away from the woman's face. 'It's at Radhika's place, Dad. Call for an ambulance but you'll be here quicker.' He shoved the mobile away.

'Where do you hurt?' Tony whispered close to her ear but she only mumbled.

'Help me, Ivor. I'm going to try to hear anything she'll say.' Head to head, they bowed over her and Tony said, 'Any pain or numbness, Radhika?'

He pulled the hair completely away from her face and she shook her head, no.

'Want to die,' she said very softly. 'Better.'

The two men exchanged glances.

'I'm going to try to get a better look,' Tony said. The blood on her face had dried, both of her eyes were swollen almost shut. The bottom lip had a deep cut and blood from her nose had streamed over her lower face. She said nothing more and kept her eyes shut all the way.

'Dad's got the ambulance coming, but we'd better call the police.'

'No! I cannot. I must not. Please, no police. Leave me here.' Radhika forced out the words as if summoning up her last reserves of energy.

Leave her there to die?

She had feeling in all of her extremities, but that was about the best that could be said for her condition. Giving her shoulder the slightest lift, Tony waited, and when she didn't make a sound, moved her another inch or so. Gradually, with Ivor bearing a lot of the slight weight, he turned her over and settled her down again.

'We need a board,' Tony said, and looked up at the sound of an engine prowling in from the main entrance to the little clearing. He stood and ran to flag his father down.

The older man shot out of the car, Hugh did the same from the back seat and Alex swung her legs from the front passenger seat and struggled upright.

'Radhika's been beaten,' Tony said. 'She's . . . well, there's blood and bruising and she doesn't want to talk. I think we'd better try to keep her away from anyone else for a little while – unless she really needs the hospital. I think it might be a fight to get her there. She said she can't see the police. I'm going to the cottage to see if there's something we could improvise to carry her.'

'Boot of my car,' his dad said, tossing the keys. 'Folding stretcher and my bag.' He made amazingly rapid progress in the direction Tony had come from.

'Please sit down, Alex,' Tony said, and to Hugh, 'Let's get the stuff from the boot. We should warm her up. I don't know how long she's been out here. Reverend Davis found her when he was walking Fred.'

When they had the stretcher and Doc Harrison's bag, they came back past Alex who still stood in the same place. 'I want to help.'

Tony kissed her cheek quickly. 'She's going to need a lot of help, perhaps for more than a day or two, I think. But for now we need to get her into the cottage. She's talking about wanting to die.'

TWENTY-THREE

'Shit,' Hugh said with feeling. 'What are those two doing here?'
Frowning and walking with a lot of purpose, Harry Stroud and Vivian Seabrook walked toward the cottage from the same direction Tony and Reverend Davis had come earlier.

Tony shaded his eyes from early rays of sun and levered himself up from an age-worn wooden bench. His dad and Alex were in the cottage with Radhika and Ivor Davis had returned to St Aldwyn's for a service.

'I asked O'Reilly and Lamb to hold off. There won't be much they can do anyway if Radhika continues to say she doesn't know who did it and isn't filing a complaint.' Tony braced his feet apart and waited for the company to arrive. 'They didn't like it but they're biding their time. How the devil did Harry and Vivian get wind of this?'

'Let's see what they say,' Hugh said quietly.

When they were close, Vivian speeded ahead of Harry. Her hands were rolled into fists at her sides and there was no missing the shock on her face. 'I want to see Radhika,' she said. 'Is she still in there?'

'Yes,' Tony told her. 'But no visitors yet. Doc James is with her. Alex is in there to help if she can.'

Vivian made to push past but it was Harry who relieved Tony by holding the woman back. With difficulty, he turned her around and held her close. 'Best wait, old thing,' he said.

'She's a good friend.' Vivian's sniffling wasn't a comforting sound. 'She came here because of Pamela. Now look what's happened. *Both* of them attacked. How could anyone hurt a gentle soul like Radhika? What's happening in Folly? It's terrifying.'

Harry rubbed her back awkwardly and Vivian shrugged away. 'Alex shouldn't be there – I should. If Alex has her way, the next thing I'll hear is that I could be guilty of something to do with this.'

'Bollocks,' Hugh said. 'They've already said it wasn't Alex who called in that tip about you. Anyway, that's history, lass. Sit on the bench and rest yourself. It's a shocking thing. Meaningless. But the doctor's already said she can be cared for here, although she'll need a wee trip to the hospital for X-rays in case anything's broken.'

'It's true then,' Harry said. 'Someone . . . this is awful . . . someone did attack her?'

'They did,' Hugh agreed. 'She's so small she would have been easily knocked down and beaten.'

'Don't!' Vivian said. She sat on the bench and covered her face.

Hugh crossed his arms and asked of Harry, 'How did you hear about this?'

'We were walking. The delivery driver from George's Bakery stopped and told us,' Harry said.

Hugh and Tony both shook their heads from side to side.

The front door to the cottage opened and Tony's father came out. He shut the door behind him. 'Where's the bloody ambulance?' he said. 'Radhika's unlikely to say much but we had to let the police know what's going on; more or less. I didn't give much detail, though. That Dan O'Reilly's a sensible chap. He'll tread lightly, and he's agreed to hold off trying to question her for a bit. He told me they were off to the parish hall where his team is. Radhika can't be subjected to anymore pressure at all yet.'

Tony raised his brows in question.

Doc Harrison pulled him aside and murmured, 'Her fingers were deliberately broken. Some of the ends are crushed.'

TWENTY-FOUR

The sound of the brass knocker reverberated, but the door scraped open over a worn stone step before anyone could react. Bill Lamb looked over his shoulder at the entrance to the parish hall. 'Well, well, boss, look what the wind blew in.'

'Remember what we talked about earlier,' Dan said. 'We need co-operation in a community like this. Antagonizing people won't get us anywhere.'

He half-rose from his seat and waved Tony and Alex over. They looked bedraggled and exhausted.

Tony helped Alex with her hop-and-swing gait, but gave O'Reilly and Lamb a wave. 'At least it's not raining,' he said, nodding at the team members they passed. 'That's sun coming through those dusty windows. Busy bees in here.'

O'Reilly wanted to see a whole lot more activity in the hall. They had a ton of incidents but the leads were thin.

The windows were high in the walls. Green, yellow and red patchworks of leaded glass festooned with cobwebs. 'Come and have a seat,' Dan said, getting two more folding chairs to pull up to the desk.

'Coffee?' Bill asked, and Dan came close to guffawing. His sergeant was already on his feet and heading for the coffee maker Hugh Rhys had brought over from the Black Dog only half an hour earlier.

'Thanks, Bill,' Alex said as she dropped into a chair and leaned her single crutch against his desk. 'We came because we think we have to, even though no one's making a complaint. Doc James dropped us off. He'd like to talk to you a bit later.'

Bill arrived back with the coffee on a tray with a jug of milk and a plate of chocolate digestive biscuits. 'Who should be making a complaint? Doc James said we'd get a full explanation . . . or is this something different?'

That didn't get a reply.

'What's gone on at that cottage?' Dan asked. 'What's the woman's name there?' He started leafing through his notebook.

'Radhika Malek,' Alex said promptly. 'She's Tony's assistant at the small animal clinic here in Folly.' She narrowed her eyes to get a better look at the whiteboards the team had installed.

Case notes, photographs, comments, spiders' webs of lines joining leads and subjects of interest, but unfortunately all fairly tentative still. Alex was obviously too far away to make out anything she might not already know.

'She's been taken into a hospital for X-rays,' Tony added. 'She insists she's coming back home as soon as they're done with her but I don't think she should be in that place alone. She needs someone to care for her and . . . she's too vulnerable there.'

'You haven't said what happened,' Bill put in.

'Just what my father must have told you. She was beaten up – badly. I think she'd been lying on the ground a long time when Reverend Davis found her.' Tony looked sideways at Alex and cleared his throat. 'Fingers deliberately broken. Ends of some were crushed – the nails. You'll be the people to take some guesses at what he used to do it. I didn't see any metal gratings lying around.'

'Which hospital?' Dan said without commenting on Tony's reference to Pamela Gibbon's murder and the obvious similarity between some of their injuries. He wouldn't be tolerating further attempts at secrecy. 'We need someone there with her now.'

'I'm not sure where they took her,' Tony said. 'There was so much confusion.'

Dan was inclined to believe him. 'Williams,' he called to a woman DC, 'find out which hospital a Radhika Malek has been taken to from Folly-on-Weir.'

'On it,' the officer replied. 'Probably Cheltenham or Gloucester unless it's something really minor.'

'I can call my dad,' Tony said, punching at his mobile. 'He'll know.'

Watching the man's easy rapport with his father caused Dan a twinge of envy.

'Cheltenham,' Tony said.

'Cheltenham.' DC Williams said from her desk. 'Primary Care Center.'

'You people are quick but you won't make her say anything she doesn't want to say. She's terrified of something and she obviously has good reasons.'

Only a fool would refuse opinions from someone who might be useful. Dan rubbed the side of his nose. 'Any ideas about those?'

'I think she's hiding something because she can't afford not to,' Alex said. Her expressive eyes held the shadows of her lashes and deep anxiety. 'She thinks if she died it would be a good thing. She said so. I don't think that means she wants to die . . . I don't really have any idea what she means.'

'Tony,' Dan said, 'do you have employment records for Radhika? You must.'

'Yes, of course. I can't recite them but there was nothing that stood out negatively. She came from another veterinary clinic with good references. She's a fine employee.'

'We'll want to take a look at those records,' Bill said. 'I'll see to putting a guard on her right now.' He went to his own desk and got on the phone.

There was something he was missing. Dan splayed his fingertips on his forehead.

'When she first came here, Radhika stayed with Pamela.' Alex sounded faraway, as if she were thinking aloud.

Tony murmured, 'Didn't everyone know that?'

Dan dropped his hands to answer Tony. 'I didn't. Williams! Find out who interviewed Radhika Malek about Pamela Gibbon – after the victim died. Je-sus, not one word have I seen about anything like that.'

'Pamela recommended her to me,' Tony said. 'She spoke to me up at the Derwinter stables first. She told me her friend was staying with her and wanted to move to Folly. Radhika had done some veterinary work at a clinic in Cornwall . . . St Kew, I think that's where Pamela and her husband lived before they came here.'

Alex braced her supported elbow on the desk and frowned unseeingly at Dan. 'It doesn't take a great brain to work out there are connections and similarities here. How are you doing with the things that were left in the tower at Ebring Manor? Have you traced any of them?'

Bill cleared his throat. 'We can't discuss those details.'

Tony shot out his feet and leaned back in his chair, clasping his hands behind his head. His smile set O'Reilly's teeth on edge. 'Okey dokey. Alex and I were really taken with the binoculars. Expensive and left behind in an old bag like that?' He tutted. 'They must have had other fingerprints on them, in addition to Alex's and mine.'

O'Reilly looked at Bill who gazed blankly back.

This was touchy. 'Binoculars?' he said.

'Zeiss. Fancy – very expensive.' Tony was giving him a puzzled look. 'In a green canvas bag.'

Alex shifted irritably, or more likely she was uncomfortable. 'In the bag in the tower, with some glacé chestnuts or something. There was a box of those.'

'Shit,' Bill said, 'We didn't find a bag, or any binoculars.'

TWENTY-FIVE

What looked like a large white napkin, sunshine turning it luminous, fluttered from an upstairs window at Leaves of Comfort. Walking along Pond Street, past the tea rooms, was the shortest route from the parish hall to the Black Dog.

'Are they surrendering?' Tony said when they had a better angle on the building and could see Harriet clearly.

'You were a facetious teenager,' Alex said, trying not to show how fatigued she was. 'Forever young, that's you, Harrison. I can't hear what Harriet's saying.'

Tony waved. 'We don't need to hear. We're being summoned. Should have called someone to pick us up from the parish hall.'

'It isn't far to the Dog.' She was glad of his arm around her, his hand firmly gripping her waist. 'I might even go for a shot of very good brandy.'

'Me, too. But let's see what the ladies want. Then I'll have someone drive my vehicle over for me and take you home for the brandy. You don't need to be at the Dog today, do you?'

'Tony! Alex!' Harriet had pushed the window wide open.

'Coming,' Tony called, then under his breath said, 'you never know, they could have heard something useful, not that I'm sure I should be allowing you to keep poking your nose into all this.'

'Me?' Her voice broke off in a squeak.

He grinned down at her. 'Does the name Gidley-Rains mean anything to you? Looked like it said Bourton underneath. Bourton-on-the-Water, I assume.'

They turned in at the Burke sisters' gate. Encouraged by the sunshine, a profusion of yellow and purple pansies was starting to open along the pathway. 'I don't know,' Alex responded. 'I'll have to think about it . . . but what did you say about me poking my nose into things? Didn't you take a sneaky read of the whiteboards at the parish hall? Isn't that how you found Gidley-Rains' name?'

'Hurry, you two. Come right on in. The coffee's getting cool. And we've got a houseful waiting for you.'

'What's she talking about?' Tony muttered. 'They didn't know they'd see us.'

He opened the blue door, pushed it wide, and got Alex inside. Seconds later Harriet appeared in the doorway at the top of the stairs to their flat and Katie tore past her. Tongue lolling, whining with ecstasy, she barreled into Tony. Bogie appeared from behind Harriet, his entire body wiggling.

'Hello, my friend,' Tony said, rubbing Katie down. 'What are you doing . . . here?' He narrowed his eyes. 'I left her with Radhika, of course I did.'

'Lily brought them,' Harriet said. 'Would you get that girl up the stairs, Tony Harrison? And I don't mean your dog.'

'Yes, madam,' Tony said, and enjoyed lifting and carrying a scowling Alex despite her rigid body.

'Lily had to go over to the Slaughters for some local art sale.' Harriet scratched Bogie's head and pushed both Oliver, and new boy Maxwell Brady back into the flat. He wore a black eye patch and seemed comfortable with it.

'What did Mum say about having Katie?'

'She turned up at the Dog, trailing her leash, around midnight,' Mary called from the ladies' sitting room. 'We think Radhika must have lost hold of her when she was attacked.'

Tony leaned against a wall and returned Alex's puzzled look. They both shook their heads. 'Let me get you settled,' he said. 'Then we'll start the inquisition. We're ready for a warm, fresh roll or two – with or without anything on them.'

'I'll heat something up for you,' Harriet said. 'Put Alex on the couch.'

The sagging, faded pink velvet couch wasn't the most comfortable but Alex settled gratefully. The sisters' sitting room folded any visitor into its pink warmness. Faded, fringed puce velvet drapes framed thick-paned windows and pink and green carpets, worn to silky shine, covered much of the dark oak floors.

Swathed in a green shawl and rocking gently in her favorite spindled chair, Mary Burke faced the window over St Aldwyn's churchyard. She pointed a thin and elegant finger at Tony and Alex. 'I'm disappointed in you two.'

Alex raised her brows. 'Really?'

'So much going on. So much you obviously don't yet know. But you didn't come to see if we might know something useful. You came quickly enough when you needed us for . . . when you needed us the last time.'

'I want it all to go away,' Alex said. 'It's unbelievable that we've had another murder in Folly – or near Folly. And it's been a whirlwind, Mary. You know we always want your opinions.'

Settling in front of the small fireplace with her nose on her paws, Katie watched the cats warily while Oliver and Maxwell eyed her from either side of the hearth. Bogie leaned against the couch where Alex lay and cast baleful looks at her.

Harriet had been into the kitchen and returned with a steaming kettle from which she added water to the china coffee pot. Retracing her steps, she came back without the kettle but carrying a platter of steaming cottage rolls, a bowl filled with small pots of jam and with a butter dish balanced beside the rolls. 'It's too early for today's fresh delivery but you'll enjoy these.'

While Harriet dealt with putting rolls, butter and pots of jam on plates, Tony squished in by Alex's feet, lifting them onto his thighs where they felt very comfortable.

'Harriet?' Mary said. 'What about . . . you know?'

'Oh, my, yes.' Producing a package from behind a cushion like a conjurer whipping a rabbit from a hat, Harriet presented it to Alex. 'Don't open it too quickly. Do you know who Sarah Chauncey Woolsey was?'

Alex squinched up her eyes. 'This is a book. It must be a children's book.' She collected them. 'I've been too distracted to think of them this year.'

'We'll talk about what all this is doing to you later,' Tony said.

His feelings for her showed. He wanted her to be happy . . . and he just *wanted* her. Her body tightened and turned warm. She smiled at him. 'Perhaps we will,' she murmured.

'And from what I hear you've been too distracted to paint, too, Alex.' Mary looked disapproving. 'You shouldn't squander so much talent. Now Sarah Woolsey . . .'

Alex tipped her head back and grinned. 'It's Susan Coolidge, of course. She was American but I read all the Katy books when I was a child.' She couldn't wait any longer to tear the paper away. 'Crikey! *What Katy Did* and it's really old. It's . . . no, it can't be a first edition. It is!' The book had a gold-colored board cover with a little band of ants, or crickets – she wasn't sure – scampering across the front. But the publication date was 1872. A first edition. 'You can't

give it to me, ladies. Whew, how much do I owe you. I know you
must have bought it.'

The ladies exchanged a glance. 'Shall we tell her?' Mary said
and when Harriet nodded, added, 'We found it in a box of things
from when we were children. I hardly remembered it.'

'You should keep it,' Alex said. 'It must have a special meaning
for both of you.'

'There are just the two of us. No family to pass things to. And
if the book can bring out that smile, my girl, it's in the right hands
now. Anyway, it's ours so we can give it to you. End of subject.'

'Thank you both,' Alex whispered.

'OK,' Tony said. 'I hate to change the subject but Katie went to
the Dog and Lily took her in, right? Didn't anyone go to find out
if Radhika was all right?'

'Juste Vidal called her. She said Katie got away from her and
she was glad the dog was OK. Lily offered to keep the dog
and Radhika didn't argue. She hung up on Juste.'

Muscles in Tony's thighs had flexed beneath Alex's ankles. 'How
did you find out Radhika had been hurt?' she asked.

'Your mum told us when she came this morning. We need to find
out when Radhika was attacked. Juste told us she only gave one-
word answers. So what was the timeline?'

Alex suppressed a smile at Harriet's ease with detection.

'After your mum left, we knew to watch for you because you
would probably walk back to the Dog from the parish hall,' Mary
said. 'Doc James dropped you there, correct?'

'Mm,' Alex said.

Mary suddenly pushed up from her chair and stood, holding the
walker with one hand. She faced Tony and Alex with an air that
suggested something momentous to come. 'Harriet and I are going
to take Radhika in here, aren't we?'

'When she's discharged from the hospital,' Harriet said. 'I'm
going up to visit as soon as they'll let me. I want to tell her we
won't hear of her going home to that cottage alone. We're hiring
Prue Wally to come and help out. With Pamela Gibbon gone, Prue
needs the extra.'

Alex feared the idea of Radhika being alone but she wondered
how it would work for her to be here. Would it put Harriet and
Mary in danger, too?

'She's going to have my room,' Harriet said. 'It's got an en suite bathroom. I'll move in with Mary. She's got twin beds in there. We may have to ask you to help us get her settled.'

There didn't seem anything to argue about and with plenty of people around at the Burke's, Radhika should be safe.

'That's good of you,' Tony said. 'Alex can also help persuade Radhika – she's very fond of Alex. And I'll help out with everything. But we'll have to clear this with the police and make sure the three of you will be OK.'

'I hope that lovely Dan O'Reilly comes to see us. I've got a few questions for him.'

Hiding a smile behind her coffee cup, Harriet said, 'Mary always had a soft spot for a good-looking Irishman. What I want to know is why they're taking their time the way they are. Young Jay Gibbon was in yesterday and he said as much, too. We hadn't seen him since . . . well, I suppose it was when he was coming to see his father years ago. He's changed a lot. Looks a bit down at heel.'

'You knew Jay?' Alex said slowly. 'I didn't remember him at all.'

'It would have been when you were away,' Harriet told her. 'You weren't around much for some years after you went up to town for school.'

Alex didn't want to talk about all that. 'But Jay came by yesterday? Just for tea?'

Mary turned the full effect of her ice-cube thick glasses on them. 'He had tea but we asked him up at closing time. After all, he's been through a lot, too. He seems a bit shocked. I was surprised he's staying at Pamela's though, even if it was once his father's, too.'

The scent of lilacs wafted from a bowl of potpourri near the fire. Alex let her eyelids close a little while silence slipped softly around her. When she opened her eyes again, Maxwell stretched, arched his back and edged close to Katie. The cat settled in, back to back with the dog and closed his one eye. Evidently a bond remained from Katie's nursing efforts when Maxwell was injured.

'So what exactly did Jay have to say?' Tony asked at last.

'According to Jay, the solicitor hasn't sent out the will yet. Apparently the man's been on vacation.' Harriet set down her cup. She got up and opened the window, let in the scent of loamy soil and thick grass recently mown beneath the trees. 'He still thinks there's something funny going on but he doesn't know what.

Apparently his father always said there would be a provision for Jay when he was forty, even if Charles Gibbon was dead and Pamela had inherited. He looks older but he turned forty a week or so ago and he didn't hear a thing.'

'He hated Pamela,' Mary said. She was looking at her roll from all sides as if it were something she'd never seen before. 'She had everything and he could never get a break.'

'Mary,' Harriet said gently, 'he never said he hated Pamela.'

'You could tell he did,' Mary said, a stubborn purse to her pale lips. She turned to Tony and Alex again. 'Haven't the police talked to the solicitor yet? You'd think they'd do that right away.'

'They don't tell us what they're up to,' Tony said mildly, although his eyes were steely when they met Alex's. 'Hang on. Let me just look something up.' He took out his mobile and whipped his thumbs over the touch screen.

'Venetia Stroud was the one I was surprised to see,' Harriet said. 'She joined Jay when he was at a table downstairs. It was strange, almost like she'd been waiting to follow him in.'

Absently, Tony patted Alex's ankles. She'd stiffened automatically at the mention of Venetia.

'What time was that?' Alex asked. The little room felt too warm and closed in.

'Just before closing time,' Mary told her promptly. 'That's why it wasn't awkward to ask Jay up to our flat. Venetia went out first and I told Jay I'd saved something for him.'

Tony smiled at Alex and frowned afterward. 'You OK?' Her anxiety must show. She nodded at him, yes. Surely he had worked out that Venetia came to Leaves of Comfort while Alex was locked in Harry's flat. 'Found what I wanted in Bourton-on-the-Water. The name on the whiteboard at the parish hall. It's a solicitor.'

Which meant the police were very aware of needing details of Pamela's will. Why hadn't she and Tony thought about that?

Bright as ever, Mary said, 'Do you mean you've found Pamela's solicitor? Couldn't we think of an excuse to call his office just to see if he's really away?'

'No,' Alex said flatly. 'Your lovely Dan O'Reilly would have our heads.'

'Did Jay say anything about Venetia?' Tony asked the sisters. 'I wouldn't have thought they knew one another.'

'Venetia and the major met Jay on his first trip to Folly. He was looking for his father's house and stopped at the Strouds' to see if they could give him directions. He was only a little way off. Cedric Chase is very close.'

'So Venetia supposedly saw Jay coming into the tea rooms and followed just to say hello?' Tony looked skeptical.

'We decided she followed him here, didn't we, Mary?' said Harriet. 'It might have been a chance that she saw him, but she's never been here before so why now unless she was looking for Jay? And she was all dressed up. I've never really had more than a word or two with her but she was always quietly turned out. A lot of make-up yesterday, too. She was excitable as if she was on the verge of something momentous.'

Just as Alex had seen her and the times probably meshed. Venetia must have left the Stroud house, seen Jay, and watched to find out where he went.

'She wanted to know if he had met you yet, Alex,' Harriet said, 'and whether you had said anything about Harry. He got the feeling Venetia didn't like you, or trust you and she warned Jay to be careful what he said around you about Pamela and what might have happened to her.'

Tony whistled, long and low. 'That's preposterous. Why is she singling out Alex?'

'I'm not sure, but Jay wonders if Venetia thinks her son has done something he shouldn't have and she's trying to cover for him. She said Alex is a woman twice scorned.'

Alex only stared at Harriet and forced a swallow to calm her thunderous heartbeat.

'You are not to get upset by this,' Harriet said.

Mary shook her head emphatically. 'Absolutely not.'

'She said you'd been scorned by your husband, and now she thinks you've been scorned by Harry and you've got plans to punish him. She told Jay not to take anything you say seriously.'

TWENTY-SIX

I'm getting closer and it would be too easy to rush things.

They fall for every crumb I throw them – fucking incompetents and amateurs. But I can't let down until I've got what I need. If my little Sherlock Holmes clones had stayed out of it, this could all have been over by now. You'd think they would have learned from that last near mess that they shouldn't meddle. Alex almost died. Too bad she didn't.

Success has a taste, not sweet, not spicy – it's exciting! It's like the tang of a lover's body when she's surrendered and you've won. I've known that taste well and I can swallow it again in my mind. This could all have been so different if Pamela had only admitted how much she loved me. We would have had everything together. Love and hate are such close companions.

This is no time for dreams, or regrets.

This one is dangerous to me now, but she isn't afraid often enough – and that makes her the perfect victim.

I'm walking behind you, Alex.

TWENTY-SEVEN

A t home with Alex.
  In the middle of the day.
  In the middle of all the chaos, and he felt peace. This was right.

'Do you still feel like that brandy?' he asked, assessing her pale, tired face, the withdrawn expression, and that other thing he sometimes saw in her – insecurity?

She nodded, yes, and rested her forehead on the back of her hand atop the kitchen table. 'I should go home and check out the house,' she said, her voice muffled.

'Lily thought about that. She checked already. All fine there, and Prue Wally will go in and freshen things up.'

'Prue is going to be a very busy woman,' Alex said, straightening up as Tony put a glass of brandy beside her. 'I can't get over the gift from Harriet and Mary. The book is a little gem.'

He ran a hand over her curly hair. 'You're special to them.' A glance from those almond-shaped green eyes and he was sucked in. And he was glad of it.

'Why would Venetia make a crack about my being twice scorned? She knows there's never been anything between Harry and me.'

'Do you think Jay's got a point and the woman's afraid Harry's done something criminal? You said she was an odd one. She could be half out of her mind worrying about her baby boy and trying to cover for him.' Bogie rose from beneath the table and stood beside Alex, staring into her face with what looked like a deeply worried frown. 'Your boy needs reassurance,' Tony added.

'I'm sorry,' she said reaching for his hand and lacing her fingers with his. 'This is a strain on you, too. We'll come through it.'

The wall clock ticked loudly several times before he squeezed her hand. 'I meant Bogie, but I'm glad to be your boy, too.'

She turned slightly pink and laughed. 'Poor Bogie.' At the sound of his name on his beloved mistress's lips, the dog pushed his head on her lap.

The house phone rang and Tony picked it up. 'Harrison.'

'This is Lily. Are you two OK? I want to see Alex as soon as I can. Would she be better at Corner Cottage, do you think? We could make sure she rests and have someone there all the time, at least when you and I have to work at the same time.'

'Just a moment.' Tony put his hand over the mouthpiece. A better man wouldn't have thoughts of refusing the offer and making an excuse to Alex. 'Your mother wants to know if you'd be better at Corner Cottage. It's up to you.'

He made what felt like a good hangdog expression. Being a better man was a pain in the ass sometimes.

Alex took the phone from him. 'Hi, Mum. I'm doing better.' She listened quietly, then said, 'I think I'm good here. But I reserve the right to change my mind.'

Her smile suggested she'd amused her mother. 'I know,' Alex said. 'As soon as they say we can, we'll go to the hospital. We've been told to wait until Radhika is strong enough. Mm. Later. Love you.' She handed him the phone and he hung up.

'Drink the brandy,' Tony said. 'Then I'm taking you to bed.'

Wearing one of Tony's shirts and propped against a pile of pillows in his bed, Alex watched him move about the room. Sun still poured through open curtains and a maple tree waved gently outside the window.

'Tony, may I take—'

'Nope, you can't take a shower yet. Not without me in there to help you. That would take a long time and you're too weak.'

Did he think having him help her out of her clothes and into his shirt had made her feel less wobbly-legged?

'I feel filthy. I am filthy.'

'You're not.' He advanced on her with several damp flannels and a towel. Ignoring her protests, he wiped her face and neck, and gave her ears a wipe.

'Ew, Tony!'

He snickered.

Another washcloth went under the shirt and made an unspeakable, if gentle, passage over her body and he followed up with a towel rub. 'Don't tell me that doesn't feel better.' He pulled the sheet up from her feet and gave them a good washing.

'That's it, thank you,' she wailed, clamping the sheet tightly around her body. 'You'll be punished. I'm going to wait till you're asleep one night and do that to you.'

Smug – that covered the look he gave her. 'Really? That's wonderful. Hurry up and get well enough to do it.'

He piled the flannels on top of the towel, rolled the whole mess together – and set it aside.

His own clothes more or less hit a plaid-covered easy chair in the corner of the mostly shades-of-green room until he stood before her, unselfconsciously naked. She snapped her open mouth shut but couldn't do a thing about her flipping heart. It ought to be a sin to hide that body under baggy, country clothes.

'Don't want to tease you,' he said, 'but I'm for a quick shower.'

Just like that. She heard the shower come on and saw steam creep past the edge of the bathroom door where he hadn't quite closed it.

And she let her eyelids droop, floated, cocooned in Tony's lovely, comfy bed.

Tony slid carefully under the covers with Alex. He had closed the curtains, careful to make very little noise. Propped on an elbow, his head braced on his hand, he studied her. Asleep she looked ridiculously young.

Was he wrong to encourage their lives to become locked together? It was happening, if it hadn't already become close to complete.

They were slipping into depending on each other. He liked it that way. But was he any good at relationships? Did he have what it took to give her what she needed? He hadn't kept Penny happy.

And Penny was a whole other issue – a thorny one.

He moved cautiously closer. She was already more comfortable with the immobilized foot. Her clavicle would do its own thing and that could be a long or short recovery depending on the crack and her ability to heal. The image of putting her into his shirt was nice.

She had been straight-faced and stoic and he'd managed to put on a pseudo clinical attitude.

There hadn't been an instant when he'd felt remotely clinical and he didn't now. The hand he placed softly on her stomach on top of the shirt, automatically inched gently to her hip and then her waist. That should be the stopping point. His brain and body made no secret of where they wanted to go.

With not enough guilt, he covered her soft breast and felt her react.

Her eyes flickered open and still he didn't feel any guilt. When her back arched away from the mattress he inwardly cursed the damn sling.

His mobile rang. It was a conspiracy to get in their way! After five rings, it stopped, but Alex was wide awake and blinking.

And the phone rang again. Tony swallowed curses and answered.

One of the Derwinters' mares was foaling. 'On my way.' He canceled the call. 'I don't believe this. I've got to get to the Derwinters and help with a delivery. Horse. Stay where you are, love. With any luck this'll go well and quickly.'

Getting herself into the shower wasn't so difficult, apart from having to stick her wrapped ankle out of the stall and try not to move her left arm. The shoulder felt a bit less raw – or maybe it didn't.

Fortunately all she had to do to her hair was run her fingers through it wet and flip a comb into the curls when she got out of the shower.

She turned on the water and luxuriated, turned her face up to the hot water. Using Tony's soap appealed to her, not that she had a choice. Soaping all over felt wonderful . . . until Bogie decided to push open the bathroom door and bark at her. He didn't like water much and apparently assumed she was being tortured, the way he was tortured by baths. Alex peeked at him around the door and he took off, looking disgusted and still barking and turning in circles.

Laughing into the water, she turned up the heat as it cooled, all the way up as it got colder, and sucked air through her teeth when she was sluiced with an icy deluge. 'Crickey!' She cranked it off and stood, shivering and catching her breath.

Before she got in, she'd opened the window and a cool breeze only encouraged the rash of goosebumps that shrank her skin all over. When she landed on the bath mat, a desperate grab at the edge of the shower door kept her good foot from sliding and taking her down.

Wrapped in a huge towel, Alex rubbed at her skin.

Bogie's bark kept going.

Alex scooted until she could open the door wider.

The dog didn't sound normal. There was a hysterical note tearing from his throat – but it was muffled. There could be an intruder in the house, or trying to get into the house.

Alex fumbled in her haste. Tony's shirt and her panties went over her still damp body and she slid on the sling. Somehow she'd managed to soak the strapping on her ankle. She would have to change that.

Bogie was hurt. Fighting against the jumpy, panicky sensations that slowed her down even more, she decided against the crutch and damn the pain. Hopping, grabbing at walls, furniture and door-jambs as she went, she got to the top of the stairs.

'Bogie,' she called. 'Here, boy. Come here.'

He kept on barking.

Could he have got outside and be trying to be let in again? Tony's house had thick stone walls and heavy doors that could dampen noise.

Clinging to the banister, Alex hopped slowly downstairs . . . just in time for the front door to slam open, letting in a rush of wind, old leaves and a smatter of rain.

She slammed a hand over her heart and yelled, 'Get out.' And closed her mouth tightly as it registered how foolish she sounded.

'Bogie?' she said tentatively, but it was Katie, not Bogie who tore into the house with Tony close behind.

'What are you doing here?'

He shoved the door shut behind him. 'I live here,' he said. 'What are you doing? Where's your crutch? You're sopping, Alex.'

She waved him away and turned toward the back of the house. 'Bogie's either got stuck outside, or he's trapped in here somewhere. Do you have your hot water on a timer?'

'Stop!' Tony pulled her close and held her still. 'I don't under-stand you. Explain, please.'

Bogie's deadened bark started again. He sounded frantic. 'Hear that?' Alex said, glad of Tony's solid, stable body beside her. 'I have to find him.'

'He's in the kitchen by the sound of him,' Tony said. He got her through to the kitchen and let her down in a chair. 'Sounds like the laundry room.'

The laundry room was in a hallway off the kitchen. Quickly, he threw open a door to reveal the washer and dryer – but no Bogie.

Katie trotted straight past the laundry room and farther along the little passageway toward a rarely used outside door. More mechanical stuff was in a closet and a tiny mud room with a sink lay beyond that.

Tony's dog whined and fussed. Alex could hear her snuffling

along the old terracotta floor tiles. At the sound of frantic scrabbling, Tony darted after Katie and Alex pushed and pulled herself upright. Hopping on her good foot she headed for the hallway Tony and Katie had taken.

Bogie, darting at her with wild eyes, almost knocked Alex over. She made it to the doorjamb and held on. 'Where was he?'

'Shut in the cupboard,' he said, reappearing. 'I don't get why he was in there.'

An unexpected clap of thunder overhead jolted Alex. She leaned against the wall. 'Bogie came in while I was showering. He was barking then and he ran back out of the bathroom. It scared me so I got out of the shower and came looking for him. Do you leave that cupboard door open? He must have run in there and accidentally closed it.'

'I don't leave it open,' Tony said. He helped Alex back to her chair. 'How would he close it?'

Alex's head began to ache. 'I'm mad at myself.' She was. Any small deviation from the norm and she threw herself into some sort of conspiracy mode.

'For getting upset?'

Lightning flashed beyond a window in the little outside door.

A barrage of rain slashed across the glass.

'I thought it would be a lovely day,' she said. Changing the subject would be the best course. Hadn't she learned to move away from conflict? She didn't often think of her marriage but in this unsuitable moment she almost heard Mike's voice telling her to 'cool it.' He watched too much American TV.

'Alex, I asked you a question. What are you mad at yourself for?'

'I second guess everything that happens and it's stupid. I get myself into tight spots and look at me.' She indicated her battered limbs. 'All for nothing. You'd think I would learn. So Bogie barked then got locked in somehow. And I decide a mad killer is lurking down here – possibly with designs on my dog. I'm sorry. I probably need to calm down – sleep maybe.'

'OK.' Tony's wavy hair was damp and wild, but his blue eyes were steady. They studied her closely enough to make Alex very uncomfortable. 'First, what did you say about the water being on a timer?'

'Just that. I wondered if it was on a timer. It went icy cold while I was in the shower and I'd only been there a couple of minutes. Forget it. It's nothing.'

Raking his fingers through his hair, he turned back into the hall and opened the cupboard again. There was barely enough room for him to step inside. He checked something she couldn't see, screwing up his face in concentration. 'Light would help,' he said, flipping a switch. 'That would explain it. The hot water's been turned off. You got what was left in the pipes, then the cold stuff. Sorry about that but I didn't touch anything here. You saw me take off in a hurry.'

'So you think someone turned off the hot water to give me a shock?'

'Yes. And Bogie couldn't have shut himself in that cupboard. It closes from the outside and he's not Houdini.'

Alex shuddered. 'I wonder if you came back sooner than they expected. Who knows what else they had planned?'

'We'll never know and that's just as well. Now we're on our guard.'

She remembered the mare. 'Was the foal already born when you got there? Must have gone fast.'

'If I hadn't been so caught up in our latest drama, I'd have remembered she wasn't due for several weeks. I walked in and they didn't know why I'd come. No one had any idea why I was called. I assumed it was one of the stable hands, but I couldn't find out who.'

'We know,' she told him evenly. From now on she would be keeping a level head. 'A silly trick to get you away from here and pull a stunt to scare me. Whoever turned the hot water off, shut Bogie in. What are we supposed to take from that? A warning they could kill me or Bogie?' She shuddered.

'Acts of desperation,' Tony said quietly. 'Annoyances pulled off because they want us to stay out of whatever's going on.'

'Pamela's murder and what they did to Radhika can't be called silly tricks, though. And we aren't going anywhere. At least, I'm not. What's that?' She pointed to his left hand, holding a wad of tissues and almost hidden behind his back. 'Come on, Tony. Give.'

'A sausage,' he said sharply. 'I'm going to deal with it so don't pester me.'

'You amaze me,' she said, and jabbed him in the chest with a forefinger. 'Where was the sausage? Show it to me.'

Reluctantly he opened the tissue's to reveal a piece of a Cumberland sausage.

'On the floor in the utility room,' Tony said, grimacing. 'I'll test it myself.'

'For poison?'

'Right. We'll watch Bogie but it doesn't look as if he touched it. I think the main reason for leaving it was to round out their nasty picture. So, do we mention this to the police?'

'Not without more evidence that anything really happened,' Alex said. Hopping and holding on, Alex got herself to the back door. It opened easily and she looked at the handles on both sides, and the lock. 'Anyone with a hair grip could open this. School kids have been doing that forever.'

At least he had the grace to look awkward. 'It'll be fixed today. That and all the locks in the house will be changed. I'd better get an alarm system in.'

'I don't like them,' Alex said. 'I've got one and it nearly shocked me to death if you remember.'

'I'm still doing it. But I'm tempted to send you away to some place safe,' Tony said.

Alex snorted. 'I'll assume that was a joke, Tony. You know you don't get to send me anywhere. If you said you thought we ought to work harder and faster, I'd be on board.'

He let out a long breath. 'I wouldn't be comfortable leaving you on your own. Do you agree you should have someone with you all the time?'

'I won't do anything—'

'Do you agree, Alex?'

'Put that way. No.'

TWENTY-EIGHT

His boss was either pulling rank – which he had a right to do – or testing him. Bill Lamb walked along the hospital corridor avoiding any eye contact, especially with patients on gurneys or in wheelchairs, or walking with IV poles.

Nothing good had ever happened to him in a hospital – or nothing good that wiped out memories of the other: deaths of people he'd cared about. Dan O'Reilly knew that.

He reached the right place and flipped out his warrant card. They had Radhika Malek in a private room and the copper on guard duty shuffled upright and gave a sloppy salute. 'Evening, sir. All quiet around here.'

'That's good.' The word had come through to the station at just before six that Radhika could have one visitor at a time. His boss had sent him to Cheltenham within the hour.

A nurse at the ward desk had said he could go in to see Radhika, but he mustn't stress the patient in any way. He'd seen others from Folly in a waiting room, so the police hadn't been the only ones to get the word.

Naturally, Alex and Tony had been there, and the new vicar's wife. He hadn't acknowledged them.

Bugger, he wanted to get this over with.

He tapped a small square of glass in the door but there was no answer.

Quietly, he lowered the handle and pushed a couple of inches. 'Radhika Malek?' he said. 'May I have a few words with you?'

He heard her say, 'Yes,' although she spoke barely above a whisper.

Closing the door behind him, he went to stand at the foot of the bed but made sure he wasn't too close. The patient's – or in this case, the victim's – emotional comfort must be considered.

If he had seen this woman before, he wouldn't have forgotten her. 'I'm Detective Sergeant Lamb. Sorry to disturb you but we've been waiting to ask a few questions about the attack on you.'

Her blue-black hair shone in a thick plait that lay over one shoulder. Dark eyes that must be huge when they weren't swollen and discolored looked at him steadily and he got the feeling she was doing her best not to appear frightened. Ms Malek, with her deep olive skin, was a diminutive knockout.

'Is it OK if I sit?' he said, and she nodded, yes.

Taking a chair padded in nasty pale green plastic to match the walls and the curtains around the bed, he sat down and rested his forearms on his thighs. Best to seem relaxed, or so he'd always thought. Not always easy. He hadn't earned his bulldog reputation for nothing.

'Could you tell me everything you remember about the night you were attacked?'

Her heavily bandaged hands had been resting at her sides on the white sheets. She lifted them now and he saw metal splints showing at the ends of her fingers. The woman stared at them as if for the first time, and didn't say a word.

Bill let a couple of minutes tick by.

'It must be hard to talk about,' he said. 'Even harder to think about, I should imagine.'

Those unreadable eyes met his. She nodded her head, yes.

'We know there are things that need sorting out in Folly-on-Weir. You're the closest we've got to a witness, otherwise I wouldn't be bothering you.'

Panic flashed across her features and for an instant she looked as if she was searching for a way to escape.

'Did you see who your assailant was?'

A shake, no, this time.

'Any impressions he left you with? Any ideas about his size? Anything at all could be just what we're looking for.'

'Big,' she said. 'Heavy. He knocked me down and lay on top of me. He – he banged my face on the ground. And he hit my hands with . . . I don't know. Perhaps a hammer, or perhaps a stone. I don't know.'

'Where had you been?'

This time her silence surprised him.

'Did you get any impression you might know this person?'

Another shake of the head, no, and this time she looked away quickly.

He couldn't ask her if she was lying, not now, but he thought she might be.

A nurse tapped the door and walked in. 'Are you doing OK, Radhika? Don't let yourself get tired out.'

Radhika didn't give an indication either way.

'This was hand delivered for you before I came on shift.'

Lamb raised his head to peer at the envelope in the nurse's hand but she turned it upside down, deliberately, and tucked it in the top drawer of the nightstand. 'Must be a well-wisher,' the woman said. 'I'll help you open it later.'

After the nurse left, Lamb sat back in his chair, rethinking how to question Radhika Malek. Something about her precluded any overly tough approach.

He leaned forward again. 'Can I ask for a cup of tea for you?'

'Yes, please.'

Grateful for that much loosening up, he went to the guard on the door and asked him for tea and biscuits – for two.

'Do you have any notions about who might have done this?' Again he sat down. He unbuttoned his suit jacket and smoothed his tie. 'Toss out any suggestions, even if you think they could be crazy. Anything that comes to mind. Anything at all.'

Silence.

'Did you have Dr Harrison's dog with you at the time?'

'Yes.'

'Did you let her go or did she just get away from you?' Pointless questions had been known to open up a witness.

'When I was being held down, I slipped off the leash and told Katie to go. She went to—'

'The Black Dog. Yes, we know. Why do you think she didn't go home?'

'It is too far. When she is in the village she is always trying to get to the pub. She is most happy there.'

Lamb looked more closely at Radhika. 'Are you crying, miss?' He reached for a box of tissues, glanced at her hand and pulled a couple out for her. She raised her eyes to his face and he couldn't help dabbing at them, and at her cheeks, himself.

'I have to go away,' she mumbled. 'I must go before he finds out I'm not dead. I was left for dead.'

Rather than the copper on the door, Alex entered with Tony carrying mugs on a tray and biscuits wrapped in plastic.

'Alex,' Radhika said, speaking voluntarily for the first time since Lamb had been there. 'I wanted to send for you but you are injured.

I need you with me. Tony . . . good people. I am so grateful to you for trusting me. I have loved Folly. I don't want to go, but—'

'You're not going,' Alex said.

Tony wheeled the bed table closer then found another chair for Alex.

'We're in the middle of . . .' Lamb almost said 'interrogation', but stopped himself. 'We're having an official chat. The lady isn't supposed to have more than one visitor at a time, anyway.'

'The policeman's phone rang and I volunteered to take the tray for him,' Alex said. What a master she was at the innocent looks. 'He thought you'd already left. Said he got held up in the cafeteria.'

Lamb had no doubt that Alex had engineered her way into the hospital room but he'd be having a word with the man on the door later.

'I need you to leave,' he said. 'I'm here on official business.'

'I cannot speak with you unless Alex stays.' Radhika turned her eyes to Tony Harrison and gave an apologetic smile. 'You understand I need a woman for support, Tony?'

'Of course I do. I'll be in the waiting room. The vicar's wife is out there.' Radhika looked at her hands on the bed. 'Most kind, I am sure, but I only need Alex.'

Why would Radhika choose me? Alex wondered. We aren't old friends.

Radhika continued, 'She stayed with me after . . . after it happened when she needed to be resting herself. I trust Alex.'

Lamb looked out of his depth but determined. He kept glancing at something on the bedside table, or that's how it seemed, but Alex couldn't see what that might be.

Once Tony left and closed the door, an awkward silence followed. Radhika reached out a bandaged hand to Alex and she covered it carefully.

'After the dog took off last night,' Lamb said, 'you took a call on your mobile from Lily Duggins.'

'Yes, she wanted to know why Katie had gone to the pub. I asked Lily to keep Katie for me and she agreed.'

'But you'd already been attacked?'

Radhika closed her eyes and breathed through her mouth. 'Yes.'

'Why didn't you ask for help?'

Tears slid free again. 'I wanted to manage on my own. I forgot I had my phone until it rang. I didn't want help.' Her voice rose. 'I don't want help now. I will be well and then I will leave Folly. It will be best.'

'Listen,' Alex said, drawing closer to Radhika and dropping her voice even lower. 'When there's trouble – and that's what we have now – it's best to stick together. We'll help one another. Harriet and Mary Burke are ready to take you into their home. They have a bedroom ready. You can be safe and recover.'

'I could not put them at risk. No, I must not accept their kind offer.'

'I don't see how you can refuse. Everyone knows you've said you'll go back to the cottage on your own. We would never be comfortable with that.'

'We'll guard the cottage round the clock,' Lamb said. 'That'll be best. You wouldn't want to deal with the stairs at the sisters' place.'

'You could put a guard on Harriet and Mary's place. How would that be different? Except that Radhika would have company all the time.'

For an instant Lamb looked on the verge of an outburst, but he shuttered his face and stood up. 'I have some calls to make. Please understand that you must not go anywhere without informing us of your plans, Ms Malek.' He walked out quickly, leaving behind an air of annoyance and determination to orchestrate what each of them did no matter how they felt about that.

'The police are a danger to me,' Radhika said.

TWENTY-NINE

For seconds after Lamb left, they remained, holding hands and in silence.

Alex couldn't help asking, 'What do you mean about the police being a danger to you?'

'Forget I said that.' Radhika gave Alex a small smile. 'Thank you for being with me. How charming it feels to be peaceful at last. So much pushing and anxiety all these people make. So much determination to get what they want.'

'They?' Alex asked.

That brought a long look from Radhika's dark brown eyes. 'The police, the good people around me . . . and . . . just people.'

'Can you tell me who the "just people" are?'

Radhika looked away and said nothing.

'Am I *just people*?'

'You are different. I feel that. Also I trust Tony.' She reached for her mug of tea and frowned. 'And others, of course.'

Alex lifted it to the other woman's lips and waited while she took several sips. 'Would you like a biscuit. There are digestives and garibaldis.'

'I like currants.' Radhika drew up her shoulders. 'If you unwrap a garibaldi I can hold it with my right hand.'

The blessing of opposable thumbs. Alex popped the biscuit into the pincer Radhika made. 'Tell me when you want more.'

'You are not responsible for me. Not in any way. If I can ask you to help me – and I would not take advantage – but it would be good if I could call or come to you for some small thing I cannot accomplish myself.'

A nurse bustled in and the bed curtains billowed. They jangled against their metal hooks. 'Are you all right, Ms Malek? I thought the policeman was with you.'

'He left. This is my dear friend Alex. She has traveled to see me.'

Alex saw the slight sideward shift of Radhika's eyes. Yes, 'travel' was a broad term.

The nurse nodded. 'I'll be back before long to settle you down for the night. No more visitors. It's nice to see you looking a bit better.'

Once they were alone again, Radhika stared into Alex's face. 'Please listen. I don't know how long it will be before she returns and I want to finish.

'There is much I shall not tell you – or anyone. It wouldn't be safe. One day, and I promise this, I will return and share everything with you. That will be when it's all over. If it is ever over.'

'Is this anything to do with Pamela's death?' Alex felt breathless. The room wasn't cold but it was airless and the barren walls and floors made it feel like a cell.

'Nothing to do with poor Pamela. She was wonderful to me and there was no reason for her to do so much.

'I have to get away from here. First I must get well and make a plan, but then I shall lose myself.'

A frisson of excitement tightened Alex's hands into fists. No, she didn't believe Radhika's story had nothing to do with Pamela, or other elements in play around here. The woman in the bed, who looked at her with honesty, might not know exactly what she was caught up with and that made it all the more imperative that she be watched and kept safe. Alex wondered what it would take to shake loose the whole story, but now wasn't the time to push.

'I'll help you, but I will have to let Tony know what you've said to me.'

The worried frown came back but she said, 'Of course. I know he will understand the problem.'

I doubt he'll understand it anymore than I do.

'I forgot. There is an envelope in the drawer here. Could you show it to me, please?' Indicating the bed stand, Radhika swiveled in that direction. 'I was glad the nurse put it there when she saw the policeman looking at it.'

Alex made it around the bed. She moved more easily all the time – probably because she had not had the opportunity to be still and stiffen up.

'In this drawer?' she said and when Radhika nodded, opened the top drawer in a metal bed stand made of scarred, white-coated metal. 'The envelope on top – it's the only one here.' A heavy vellum envelope, creamy ivory.

Alex turned it over and frowned. 'Warren, Frankel and Gidley-Rains. I recognize Gidley-Rains. He's Pamela Gibbon's solicitor.'

'Why would they write to me?'

'I don't know. You'd better open it.'

Something rattled against the wall in the corridor and both women stopped breathing. When the sound of receding rubber wheels came, Radhika said, 'Quickly, please. You open it for me.'

Of course, the splinted and bandaged hands made the task impossible.

The seal was well closed. Alex ran a finger under the flap and slid out a heavy sheaf of paper and a cover letter. 'What does it say, Alex? What is all that, please?'

'William Gidley-Rains is a solicitor in Bourton-on-the-Water. He was Pamela's solicitor and he writes to tell you he's enclosing a copy of her will for you to read because you're a beneficiary.'

'Pamela mentions me in her will?' Radhika seemed puzzled. 'Perhaps she wanted me to do something for her. She had been very kind to me.'

'You're named as a beneficiary, that means she left something to you.'

Radhika took the papers. 'She should not give me anything more.' She sucked in a breath and hissed it out, and her eyes overflowed. 'Being in Folly has brought me happiness and peace, and horror. I do not know what to do next.'

'We'll work it out,' Alex said and hoped she sounded more confident than she felt.

'Will you read the rest of this for me?' Radhika pressed the papers on her again. 'Or read it yourself and tell me what I need to know. It makes me so sad to think about.'

'I'll read as quickly as I can and gloss over the big words. We're going to get interrupted any time now.'

Radhika pressed her head into the pillows and said, 'Thank you.'

'OK. The solicitor will expect to hear from you. He'll want to see you when you've read all this.' She turned to the first page of the will and skimmed over the verbiage at the beginning. 'Wow. There'll be talk about this when it gets out. And it will. Harry's the first beneficiary. All manner of financial stuff . . . it goes on for a couple of pages, single spaced. She had a house at Kew in Cornwall and that goes to Harry.'

'I didn't know she kept it. We met while I was working there.'

'Harry gets a bundle. Money, houses, investments – it's endless.'

'You mean he will also own Cedric Chase?'

'Not mentioned here. She had a cottage in Windermere and some sort of place in Switzerland. And rental properties, residential and office.

'Next is Jay Gibbon.' She read through the bequest to him. 'In accordance with her husband's wishes, Jay gets Cedric Chase if he's turned forty and should Pamela as well as Charles pre-decease him. This is only for Jay's lifetime – unless he has children. If he dies without issue, the house goes . . . good grief . . . it goes to Harry, too.'

'Surely . . . well, it would seem that he had a reason . . . I shouldn't say that.'

'Plenty of others will,' Alex told her. 'Vivian is to have and look after the horse Pamela rode all the time, and a racehorse she owned. There's a bequest to cover the care of the horses. Also jewelry.'

'Radhika Malek is to receive the sum,' Alex dropped her voice and whispered close to Radhika's ear. 'My, my, my. You are going to be a wealthy woman. And Harry and Mr Gidley-Rains are to give you whatever help you want to do whatever you want. Mr Gidley-Rains is executor of the will.'

'But if I'm gone, it goes to Harry, too?'

Alex, nodded, yes. Radhika was too intelligent not to see the potential drawbacks.

'I would wish that this not be known. I will not speak of it since . . . I am in the way for some.'

'The spotlight *will* be on all this, Radhika. It'll get out. But it can work in another way to your benefit rather than the way you're afraid of. No one would be foolish enough to hurt you now.'

'No? Perhaps this is why someone already hurt me – badly? I was told I must disappear. Permanently.'

Platitudes wouldn't help. Neither would pointing out that beneficiaries of Pamela's will were all suspects in her murder.

THIRTY

'You could just come home with me,' Tony said. After a rapid drive from the hospital they were entering Folly-on-Weir. 'You've got staff to take care of things like this.'

She had been called by Lily and Hugh about a disturbance at the Black Dog. 'Someone's about to get a punch up the bracket,' as Hugh said, striking fear into Alex.

'It's my responsibility to make sure people are safe at my pub,' she said. 'I don't want anyone driving drunk – or getting into a fight and hurting other customers.'

'What would you do about it? Throw Jay out?'

'You can be so facetious. I want to get there and assess what's going on.'

'And Hugh can't do that?'

'Yes, but he works for me.' She fidgeted, ready to pull off her seatbelt. 'I'm the one in charge. I told Hugh not to do anything until I get there.'

'You aren't up to this,' Tony said, but rather than make the left turn uphill toward the Dimple and home, he carried on and turned into the alley that led to the parking behind the Black Dog.

The moonless, blustery night seemed ominous. Each gust brought a smattering of big raindrops. The wipers intermittently screeched across the windshield, leaving streaks that didn't improve visibility. The colored lights outlining the pub's roof didn't lift Alex's spirits, but glowing windows, curtains drawn, were patches of familiar reassurance.

'I'm not going to hesitate to call the police. I don't understand why that hasn't been done already.'

'Don't you? Come on, Alex, everyone's treading on broken glass at the moment. They're all afraid of making waves. Anyway, aren't O'Reilly and Lamb still staying at the Dog?'

That was true. 'They are.' Alex frowned. 'If there was a disturbance, wouldn't they go down and do something about it?'

Tony pulled into a parking spot behind the building, the vehicle tires grinding through damp pea gravel. 'I would have thought so.

Unless they've got some rule about not interfering unless they're asked to.'

'I am so tired,' Alex said, leaning against the headrest for a few seconds before pushing the door of Tony's car open. The back of the building was a hulking dark outline. 'I'm going to take my mum up on her offer of sleeping at Corner Cottage tonight. I think I've just about got what it takes to totter across the street with Bogie and collapse.'

She didn't look at Tony, but felt him withdraw.

'You don't need to go into the pub at all,' he said. 'Stay here and let me deal with it.'

Alex shrugged upright. 'Thank you for being my rock, Tony, but I've got to go in and see what's up with Jay Gibbon. He's been through a lot, too. I don't think it's anymore than his getting drunk and some others who shall remain nameless enjoying the mix up. Probably mixing it up some more.'

He sighed loudly. 'You haven't even told me what happened after I left Radhika's room tonight.'

She felt guilty about that but she had needed the time to think about her conversation with Radhika. Just what she should and should not say wasn't clear yet. 'We'll talk about it later. Maybe tomorrow. Depends on how long this takes.' What she already feared was that the will had something to do with Jay kicking up a fuss in the bar.

Tony's silence said more than if he had complained about her withholding information. He had to assume she knew more than she was saying.

Alex slid from the vehicle, propped herself on the crutch and made her way into the building via a back door. Tony followed closely behind her.

The kitchens were empty but a buzz seeped through from the bars.

'Let me do this for you,' Tony said.

'I'd feel as if I'd wimped out. Mum called me and so did Hugh. I'm supposed to come and take over. You understand, don't you?'

Tony pulled her to face him. When she wobbled, he caught her against him until she found her balance. 'I understand because I understand you. I suppose you're strength is one . . . one of the things I love you for.'

Afraid to speak, or not to speak, Alex held him by the arms, looked up into his face. She had to respond. 'Careful, good friend. I might take something you say seriously.' Making a joke out of a serious moment might be a coward's way out but it was the best she had for now. 'We're both strong. That's what makes us a pretty good team. I'm going in there now. It may be nothing at all. People overreact sometimes.'

She felt his reluctance to release her but kept straightening, moving away from him.

The first thing she noticed was that no one was working behind the bar. The next was the absence of music. No constant pinging came from the fruit machines. But there was no lack of noise, although there were only one or two voices that rose repeatedly, angrily, from the main bar.

Alex swung and hopped her way through until she could see the bar. Lily stood in the entrance to the restaurant as if guarding it from intruders. She saw Alex and pointed toward Jay Gibbon, who sat at a table next to Harriet and Mary's – who would normally have left a long time ago – and gripped the handle of a beer glass in one hand and a large, crumpled and grimy white handkerchief in the other.

Approaching from her right, Hugh stepped lightly but with purpose, his features set. 'Just give me the word and I'll get the coppers in,' he said when he got close to Alex. 'There's a search going on around the Ebring Manor area though I don't know what they'd find at this time of night. O'Reilly and Lamb are up there. They left here as if they were going to a fire. Now that we don't have a local constable anymore these little scuffles turn into bigger deals than necessary if we're not careful.'

'Someone should be behind the bar,' Alex said absently. 'I thought Juste was here.'

'He just saw two women to their car – they were anxious because of all this, I suppose. He should be right in. Too bad Kev doesn't leave. That man enjoys a dust up a bit too much. Any excuse will do.'

Kev Winslet never changed. Alex supposed he must be irreplaceable as the Derwinters' gamekeeper or he would have been fired long ago. He was a loud, argumentative tough when he'd had a drink or two. A big, florid man, the more intense he became, the lower his bushy brows descended toward his eyes. He made the picture of a quintessential country man. Tonight he'd probably had a good deal more than two drinks. Rolling on the heels of the rubber boots he wore with corduroy trousers tucked inside, he thrust his red face forward, his attention firmly on Jay.

An abrupt stream of garbled words poured from Jay who appeared to address the bar in general. His closest listener was Major Stroud, his face a fearsome shade of purple, who hovered beside Jay's table, listening and swaying slightly in his suede brogues.

'Do you think Harriet and Mary are too afraid to get up?' Alex asked Tony quietly.

He gave a short laugh. 'I think they're too afraid that if they do get up they'll miss something.'

'Those dogs are as bad as they are.' Alex inclined her head at Katie and Bogie who sat, one beside each sister, looking bright-eyed and pleased with themselves. 'You'd think they'd be over here giving us a mad greeting.'

Tony laughed. 'Ungrateful pair. Everything seems suspended to me. Can you make out anything Jay's saying?'

Alex shook her head, no. 'But I think he's said plenty already. Look at these people. They're straining for what he says next – that they can understand, that is.'

'If he was a man he'd come and meet me,' Jay said clearly.

'Pissed as a newt,' Kev hollered and staggered about snorting and shedding tears at his own witticism.

Ignoring Kev, Major Stroud said, 'And listen to a drunk calling him out? I bloody don't think so, Gibbon.' He raised his voice. 'I ordered a drink, where is it?'

Juste came in at that moment, bringing a rush of unkind night air with him.

'Keep an eye on things,' Hugh said, going behind the bar to pour a double Glenlivet.

A tight knot of regulars stood a short distance behind the major and Kev. Liz Hadley's husband Sam – Liz only came in when she was due to work – Frank Lymer from Underhill, another Derwinter worker, and several members of the dart team who had played earlier. Mary Burke still held a place on that team, throwing, Alex believed, almost purely from instinct and with her walker placed firmly to the side.

'Evening, Jay,' Alex said, making her awkward way to the man's table and sitting down. 'What's up?'

He looked sideways at her with bloodshot eyes. His thin straight hair hung over his brow and his scalp shone through the strands. 'None of your business,' he said. 'You don't know me.' With the grubby handkerchief, he wiped his face and eyes. She realized he was close to tears.

'You're going through hard times,' she said quietly, hoping she was hitting the right note with him. 'Are you tired? You look very tired. Do you want a ride home?'

He gave her something between a smirk and a leer. 'Got a home of my own now. Right on his turf. Bet he's fucking browned off about that.'

'You don't have to listen to this, Alex,' the major said, slurring his words together. 'Bloody disgrace is what he is. Coming in here shouting about who knows what. Calling out my son who doesn't even know him. Why should Harry want anything to do with this piece of rubbish?'

'A right rollicking is what he needs,' Frank said. 'Throwing his weight about. Calling us all names like he's somethin' special.'

Jay staggered to his feet, pulled back an arm and made to punch Frank Lymer. The fist swung wide even before Tony grabbed and stuffed Jay back in his chair. Kev Winslet was already winding up to deliver a blow of his own and stumbled sideways under his own momentum.

'Don't give a monkey's arse,' Kev said expansively, waving his arms for balance. 'I'm gonna lamp 'im. Greasy little bugger. Never laid eyes on him till he thought he had somethin' comin' to him.'

'I think it's time for that phone call,' Tony said. 'I'd like you out of here, Alex.'

'I know you would,' she said very quietly. 'Don't worry, I'm OK.'

Jay fluttered his nasty handkerchief. 'Get me that Harry Stroud. Too much 'splaining needed. How did he do it, that's what I want to know. I'm not letting him get away with it. I'll ch-challenge, I tell you.' He poured the rest of the beer straight down his throat and waved the glass around for more.

'What's the man talking about?' Stroud asked.

She was on her own with this. Only she knew Jay was reacting to reading his copy of the will. And he wasn't taking what had been bequeathed to Harry well at all.

'Coffee, Hugh, please,' Alex said. Fortunately Jay either didn't register what she'd said or thought she wanted it for herself. He concentrated on returning his glass to the table, squinting from side to side as if things weren't staying still for him.

'I'll take you home, Jay,' Tony said. 'Cedric Chase isn't far but you're tired out. Let me give you a lift.'

'Not bloody going home till I tell Harry Stroud I'm on to him.' He slammed the table. His glass slid and hit the floor, smashed into half a dozen pieces. 'Now look what – what you've done. All of you. Watching me like I'm a bug under a fucking glass. Bugger off, all of you. Get me Harry Stroud or I'll go get him myself. S'got a lot to answer for. Time he was asked questions.'

'Jay, you're not making much sense,' Alex told him. 'Whatever's on your mind won't seem so raw in the morning.'

Using a broom, Juste swept broken glass away from the table and into a dustpan.

'That's what you think. He's done something, I tell you. If you were all upstanding like you reckon you are, you'd want to get to the bottom of it, too. What's gone on here's not right, I tell you and he's not getting away with it.'

'Time to call the police, Alex,' Harriet Burke announced in ringing tones. 'We want him out of here and off the streets before we all try to go home. He's a menace.'

Ignoring her, Jay let out a huge belch and tried to straighten in his chair. 'Let's ask him why?' he said. 'Why him? How did he make her do it? Sodding tosser.'

'That's enough,' Hugh said, coming from behind the bar. 'I'm taking you home.'

'You fucking won't,' Jay said. 'Got myself here. Get myself back. I live in Folly too now. S'my village so get used to it. And when I get to the bottom of what's gone on here, it'll be even more my village.' He pointed an unsteady finger at the major. 'I'll be calling the shots.'

THIRTY-ONE

*T*his was according to plan. The beginning of the end and it couldn't come soon enough.

Another blast of wind blew through heavy trees lining the long driveway to Cedric Chase. Heavy branches bent under the onslaught and more rain fell in big, cool drops.

So much the better. The more noise, the better.

With the car pulled well to the side and the headlights off, even with the engine running – the powerful, quiet engine running – if the stupid lout was as wasted as he was supposed to be, he wouldn't hear the Mercedes. Thank God it was black, like the night.

The rain got heavier and the trees didn't keep anything dry. Pressed back between the trunks, waiting, the passenger side door cracked open to make things easier, the plan seemed perfect as long as not one tiny thing went wrong – or unless the man managed to pass out before he got here.

With a pelting sound, heavy skies broke open to pour their burden down. Off to the right, water squelched, the sound only vaguely heard through the beat of the rain and the lashing of the wind. A man's irregular footfalls into an inch or so of mud mixed with gravel, and his muffled curses.

He cried out and the sound of him falling came clearly. Now he was getting closer.

There he was and he'd seen the car. His head swiveled from side to side, adjusting his vision to the glimmer off the car's immaculate paint in the darkness and a brain thickened by drink.

No more swearing. Stumbling, sliding, he approached the car and, amazing but true, the passenger door swung open wide for him.

He was too slow to react and a shove to the back sent him head-first across the seats.

Shut him in and get behind the wheel.

Bugger, bugger, bugger. The fool was bleeding all over. He'd smashed his face into the gear stick and lay, moaning, and rubbing at his eyes.

It wasn't far. Hold him off. Stay out of the range of his grappling hands. Slip the car into gear and ease forward. Forward for no more than a hundred yards and into the garage. The little luminous ball hanging from the rafters on a string tapped the windshield. That was the warning to stop.

The vodka had been opened in readiness. Press the bottle into his slippery hand and upend it to his mouth. He didn't fight it, just parted his lips and sucked at the stuff.

With a thud, the vodka hit the floor.

He'd passed out.

He gave his blood – use it. Fitting his hands over the wheel wasn't easy. Sliding them around and smearing the center console and seats with the blood so generously supplied took an age.

Get a move on. The fool's unconscious already.

Slam both doors.

Where . . . the hose was there, right where it had been placed. Put one end into the exhaust, the other end through the slightly open back window of the car.

Breathing got more difficult.

It would get impossible for the sot left behind.

THIRTY-TWO

Sneaking around irritated Alex, and perhaps also vaguely amused her. She drove with pained attention, just fast enough not to draw any attention and alternately grumbled and smiled to herself. When she borrowed Lily's silver Fiesta, there had been dire threats about what would probably happen to her if she insisted on driving, 'in your condition.' Lily's fussing was a small price to pay for not having to struggle up to sit in her own vehicle, or risk being noticed leaving the village in the Land Rover.

The roads were still damp but the day showed signs of being showy bright. Steam rose from winding dry stone walls where the sun warmed them. Horses ambled to poke hopeful noses over the top at the few passers-by on foot.

Tony had done his best, and failed, to be sanguine about Alex spending the night at the cottage. Thinking about the question in his eyes, before trying to shut out visions of Jay Gibbon's performance, turned her stomach. At least staying at the cottage made leaving the village unseen even easier.

She had slipped her arm out of the sling to rest her hand on the automatic gear shift. Never again would she sneer at those who didn't drive manual transmissions.

The foot was more of a problem than her shoulder. The main thing was to avoid pressing hard or suddenly on the accelerator, that and using her left foot for the brake. Her greatest fear was an unexpected brake when she might forget and slam the wrong foot down.

Her mum was a gem, best mum in the world. She wouldn't let on that Alex had left the village, even to Tony who would be trying to catch up at the clinic and needed to visit three farms later, fortunately. O'Reilly wanted to see her. He phoned Corner Cottage shortly before she left but she'd listened to his message without picking up.

On the run. That's how she felt. Avoiding O'Reilly and putting off what she'd avoided last night: telling Tony about the will. She had promised Radhika that she wouldn't mention it to anyone – but increasingly doubted Tony had been included in that, Radhika had said as much.

Be honest with yourself. You're afraid he'll try to stop you from digging any deeper into 'police business.'

Alex drove along a single lane, pass-at-your-own-peril, road between broad sweeping fields that would turn pinkish purple with lavender in July. Even thinking about lavender harvest time brought the ghost of the heady scent that would slither through open car windows for miles around.

Half a pint of a Donnington Ale and a ploughman's lunch while she looked out over the hills and valleys sounded perfect. From the Mount Inn she'd have a panoramic view of the surrounding villages with sheep on hills, legs skinny beneath ballooning coats, and crops starting to look serious about getting ready for eventual harvest.

The only vehicle ahead of her was a mud-caked green tractor, bouncing along with its driver riding the high seat as if he were on a horse at an easy walk. He rocked onto the verge to let her pass.

She needed to get away, to have time to think. Being under what felt like constant surveillance frazzled her. 'Ouch.' Her ankle complained bitterly when her mind wandered and she did forget to use the opposite foot instead.

Some said the village of Stanton was the most distinguished, the most picturesque in the Cotswolds. If asked she would have to put in a few words for her beautiful Folly-on-Weir. But once on the outskirts of Stanton the world seemed to slip away, or perhaps she'd driven straight through Alice's looking glass.

Stanton's cottages, built of honey-colored stone, most of them thatched, bulged, sometimes seeming to hang over the road, along the winding streets. She had to give a long look at one particular cottage she passed. It had a window with its sill almost touching the pavement and a short door that rested at the same level, only with the threshold beneath the surface of the street.

Vines grew thick over doors, their popping leaves shiny.

Her mirror still showed no sign of following and familiar vehicles. Alex relaxed a little. Her fear had been that O'Reilly, who was an habitual early riser, or Tony, would see her leave and follow.

The Church of St Michael and All Angels, a late Norman building, had to be in the perfect spot and with the perfect soil for roses. Along an aged wall, emerald green buds with peeping hints of petals, would soon bloom coral and yellow, and pink. Alex knew how seasons changed the gardens, could see the colors in her mind.

This wasn't a day to stop. Her destination was the pub, the Mount Inn. From its elevated position, the name must have been an easy choice. Alex reached the place where luncheon trade spilled onto a side porch and hovered in clumps at the main door. The soft day must be drawing customers outside, that and the urge to smoke.

Alex drove past the building and turned left up a steep drive and into the parking lot at the back of the building. Some workmen were busy with paint while another worked on the gardens. She knew all too well how much effort it took to keep up a pub, especially with long open hours being the norm.

With the sling back in place and her crutch beneath her arm, although she expected to prefer hobbling without the crutch shortly, she went through the back door of the pub and into the main bar. The place was crowded but a man sitting alone at a corner table glanced at her wounded body and nodded before taking his plate and glass outside.

Even on a dry day, horse was the predominant aroma in these parts, with a strong whiff of beer and hot pub grub mixed in. Alex slid into a chair facing the windows. This was the place to come if you wanted to study tweeds, breeches, and riding boots that showed wear and wore it well. Most patrons kept their laughter and conversation to a refined hum but the guffaws tended to break out from time to time.

She ordered a half of Double Donn and settled for a ham and cheese sandwich. Her hunger had faded and the ploughman's would be too much. This was where she'd chosen to come to try and work her way through what they did and didn't know about Pamela Gibbon's death and what was obviously an unfolding case that wouldn't be over while the key player remained on the loose and determined to get what he wanted.

A conviction she didn't much like was that Venetia Stroud would be worth another visit. Her behavior toward Alex, and the way she'd followed Jay to Leaves of Comfort, raised too many questions to ignore. Going alone for a second time was a lousy idea, but if she mentioned it to Tony he was likely to want to involve the police. They didn't have a good excuse to tell them about Venetia, not one with a solid foundation.

Through the windows, Alex looked downhill to the roofs and

towers of Stanton. In the distance, fields of acid yellow rapeseed rolled out between other crops. People either loved or hated the stuff and its smell, so like its cabbage cousin, but she couldn't help getting a charge from the unabashedly carnival brilliance.

'How are you managing to drive like that, Alex?'

She gritted her teeth and swiveled to look up into Harry Stroud's grey eyes. With the bottom of his hacking jacket pushed back and his hands sunk in the pockets of tan twill trousers, he fitted into the Mount perfectly. A finely checked shirt and solid green tie completed the outfit. Sometimes there was comfort in seeing these familiar solid types but not this one and not now.

She shook her head, amazed to see him there. 'I'm driving just fine, thanks.'

'May I join you?' He was already lowering himself into a chair opposite hers. 'I'm not going to lie. I saw you leave the village in Lily's car and I followed you. Took me a while since I stayed a long way back. Then I had to get up the nerve to follow you in here.'

Alex bristled. 'You still think that was a good idea?'

'Be gentle with me,' he said and gave a lopsided smile that didn't charm her. 'I was a fool that night at my place. My only excuse is that I'd been through a lot already and you were a surprise. I feel as if the whole village is against me.'

'Really? Why? I hadn't noticed you being treated any differently from normal.' Had the major told his son about Jay's ramblings?

'Oh, God.' Elbows on the table and fingers driven into short dark curls, he bowed his head. 'This gets more bloody awful by the moment. I don't know what's going on. Do you?'

Ah, he had no idea she was aware copies of the will had been circulated to beneficiaries. 'How is your mother?' She could also play frustrating games when she had to. 'Did she enjoy the ballet that night?' *Did she ever get there after nailing Jay Gibbon at Leaves of Comfort? Did she intend to go at all?*

'You won't forget that in a hurry.'

'No, I won't. Before you start interrogating me, why not give me a sensible explanation for your mother's, and then your own behavior? Shouldn't you be in the City at your office?' He didn't seem to have any particular schedule and never had.

'I do most of my work directly with my clients. At their homes. They prefer it that way and so do I.'

Alex shrugged. She thought he looked a little wild, disoriented even. But she tensed at an impression of excitement barely tamped down. And then, why wouldn't he be excited? He was to be a very wealthy man.

A waitress brought her beer and sandwich and looked at Harry who said, 'I'll have the same,' in an expressionless voice.

'If I tell you what I think will you keep it to yourself?' he asked.

Before she could agree or disagree, he went on.

'My mother isn't the most stable woman in the world but I love her. She has always cared about me which is more than I can say about some people. I don't know who planted the doubt, but I do think she's worried that I might have had something to do with Pamela's death. It wasn't supposed to be common knowledge that we saw each other sometimes, but with village life . . . well, I don't have to finish that explanation, do I? When you came to the house, Mother probably wanted to convince you there wasn't any truth in the rumors.'

The beer was perfect and crusty wheat bread had been cut into thick slices for the sandwich. 'And locking me into your rooms was the way to do that?'

'She said that was an accident. She told me what you said, about supporting me. It was pretty much what you said to me. That you didn't think the attention I'm getting is fair and you wanted to reassure me of that. If what happened was deliberate it was wrong, but couldn't she have been afraid you'd leave without seeing me? Or change your mind before you could back me up?'

His eyes became earnest, the expression vaguely sad and very worried as they gazed into hers.

'She could have been, but she went about everything the wrong way. And you didn't help, Harry. You behaved badly. You scared me to death and I'm not sure that wasn't what you wanted.'

'Well it wasn't. I blew it. Simple as that. I want to make it right with you, Alex. And I want you to help me out – there, I've said it.'

Skin across Alex's back tightened. Her scalp prickled. It was nothing – she must remember that these sensations came when she was upset and in an unfamiliar situation. Like when she was closing in on the body of a dead man in the snow last winter, and listening to that man's dog howl the death wail she could not mistake . . .

A premonition of danger.

'Is there anything else you want to say?' Alex stared at him, watched the pupils of his eyes contract and a pulse beat visibly at his temples. He might not be lying, but neither was he telling all of the truth. He wanted far more than to tell her he regretted that nasty night.

'You were with Radhika at the hospital yesterday. I saw you go in with Harrison. How is she?' Muscles in his jaw flexed.

If there were such things as warning bells, they would be jangling. One of the reasons for her slipping away from the village was to allow her to decide how to tell Tony what Radhika had said without sending him directly to the police. And the will . . . the woman had begged her not to tell anyone about the will.

Harry had followed her purely to ask about Radhika, she was sure of it. What she didn't know was why he would have any interest in the other woman. It even seemed a stretch that he'd care about her or the attack on her at all.

Damn it, she must be losing her mind. He wanted to know if Radhika had seen Pamela's will by last night and mentioned it to Alex.

He wanted to find out if she knew what was in that will.

'Alex?' Harry prompted. 'How's Radhika. How are her eyes? I wasn't allowed in to see her. They said it was too late.'

'She's not in the best shape but she'll be OK.'

'Pamela thought a lot of her, y'know. She helped her get started in Folly. Is it true she's probably going to move away? I'd like to help her – for Pamela.'

Keeping him at bay without giving away how much she knew could get sticky. 'I don't believe so. She likes it here. She has friends.' He was being fed information by some source that wasn't obvious – how else would he know Radhika Malek was talking about leaving Folly?

'When will she get out of the hospital?'

The arrival of his beer and sandwich was a welcome break to let her collect her thoughts a bit.

'Good beer, Donnington's,' Harry said after a first, long swallow. 'When's Radhika going home?'

He wasn't going to let it go. 'I don't know. She's pretty badly banged up.'

'You were in there with that detective. What did he ask her, apart from the obvious?'

'He didn't question her much in front of me.' That much was true. 'He left pretty soon after I got there.'

'Will she go back to her cottage when she's discharged?'

Didn't he realize his blunt questioning sounded suspicious? 'If she does she'll need help for a while. Her fingers will be splinted and bandaged for some time.' There couldn't be anything wrong with saying that.

'Poor girl,' Harry said, shaking his head slowly. 'Who would do a thing like that to her. She's . . . she isn't anyone you'd even notice. Why her?'

Harry obviously hadn't really looked at Radhika Malek when she was her exotic self.

'What are people in Folly saying about me, Alex?' Harry asked, leaning toward her earnestly. 'You wouldn't say anything to hurt anyone. But people talk to you. When I turn up, they stop talking. I want to know what they don't want me to hear.'

From the next room came the unexpected sound of a fiddle, played well. Grabbing an excuse to turn away, Alex saw people move toward the music. She recognized the piece. An old Scottish folk song, 'Lassie Wi'theYellow Coatie,' or that was what she remembered. It sounded so right here and some customers started to sway to the sound.

'Alex?'

Reluctantly, she turned back to Harry. 'Isn't it beautiful?'

'Yes, I suppose it is if you like that sort of thing. I asked you a question. Please, Alex, you were always the one who understood.'

And he had been decent enough to her as long as that didn't include taking her to his home. Childhood was gone, and it needed to be forgotten. 'I understand that I can't tell you what you want to know.'

'You had a reporter staying at the Dog,' he said. 'Name of Patrick Guest. He's tried to question me several times. I've avoided him. He's been given reason to think I'm worth questioning.'

Guest still hung around, sometimes taking off in his car for hours but returning eventually. It surprised her that there had not been more media interest, but Folly was tiny and Pamela had not been a celebrity.

'Harry,' she said firmly, 'I came up here to get away. These have been awful days for a lot of us. I can't tell you what you want to know. But I will mention that you ought to think twice the next time you're tempted to thump a woman's shoulder.' She shouldn't have said it, but she had.

His eyebrows rose. He glanced at the sling and blinked several times. 'Oh, come on. Don't try that on me. You can't blame me for something that happened to you when I wasn't even around. You said you got hurt falling down some steps somewhere.'

'In the dark. At your parents' house. And that was after you whacked a hand down on top of my shoulder. And having too much to drink won't excuse you. I haven't told anyone what really happened and I don't intend to. Neither will I forget. I don't owe you anything, Harry, so stay out of my way.'

'But—' his mouth fell open – 'but you said you understood that I've been badly treated. You came to the house to offer support. Now I'm asking you to support me. You're in the loop, I know you are. You could help me be prepared to deflect the lies they're cooking up against me.'

The tightening of her skin was familiar, nothing to do with the temperature, just detachment, and in this case, disgust.

'Will you do that, Alex? Will you help me? They say justice always gets served but we both know that isn't true. I know you could stand up for the man I really am.'

'Harry,' she said quietly, 'I'll never do anything to hurt you, but I don't *know* what kind of man you really are.' *Except scared.*

He looked at her, long and silent. 'You and Tony Harrison found Pamela's body.'

'If I could forget it, I would.'

'Where was she?'

Hysterical laughter at the next table gave Alex a momentary sensation of the world gone mad. A spray of beer droplets from a man's wide open mouth had her looking for a way to escape.

'You know where she was.' Alex clenched her hands in her lap. 'The whole village knows where she was.'

He remembered his beer, took it halfway to his mouth and put it down again without drinking. 'I was just checking you out in case they're keeping back the truth.'

'Why would they do that?'

'To see if someone puts a foot in it by letting on where she really was.'

His forehead shone with sweat. If this was when he'd decided to crack up, at least they weren't alone the way they had been the last time he went over the top. 'I was there, Harry. Unfortunately.' She swallowed. 'Pamela's body was at the bottom of that horrible shaft.'

Harry covered his eyes with both hands and rested his elbows on the table. The fiddle music continued only Alex didn't know what the fiddler was playing anymore.

She touched Harry's arm tentatively, tempted to console him by saying no one suspected him, but she didn't know that, didn't know if she believed it herself.

'There was stuff in the old tower,' he mumbled indistinctly. 'Vivian was asked about it when they took her in. They told her not to say anything but she told me that much. We hardly know each other but she's decent to me. Anything could have been put there if someone's trying to frame me.'

'Harry!' She tugged on his rough sleeve until he looked at her with reddened eyes. 'You're driving yourself insane. You've been questioned haven't you?'

'Twice.'

'Did the police say you were a suspect?'

'No, but they said I couldn't leave the area. They told Vivian that, too. And my mother, for all the sense that makes. We're being victimized for being Pamela's friends.'

'In that case a lot of us are. The plods want to be able to get hold of any number of us. Was your mother one of Pamela's friends? She didn't make it sound that way when I spoke to her.'

Harry glanced at her sharply. 'Mother likes to test the waters. She's always looking for reactions to what she says. I think she liked Pamela well enough.'

That was a great big porky, and only raised more questions.

The barmaid came to the table. 'Can I get you something else?'

They both shook their heads and Alex didn't react to the woman's significant glances at people waiting for tables.

'Tell me what Radhika said last night.' The abrupt belligerence was ugly.

'Don't try pushing me around,' Alex said. 'It won't work.'

'Did she show you something – something she got yesterday?'

She scarcely dared breathe. If he came right out and talked about the will would she be more likely to think he was innocent of any wrongdoing?

'What is she supposed to have got? All these hints are ridiculous.'

He regarded her closely. 'All right. Forget it. What was in that tower?'

'Stop it, Harry. If you want to know that, ask the police. I didn't take an inventory and I'm not in charge of the case.'

'You're not going to help me, are you?' His lips turned down in a sneer. 'You want to get back at any of us who know what you are. You're enjoying this.'

Someone bumped into the back of her chair. She winced at the jolt to her shoulder. 'I think you should go,' she said. And for some crazy reason she wanted to laugh. 'You are so narrow, so small. And you're a snob, Harry, you must be to suggest something like that. *What I am?* Disgusting, that's what you are.'

'Did you see—'

'Please go away.'

'Alex, I'm sorry. That was uncalled for. I feel helpless, that's all. Did you see a bag in the tower – with a bunch of things in it? Binoculars, maybe?'

This conversation needed to end. 'There were lots of things up there.' A lie was her only option unless she wanted to risk saying something she shouldn't. 'I don't remember anything in particular except a tarp covering a pile of stuff.'

Harry breathed in and she saw his shoulders relax a little.

The noise level grew. A big group of backpacking walkers clomped in, walking canes in hand, their faces ruddy from the sun and air. They ordered beers, laughed, rocked on their heels discussing the latest rambles and the energy they gave off brought out smiles in all directions.

'Have you lost your binoculars?' Alex asked. What could it hurt? He'd mentioned them first.

He darted a look around the bar and back to her. 'I don't know what you're on about. Let's have a real drink.'

'No, thanks, I'd better be off,' she said.

'What does that tosser want?' Harry said, surprising her with his vehemence. In seconds she was taken aback to see Dan O'Reilly approach, a grim line to his mouth. His dark, curly hair standing on end from the wind gave him a less world-weary look but from Alex's angle, the scar she'd noted months ago caught the light and still looked quite new.

He nodded at Alex and she expected him to make a crack about her not answering her phone. Instead he gave Harry his attention. 'Good thing that car of yours is hard to miss.'

'What did you do?' Harry asked with slightly bared teeth. 'Put out an all points bulletin?'

'You're watching too much TV, Stroud. I need to talk to you and I think you were told to make sure we know where you are.'

'You told me to stick around and I have.'

'Enough of that. Alex, excuse us, please.'

She almost said, *gladly*. 'I need to get back anyway,' she said, making to get up.

'If you don't mind, you and I will have a few words. And this would be as good a place than any. Mr Stroud and I won't be long.'

What choice did she have? She watched O'Reilly lead Harry toward the back entrance of the Mount and ordered coffee. O'Reilly wanted to get her on her own, away from Tony, that much was obvious.

Just out of her grasp, barely hanging onto the edges of her mind, was something she needed to recall, something she'd missed. The harder she concentrated the more tenuous and out of reach the recollection became.

Was it something someone had said?

Harry was the only one she'd really spoken to today. Alex went over their conversation but she couldn't find the trigger she needed.

THIRTY-THREE

I f Lily Duggins's car hadn't still been parked out back, Dan might have thought Alex had run out on him. A party of four men in work overalls sat at the table where he'd found her with Stroud.

He searched around and saw her through the front windows, apparently happy to prop herself against a wall and reach down to rub the nose of a damn great horse. Its rider, a strapping young chap in a body hugging navy blue jumper that showed off his flexing muscles, talked to Alex but when Dan went outside to join her, the man raised a hand in a wave and ambled off, casting a grin at her over his shoulder.

'Who was that?' he asked, and wondered why he had.

'Just an old friend,' she said. The crutch rested beside her, she kept her weight on the good foot and turned her face up to the sun.

Of course she had friends. Men who admired her. He looked to the right in time to see Stroud's Maserati whip from the parking lot. There was a muddled up chap. Muddled, mad and arrogant. Dan had already warned Bill Lamb to expect a belligerent Harry Stroud.

When O'Reilly first met Alex he'd kicked himself for being smitten. Later, when he saw how it went between Alex and Tony, he reminded himself of his less than wonderful record with the opposite sex and convinced himself he'd had a lucky reprieve.

He might need to revisit that decision. She and Harrison were close but he felt tension there on occasion.

Alex swiveled toward him and crossed her arms. She smiled, but he didn't see her heart in it. He couldn't help it if he found her a very good looking woman. Last time he'd checked, he'd still been human.

The bound ankle had led to her wearing skirts. Today a denim one that hit above her knee. Nice legs, really nice legs.

'Detective Sergeant Lamb tells me you spent time with Ms Malek at the hospital last night.'

'I'd like to sit down.' She got to a nearby wooden picnic table and sat on the end of one bench. The lunch throng had dwindled and they had the table to themselves.

Dan slid onto the opposite bench with a futile thought about how nice it would be if they weren't about to spar – and they would spar. Alex Duggins wasn't deliberately obstructive but neither was she an easy interview.

He pushed away a heavy glass ashtray brightly advertising Cinzano on all four sides. 'I heard you had a dust up at the Dog last night,' he said. 'Sorry I wasn't there to referee.'

'It was nothing.'

She wasn't a good liar. 'Never hesitate to get official help when someone gets out of line.'

'Mmm,' she said.

Which probably meant that as far as she was concerned, what happened in the Black Dog would stay there. This might be too important not to pursue. His newfound local friend had called, anxious about some of the threatening comments made by Jay.

'Did you feel . . . uncomfortable with whatever Jay was saying?'

Predictably, she looked at her hands. 'No. Not really. He was just blustering. He likes being at Cedric Chase. Seems to make him feel important although . . .' He could tell she was thinking over the previous evening and kept silent. 'There was a sort of bravado this time.'

She turned pink. There was more she wasn't saying. He could wait to press her, but not for long, not from the way things were going.

'Bill Lamb left you with Radhika Malek early last evening. I wouldn't like to think you would withhold any pertinent information.'

Her color deepened but there was more anger than embarrassment in her expression. She didn't answer.

'I think I know what you found out. Bill said something was delivered to Radhika while he was there. Did you see that?'

Her lips, pressed together, were pale.

Despite the warmth, a cooling breeze slipped by. He vaguely thought he smelled scented stocks. 'Alex, you do realize I know what was in the envelope?'

Her green eyes rested on his, but briefly. 'This seems like game playing. Or a fishing expedition. Why ask me what you already know?'

'I don't know who else you've told about what Radhika shared with you.'

'You and I seemed to have built up a little trust and understanding of each other the last time you were here. Do you think I've turned into an irresponsible big mouth?'

That stung, but he had work to do. 'Let's assume you know what was sent to Radhika. You do know what it means – other than there being a bigger pile of questions about some people around here than there already were?'

'You tell me.'

He almost grinned. 'You'll never be a pushover, my girl. I do think we have a little list of suspects in the murder of Pamela Gibbon, don't you?' Which again was more than he should say although, if by some unlikely chance, Alex had any involvement in the crime, and she knew they were closing in, it might shake something loose.

A long sigh and she said, 'You're good at what you do, Chief Inspector. I'm sure you're closing in on the murderer. Thank God.' She paused, picking at splinters in the old wooden picnic table. 'Is the post-mortem report finished?'

Few questions surprised him but he hadn't expected that from her. 'Yes.' It couldn't hurt for her to know but that would be the extent of it.

A white-haired man, stomach straining buttons on his orange silk shirt, pallid and skinny legs poking from beneath baggy shorts, maneuvered himself into a place farther down the bench, setting down a pint and a vast ploughman's lunch. The scent of pickled onions tickled Dan's nose. He hadn't realized he was hungry until he saw the slab of beef, chunks of cheese and heaps of salad and relish on the man's plate.

'We might want to finish this discussion in my car,' he said.

An emphatic and negative shake of her head didn't do anything for his ego, but, he reminded himself, snubs came with the territory.

'You're meddling,' he said neutrally. A change of approach sometimes worked.

This time she looked really angry but didn't respond.

'You don't like Stroud but you're hanging out with him.'

'I don't dislike Harry. And I'm not hanging out with him. I've had hardly anything to do with him since we were children.'

'That's not the impression I got from him.'

'What's he been telling you?' A very straight stare this time. She was growing restless.

'What has he been *asking* you? I got the impression he was pretty intense when I got here.'

'Have you done a DNA test yet?' Her mouth stayed slightly parted while she waited to see how he would react.

'What DNA test?'

'Was Pamela pregnant?'

Despite himself, he laughed. 'You're something else, Alex Duggins. You can't ask me questions like that.'

'Asking questions isn't against the law.'

'If I answered them it would be.'

She jabbed an index finger into the table and winced, trying to cover what she'd done.

'Will you look at that,' he said, pulling her hand up to look at the finger. 'You've a temper there.' A long splinter stuck out from beneath the nail. He pulled it out and held the end of her finger tightly. 'It won't hurt long.'

If she hadn't been determined to keep on her tough face, she might have said more. As it was, she hissed through her teeth and said a tight, 'Thank you. You knew I was asking about Harry's DNA. You need to watch out for moles in your camp. A reporter was the first to mention it.'

For the first time in ages, he wanted a cigarette. 'You could have been asking about anyone until you made yourself plain. And you know I couldn't and wouldn't tell you one way or the other.'

She looked a bit smug and didn't say anything.

'That sort of guaranteed-to-prick the ears comment is standard reporter fare. Must have been that smarmy bastard staying at the Dog. Like he could know anything, especially as early as he must have said it. He's got the bit between his teeth and he's not letting go. Praise be we've little other media interest so far and he thinks he's a chance of a juicy scoop if he hangs around long enough. There's no doubt he's the gift of the gab and will do a fine job embellishing it all in the end.'

Her smile stopped him.

'What?'

She had pretty teeth, strong but small. 'Nothing, except I can tell you're not fond of reporters and their ilk. That's the longest soliloquy I've heard from you.'

He was a bigger man than to get shirty over having his emotions read. 'You're right. Most of them are scum . . . well, I suppose I should say some of them are. It's always that bunch who manage to weasel their way in.'

'You won't share whether Pamela was pregnant?'

Avoidance was as good as a yes. 'It isn't in the cards for policemen to talk about suspects or victims, Alex. I think you know that.'

'OK,' she said. 'I hope you've got it straight that I came here, alone, to think. Sometimes it's easier being on your own in a crowd.'

'If Harry hadn't joined you, some other man would have tried to.' Now he was saying too much. 'Do you want to change your mind about telling me what you and Radhika talked about?'

Her eyes sharpened. 'I won't make a big deal out of the comment about my being OK with stray men joining me. You don't know me.' Her blue black curls flipped in the wind and the simple green turtleneck and denim skirt were perfect on her. Relaxed and complimentary. A very nice little body.

Blast it all but his imagination would run away sometimes, no matter how disciplined he'd become. 'Well?' he said and cleared his throat.

'Bill Lamb didn't tell you about Harriet and Mary Burke being ready to take Radhika in when she leaves the hospital?'

Bill wasn't on Dan's gold star list today. He shouldn't have left Radhika and Alex alone and neither should he have given tacit agreement to the Burke's plan without talking to his boss first.

'Well?' Alex said in a parody of the tone he'd used himself.

'Ms Malek has a right to go where she pleases, but we will have to look out for her after what's happened. It won't be so simple with people coming and going from that tea shop but I expect we'll manage.'

'You'll have help.'

He raised a brow.

'Tony and I, and probably one or two others, will make sure no one gets in and up those stairs unless they're invited.'

Bloody amateurs getting in the way. 'We'll discuss that when the time comes. I've an appointment to talk about when she'll be ready to leave the hospital. Tell me what you know about the Stroud family? If you would, that is. I know there's an older brother with a commission, and the major is always around the Dog, so I've a fairly good idea about him. It's been suggested the major's wife's a bit of an odd duck.'

'So I've heard – about Mrs Stroud. Do you have a lot of local people suggesting things to you? I don't know how you find so much out otherwise.'

'Just part of my job to find things out,' he told her evasively. 'Have you had any recent dealings with Venetia Stroud?'

Alex reacted as if she hadn't expected the interview to go in this direction. She was being careful. A farmer slowly propelled a herd of goats uphill toward the Mount and it was evident that she was glad of the opportunity to order her thoughts. The animals were mostly ginger and white, half grown ones staying close to their mothers and bleating complaints at being disturbed from a quiet day of grazing on some rocky hillside between their meadow naps.

'When was it you went to the Stroud house? Which evening?'

'Are you having me watched?' she asked sharply, sitting up straighter. 'If so, and if I went, then you know the answers.'

'You're not being watched. We don't watch people without provocation. But you were there and the thought doesn't give me a whole lot of comfort. I'd rather you not go back, at least until all this is over.'

Still she didn't give him a yay or nay response to his query.

'Alex, I'm being very serious here. Someone has died and someone was beaten up viciously. We don't have an assurance the person who did these things has moved on, which is probably just as well because we need to catch him and get him out of circulation.'

'I agree.'

'Good. Is there anything you've heard, or seen that I might find interesting? *Anything*. Is there anything you and Tony haven't told us? There's nothing too small or supposedly unimportant to pass along. Someone's life could depend on it.' He would never say, *'including yours'* but he thought it just the same.

'We thought someone got in the house and tried to poison Bogie.'

Was he hearing things? 'When?'

'The sausages weren't poisoned. It was just a silly prank to frighten me.'

'You should have contacted us,' he said, at a loss.

'Did you find the bag I told you about?'

Her repeated deflections frustrated him. 'You told us about the bag. We thanked you for your information.'

'But you won't tell me if you've found it, or the binoculars? You've asked other people about the bag. Do you know who the binoculars belong to? There can't be too many pairs like that floating around.'

Who had mentioned the bag and binoculars to her again? 'Was Harry Stroud asking you about them?' He could hope she'd either admit it or blurt out another name. He should be so lucky.

The focus went out of her eyes. She looked not at him but through him and started rubbing at the space between her eyebrows.

Dan O'Reilly held very still and waited.

Until his phone rang and he swallowed the curse on his tongue. 'O'Reilly,' he said into his mobile and listened. Bill didn't waste words but there were still enough of them to take a minute or two. 'I'll meet you there,' Dan finally responded and put the mobile back in his pocket.

'Has something happened?' Alex followed his movements as he got up and pushed herself away from the bench. 'Dan, what is it?' He could almost hear her fear.

'You'll find out anyway. We've got another body.'

THIRTY-FOUR

The ankle was stiffening and more painful. She'd overdone her first post-incident foray with a car.

Tindale Tower, or the Tooth as locals called it, stood out sharply on a high hill behind Folly, and above the Dimple and Alex's neglected house. She glanced at the tower frequently while she drove the last few miles home to the village. It felt familiar and helped keep her mind off the discomfort under her bandage. It didn't distract her from feeling sick at the thought of someone else dead before their time in the village.

She came in from the east along a rutted way, little more than a lane and dubbed Pilgrim's Way by some long ago wag. The backs of outlying cottages, yellow in the sun, stretched in dotted lines behind clusters of farm buildings on variegated quilts of fields.

Who is it?

Dan's body language had stopped her from asking, but she should have asked anyway.

Panicky fluttering crept beneath her skin. Sweat broke out on her forehead. 'Who is it, damn it?' she said aloud and her eyes stung. She was afraid, even though she wouldn't put names and faces to the possibilities she feared most. There were too many of them and two that took her breath away.

There wasn't a drivable street or lane behind the Dog. Alex drove to the High Street and made a half right turn to approach her pub.

One look ahead and she swerved to the side of the road and applied the brakes hard, with the wrong foot again. For a moment she rested her forehead atop her hands on the wheel. That hurt like hell.

When she lifted her head, the scene ahead hadn't changed. People still milled about in front of the Black Dog and the figure she couldn't fail to recognize had separated from the rest to run toward the little car.

Alex dared not drive on. With chattering teeth and every muscle jerking, she might run him over. Instead, she turned off the engine and struggled out of the car, in time to see Tony with his hair flying and arms pumping, bearing down on her.

'Alex,' he yelled. 'Alex, damn you, where have you been? I've been trying to reach you for hours.'

Her mobile. She'd deliberately turned it off before she left that morning. 'Tony, slow down,' she called. 'I'm fine. Just went for a drive.' And she'd have to elaborate on that soon enough.

But he was alive . . . and furious.

'Are you mad?' He ringed her neck and stood over her. 'You went for a drive? You can't use your right foot properly. Lily said she lent you the car . . . she shouldn't have. You take advantage of anyone who loves you.'

'No, Tony.' He was overreacting. He didn't know what he was saying. 'What's happening? I don't understand all the fuss. I only went to Stanton and had lunch at the Mount.'

'Did you deliberately turn off your phone?'

She couldn't stand like this much longer. 'Yes.' Why lie about the small stuff? 'I wanted some peace and . . . and . . . to be alone, Tony. You of all people should understand that.'

'And you included me with the people you wanted to get away from.' Flat. His voice was toneless. The high color she had seen as he ran to her drained away completely.

'May I sit in the car?' she asked him quietly. 'I think I've over-done it.'

'You bloody bet you have, Alex,' he told her through his teeth. Without another word he clamped an arm around her waist and supported her to the passenger side of the car where he unceremoni-ously deposited her inside. She could have cried when he knelt and carefully lifted her legs in front of her. As he got up, he rested his forehead briefly against hers.

'I'd better get to the Dog and let Mum know I'm OK.'

'She knows.' He slid behind the wheel and started the engine. 'She was standing beside me when you came around the corner and pulled off the road like a bad kid caught scrumping apples.'

That made her smile – a little.

'Shouldn't we go?' Alex asked. Her heart beat too hard and fast.

'You want to know why there's a crowd down there?'

'Of course.' She turned to look at him.

'We think someone else has been murdered. We don't know who or where, but rumors are flying about a body and an unnatural death.'

'I already knew.'

As expected, he gave her a blank stare.

'O'Reilly. He tried to call me this morning for another interview, I think. I heard his voice and that's why I turned off my phone. He saw me leave town and followed. Sneaked up on me at the Mount. He left when he got a call about "another body," as he put it.'

Tony tipped his head back against the rest. 'Who could expect to keep up with you? Did he say who it was they'd found?'

'No.' She swallowed. 'And I was afraid to ask. He was in one of his moods.'

'So you can work it out why I nearly lost it when I found out you weren't around. And then, after Lily said you'd driven her car, I still didn't know where you were.'

'I'm sorry,' she muttered.

'So am I. Dad's not at home and I can't get him on the phone, either. I don't know who got what information from where. I don't think it would be a good idea to go for a head count down there.' He nodded toward the jumble of people talking and watching the road in both directions.

A pair of horses cantered from the village green, across the High Street and converged on the Dog's forecourt. Alex squinted to see the riders. 'Heather Derwinter and Vivian, I think. If Heather doesn't know anything, she'll make it up.'

'I want to know where my father is, and where O'Reilly went when he left you.' Tony put on the signal and entered the road again. 'I already went by Dad's house. He's not there and his car's gone. Put on your seatbelt. I'm taking this around the back of the pub. You should go inside and put that foot up. I'll take my Range Rover and track down some information.'

'Make a U-turn,' Alex said and set her teeth for an instant. 'Either I come with you or I drive myself again. We won't be so noticeable in this.'

A single glowering glance and he spun the wheel to head back in the direction from which she'd come. 'Your mother won't be amused.'

'My mother doesn't interfere with what I decide to do.'

'Touché.' He sighed. 'I'm going to make a wide loop behind the village and get back to the parish hall. If the two big cats are away, the mice may get careless with their tongues. We need to be out of sight of the audience before we make the next turn.'

'We can take the road that runs past Wilkins' Dairy.'

'Hillop,' Tony said. 'Good idea.'

He checked the rear-view mirror several times as they approached Hillop Road. 'This'll do,' he said, and made a left. 'Should only take a few minutes to get there.'

And he would expect her to tell him about being with O'Reilly – and with Radhika the previous night. 'Harry Stroud followed me to Stanton, too,' she said. That was something else she'd have to share and it felt a bit safer somehow and made a good diversion. 'I nearly fell out of my chair when he walked in. He sat at my table as if I should be glad to see him. Then he grilled me about seeing Radhika last night and kept asking questions I couldn't or wouldn't answer.'

'He followed you?' Tony sounded incredulous. 'The man's amazing. I remember him from school – an ass, and he hasn't changed. How did he know you were with Radhika?'

The Fiesta's right front wheel dipped hard into a pothole and Alex grabbed for a handhold. 'He saw me.'

Tony looked quickly at her. 'When? Where?'

She rubbed the sore nail where the splinter had been embedded. 'He said he saw me go in.'

'At the hospital? Sibyl Davis was the only one in the waiting room, wasn't she?'

'That was it,' she said, excited. 'I knew there was something I ought to be noticing. He wasn't at the hospital so how could he see me?'

'Sibyl could have told him.'

Alex considered that. 'She could have. If he found out she was there he wouldn't hesitate to ask questions. I don't know. I can't imagine Harry and Sibyl in a conversation.'

Uneven roads divided up the farms. They sped along too fast, dropping into holes and popping in and out of ruts. A really good rain would coat everything in miserable mud but with luck, the mud would be smoother by the time it dried.

'Harry said the police are singling his mother out for attention. I don't know if I believe it.'

'She sounds unstable to me.'

'I should never have suggested to her – or to Harry – that I was sympathetic toward him.' They had almost reached Mallard Lane. 'He came after me today because he thought I was on his side and if I knew anything that could help him, I'd say so.'

A van came from behind them and the driver leaned on his horn. Tony moved over, tipping the Fiesta to a dizzying angle on a steep verge to let the white van pass. It turned down Mallard Lane.

'SOCO,' Alex said. 'Oh, no. Where are they going? Not the church, you think?'

He had set off again and was really moving too fast this time, following in the path of the official van. 'I don't know, Alex. We're going to find out.'

The van passed St Aldwyn's Church and rectory, and the graveyard.

Alex realized how close they were to the Burke sisters but at the junction with Pond Street the van turned right and she breathed freely again. They must be going to the parish hall to check in with the team.

Rather than stop, the vehicle drove straight past the parish hall where Alex didn't see either Dan O'Reilly or Bill Lamb's vehicle. Tony also drove by.

'I get it,' Alex said. 'They're doing what we're doing – staying away from the center of Folly.'

A couple of miles farther on the van made a left to a point where the High Street was known simply as the main road, the same one that eventually went through Underhill.

'This may have nothing to do with us,' Tony said.

But at the main road they turned left again, back toward Folly.

'The Stroud place?'

No sooner had Tony made the suggestion than their quarry made a swift right up another driveway, this one before the driveway to The Vines.

'Cedric Chase,' Alex and Tony said in unison.

Neither of them spoke until SOCO passed through the wide gate to the long drive that led to the house. 'We may have trouble getting in,' Tony said as a policeman walked out, hand held up to stop them.

The man ducked down at the driver's window and Tony said, 'Dr Harrison, I'm expected,' and they were waved on.

Inappropriate it might be, but Alex snorted with laughter and put a hand over her nose and mouth. 'You keep on surprising me,' she said. 'I thought you were too straight to do something like that.'

Driving very slowly, Tony turned a ludicrously innocent face toward her. 'I don't know what you're talking about. I am Dr Harrison and I don't think anyone we know up here will be shocked to see me . . . or you.'

Alex shook her head, but she sobered and looked ahead. 'Should we park back here and . . . walk?' They drew level with officers searching the bushes beside the road. 'We're just about there. On foot or driving, they can tell us to get out just as well. You're better off in the car.'

'It's probably Jay, isn't it?'

Tony took in a deep breath and held it, then let it out slowly. 'Another mistake? Someone should have seen him home last night.'

An assortment of official vehicles crowded around the front of Cedric Chase, Pamela Gibbon's red brick Victorian house. The garage doors stood open and androgynous jump-suited people went purposefully in and out. Doc James' Mercedes was parked beside a small, battered car missing most of its paint.

'That's Prue Wally's car next to your dad's,' Alex said. 'I imagine she still cleans the house.' Her stomach made revolutions again.

They parked near the Mercedes. Tony got out. Alex was slower but made it and put the crutch firmly under her arm.

'Do we go in through the front door or approach from the back?' Tony said.

'They're going to stop us either way,' Alex said. 'I vote for the front.'

'Me, too.'

Barely through the front door and into an expansive entry hall with a black-and-white checkerboard floor, they saw Prue Wally carrying a tray of mugs. Round, with thin brown hair and bright black eyes like a robin, her small mouth was turned down and she'd obviously been crying. She saw them and nodded to a door on their left.

'In there,' she told them. 'Doc's waiting for those police to come back – like me. This is an unlucky 'ouse. That Jay Gibbon's 'as been and gone and done for hisself.'

THIRTY-FIVE

'No sign of him yet, guv,' Bill Lamb said, pocketing his mobile. 'And there hasn't been a single sighting of that flashy car of his.'

'Fuck,' Dan said with almost as much frustration as he felt. 'I told the silly sod to get back here without going anywhere else. He seemed OK with that.'

'Could be why he's gone somewhere else, though,' Bill said, studiously watching Dr Molly Lewis contort herself as close to the corpse as she could get while it was still in the car.

'Clever,' Bill told him, holding back from losing his temper. 'The man must be a fool if he thinks this doesn't look bad for him. Even if a DNA test proves he's the father, it doesn't have to follow that he's done anything against the law. Running away changes that.'

'We'll find him. Let's hope he doesn't decide to check out permanently, too. We're losing suspects here.'

'With what he stands to inherit I doubt he'll be away long.' Bill ducked to peer inside the black Mercedes. 'And he knows the will gives him a damn good reason to like the idea of being the only surviving beneficiary. Or even close to. He'd have to have a screw lose to lead us right to him for the wrong reasons.'

'Wouldn't be the first greedy tosser to try reverse psychology,' Bill remarked.

Braving the probability of cutting comments from Molly, Dan went to stand behind her. 'Any ideas, Molly? Looks straightforward, doesn't it.'

Indecipherable mutterings issued forth. He put his head closer, 'What was that?'

'You've never brought me anything straightforward, Dan O'Reilly. I'm not making guesses on this one but I've got some thoughts. I'll know more when I get him on the table.'

Prue sat in an overstuffed blue-and-green velvet wingback. She sank into the upholstery as if trying to push herself out of sight completely.

Doc James, his thick white hair awry, swallowed gulps of tea.

'They're all in the garage?' Tony asked. Neither he nor Alex could believe they still hadn't been chucked out.

'Picky work,' Doc James said. 'They can't afford to make any mistakes before they break down the scene.'

'Do you think the kettle's still hot, Prue?' Alex said. 'I could sneak into the kitchen for a couple more mugs of tea.'

'S'electric. Boils quick.'

Alex went to the door, stood to one side and peered out. Not a soul. She slid into the hall and limped back in the direction from which she'd seen Prue come.

By the time she reached the kitchen, both Tony and Doc James were close behind her. Apparently Prue was a rule follower and not about to leave the drawing room again. Or perhaps she was too worn out and upset to move.

Alex was about to switch on the kettle when Tony held up a hand and said, 'Ssh,' very softly. He jabbed a forefinger in the direction of a door. Muffled voices came from the other side. 'Garage,' he mouthed.

Doc James gave a tiny groan when his son slowly turned the door knob and eased the door open just enough to rest on the catch. But the GP, and Alex, were right with Tony in seconds, standing as close as they dared to the infinitesimal crack through which voices had become marginally clearer.

A woman's familiar voice said, 'Depends on what came first, booze or the other. How capable he was or wasn't of dealing with the hose and getting back in the car. Trouble is we may have difficulty with that, depending on how much he inhaled before he died.'

'How do you decide that?' Bill Lamb said.

'With difficulty.' This was Molly Lewis, the pathologist, Alex realized. 'Percentages have to be marked enough to give us a clear picture.'

The kitchen crew exchanged meaningful if confused glances.

'Prue's outside,' Alex whispered, indicating a courtyard beyond the kitchen, lushly planted and bordered on all sides by what resembled a covered ecclesiastical walkway. A central swimming pool and a lot of elegant wicker furniture seemed out of place, if enticing. Prue talked on her phone in clear sight of the kitchen.

'She'll draw attention,' Alex said. 'We don't want that.' And she pushed open a window.

'He done hisself in,' Prue was saying. 'I already said that. 'E killed hisself somehow in Mrs Gibbon's car. Nah, I'm awright. Gotta wait till they say I can go. Make sure you go 'ome for a bit and let the dog out. Yeah, I'll call again.'

When she turned, Alex waved frantically and beckoned Prue to join them.

'I don't suppose it matters what Wally says about all this,' Doc James murmured. 'But it'll mean another round of chatter and mystery and if this is murder, it'll all get even more muddled out there.'

Her phone nowhere in sight, Prue sidled into the kitchen. 'Want 'elp wiv the tea?'

'Were you talking to your husband?' Tony asked gently, quietly and carried on without getting an answer. 'Didn't I see him at the Black Dog earlier?'

She turned bright pink and her mouth trembled. 'I 'ad to tell 'im somethin'. 'E was gettin' worried about me. No 'arm, is there? 'E's still at the Dog.'

Alex sighed. 'So now they'll all have part of the story and go running off in all directions. Not to worry, Prue. It was bound to happen.' Although it would be better if the news broke when the authorities were sure whether Jay's death had been a suicide or a murder. Or it might be.

O'Reilly's raised voice, sharp and irritable, said, 'What do you want, Short?'

'Sorry to interrupt,' a new voice said. 'Thought you'd want to know what we've found out about Harry Stroud. He was with Lark Major off Cheapside. Gutter Lane. But we already knew where he worked.'

'Was with?' O'Reilly said.

'Not anymore. They let him go almost two years ago. They're mostly in big vacation and travel investment projects but they do other stuff when they come on something they think is good. They're too busy protecting their reputation to talk about details, but Harry was into something different. All they'll say is that there was a difference of opinions and he's no longer with them and they have strict client confidentiality responsibilities.'

'Good work,' O'Reilly said. 'I want him found and brought in. Sounds like he could be an all around shit but we've got enough on our hands with the case here.'

Tony put his mouth to Alex's ear. 'We could be doing a public service if we follow up on friend Harry's secret life.'

She nodded, yes, but didn't feel so enthusiastic. How would Harry's failed career help them? She thought it could play a part in his desperation to get his hands on large sums of money to build himself up again, but that was already obvious.

Prue had assembled more mugs of tea on a tray and pointed a meaningful finger in the direction of the drawing room before leaving the kitchen.

'They will have talked to Venetia Stroud,' Tony whispered. The activity in the garage was enough to overcome most sounds from the kitchen. 'But you might get more out of her.'

Doc James didn't look happy and Alex was amazed at the suggestion . . . coming from Tony.

He shook his head as if reading their minds. 'I'd find a way to be one step behind you.'

Doc James said, 'It would change everything if Radhika had seen who attacked her.'

'Mmm.' Tony didn't look at his father. 'She'd probably be dead by now.'

'Radhika . . .' Reaching for Doc James's sleeve, she dug her fingers into the rough fabric. 'Did Harry see her after she was injured?'

'No,' he said. 'She was inside the cottage. I heard Harry and Vivian came to the cottage, but they were already gone by the time she was put in the ambulance.'

'I've got to do this,' Alex said, skirting the granite-topped kitchen island and throwing open the door to the garage. Only faintly did she hear Tony and his father gasp. 'O'Reilly? Dan. I've just remembered something.'

The light-blue suited figures around the car froze.

Lamb spoke first. 'What are you doing in there, damn you? How did you get into the house?'

She felt Tony move and gave him a warning glare. 'We walked in, Detective Sergeant. Through the front door. We were worried about Jay.' She couldn't see much inside the black Mercedes but the probable shape of the pathologist working over something. Alex fastened her attention on Dan.

'This morning at the Mount. I told you there wasn't anything else to share about Harry, but there is.

'First I should tell you I saw Pamela's will at the hospital. Radhika asked me not to let anyone know but I can't keep quiet about it any longer.' Feeling Tony's hand on her shoulder was a relief. They didn't need antagonism between them.

'Now I've remembered something Harry brought up at the Mount.

He asked me about Radhika's eyes after she was attacked. He wanted to know how they were doing since they were such a mess.'

Dan approached and pushed back the hood on his jumpsuit. 'And that's significant?'

'He didn't see Radhika like that – with her eyes swollen and black. At least, I didn't think he did.'

THIRTY-SIX

*I*f they knew what they're going to make me do, they'd stop. I lost what I really wanted but I almost had the one thing left to me in my grasp. Too much interference from people who won't mind their own business has slowed me down. It will work out but it's taking more time than I wanted. I've already waited too long.

I've thought it could become necessary to do more than I originally planned. Now I'm sure. But I've got to stay ahead of them all.

It's hard now. I must stop as soon as I've finished the job, but I don't want to. How easy it is to get rid of these people. They are foxes to my hound. Scrabbling and screaming and only digging themselves deeper into traps. Each time I feel as I never did before. I'm more aroused with every kill. Triumphant and excited for the next time.

So little more to do, really do, but I know I can't leave the other one behind. She won't stop, she'll keep on poking and so will that man of hers.

It becomes clearer that I can deal with both of them. Take Alex Duggins first and make sure Tony follows her. He always follows, like a slavish dog.

It could be perfect – the police are moving too fast now and a new angle would throw them off, give me the final way out I need.

And the thrill of seeing them watch each other die . . . oh, yes.

Tony drove into the parking lot behind the Black Dog. Alex rested a hand on his thigh, a sensation he liked a lot. 'They'll all be inside,' she said. 'We've got to be careful not to give the impression we know more than they do.'

'Right. But we're not staying long. Then I'm taking you home, yours or mine, your choice, and you're going to get a decent night's sleep.'

He parked but Alex made no move to leave the car.

'You ready?' he said.

'After we leave here, I've got some things we need to talk about.

I want to give you a complete rundown about this morning with Harry and Dan, and it's time you knew exactly what went on in Radhika's room last night. I've told Dan.'

'I wondered when you'd get around to that.'

'It's been a struggle because she asked me not to tell anyone but I have to think she didn't mean you and whether she did or not, you've got to know.'

'Why not tell me now.' He ducked to see her face in the gathering gloom. Lights popped on at the back of the pub and the door opened.

'That's my mum,' Alex said. 'There's a lot to say. Let's get home as soon as we can. Mum has a right to a bit of my time.'

Bogie and Katie squeezed in beside Lily at the doorway and peered around. Their bosses were not supposed to drive a Ford Fiesta.

'They're looking for us, too,' said Tony.

Reasonable as usual, Lily was satisfied with a brief explanation for Alex's long absence but she looked pinched and agitated. 'Can you face the bar? They're all hanging around hoping you'll show up with news, both of you.'

'We'll do our best,' Alex told her. 'But we've been sworn as close to saying nothing as we can get. Best for us to do our "know-nothing" act. Doc James will be along after a while. The police spent hours grilling us and now it's his turn, although what made them mad at us had nothing to do with him.'

They followed Lily inside while Katie and Bogie yipped for attention and waggled excited tails.

'Is the major in there?' Tony asked.

'Oh, yes, and barely containing himself. He's obviously putting on his usual bombastic act because of Harry, but he's an angry man.'

'We'll tread very carefully there,' Alex said. A member of the restaurant kitchen staff came through, took a large prime rib from one of the refrigerators and quickly left – with downcast eyes. 'Everyone's on eggshells,' she remarked, and said to Tony, 'If the major's here, would this be a good time for me to go and see—'

'No,' he cut her off. 'You've already pushed yourself way too hard. We've got enough on for now. Alex is coming up with me afterward, Lily. She needs some uninterrupted sleep.'

Lily turned away, but not before Alex noted the ghost of a smile on her lips.

Great, a private life was impossible in a village.

An ancient recording of The Yetties piped out old country songs in unmistakable West Country accents. Fruit machines whirred, pinged and rang while pool balls clicked clearly from the pool room where the door must have been left open so inhabitants could stay tuned in to happenings.

'There was a pickup dart match tonight,' Lily said. 'The bunch from The Trout and Sheep showed up unannounced and reckoned they thought they had a scheduled match. Good excuse to poke around and find out what's going on here. Too bad we had all of our best players here. Cleaned their clocks. Mary was in rare form. Word of warning. Those two are still here and if you notice what looks like a tartan shopping carrier with mesh windows – well, we have dogs all the time, why not a cat? Mary says Maxwell gets lonely at home because Oliver ignores him.'

Alex had to smile and Tony chuckled. 'Bit of local color,' he said. 'Not that we've ever been short of that.' He pretended to take a huge breath. 'Ready? Here we go.'

Both Hugh and Juste were behind the bar, serving at a brisk pace. The place was packed and there were a good many faces Alex didn't recognize.

A panicky tremor climbed up her back and she whispered to Tony, 'Seriously, what better time to go and beard Venetia. I don't know how deep she is in all of this but I'd bet she knows the lot. Honestly, well, I shouldn't say it, but there's something sick enough about her that nothing would shock me. I think she'd do anything to protect Harry.'

He surprised her by taking her hand and squeezing. 'Humor me, Alex. I know it was my idea for you to go but we don't know where Harry is. He could well be at that house. I can't . . . Please don't insist on going tonight.'

Their presence had been noted and the crush at the bar grew dense.

'I don't really want to anyway,' she said with a sheepish smile. 'Thanks for giving me a perfect excuse. I can't go because I don't want to worry you! Let's get through this.'

'Glad to see you,' Hugh said with a genuine smile. 'What can I get you?'

She should probably stay very sober, not that she wouldn't like to anesthetize her brain. *What the hell.* 'I'll have a Courvoisier, please.'

'Sounds good.' Tony kept hold of her hand. 'Make it two, please, Hugh.' And Tony being Tony, he pulled money from his pocket and put it on the bar. 'Have one yourself, Hugh, and Juste. And Lily, if you can find her.' Lily had already slipped away and would be checking out the restaurant and inn. They had several guests and she insisted on giving them personal service.

The instant Alex eased from behind the bar, Major Stroud placed himself where she couldn't avoid him. Tonight his eyes were clear, his face on the pale side, but he held himself rigid and a nerve beside his left eye jerked convulsively.

'Evening,' she told him, managing a smile.

He started to speak but was drowned out by questions on all sides. Wally – if people remembered the first name of Prue's husband, they never used it – showed mellow but unsteady signs of having been at the Dog most of the day and planted his feet apart in front of Tony and Alex. 'Is it true Harry Stroud made Jay Gibbon's life so 'orrible he did for hisself? That's what I'm hearin'. Harry thought Jay didn't have no right to be in Pamela's house and told him so.'

The major slammed a full glass on a table, slopping beer. 'Keep your bloody mouth shut, Wally or I'll keep it shut for you. Absolute tripe. When the wine's in the wit's out, or whatever else you've been tipping down all day. Another suggestion like that and I'll sue.'

'It was Harry who suggested Jay stay there,' Tony said quickly before casting a questioning glance at Alex. He was wondering if he should have revealed anything at all that he knew. 'Please calm down. We'll all have to wait for the official notification. Now, excuse us, please.'

'That's right,' Alex agreed in passing. 'Harry's a generous man. He knew Jay was related to Pamela. There was no one using the house and Harry couldn't see any reason for Jay not to be comfortable.'

'That's Harry,' Stroud said. 'Always looking out for the other fella.'

Wally let out a deflated sigh. 'If you say so. But summat made that Jay kill hisself.'

Under his breath Tony said, 'It's not up to us to give any details of the death.'

On their way to Harriet and Mary's table, they fended off questions with noncommittal shakes of the head and mutters, keeping their faces bland.

Harriet saw them coming, looked at their joined hands and gave a beatific smile. Both sisters' faces were highly pink from the fire to which they sat too close. Even on a warm night, everyone expected wood to be crackling away there.

'We've saved these for you,' Mary said, patting a dark wood captain's chair. 'Sit down with your backs to this gaggle. We need to talk to you.'

Before they could settle, Major Stroud arrived again. 'Did you see Harry today?' he asked, skewering Alex with a penetrating gaze. 'Speak up, now. I won't bite your head off.'

She squeezed Tony's hand on the table to keep him quiet. 'Why would you think I saw him?'

'I asked you a question.'

'Now I've asked you a question. Major, forgive me, but you don't seem yourself lately. You keep suggesting I know things I don't. And you don't take my word when I give it to you. Tony and I have been tied up for hours.'

He moved closer and leaned over her. 'A friend of mine saw you and Harry together at the Mount. Where is he?'

'The local grapevine is a pain in the neck,' she said. 'That was early in the day. I happened to be there when he arrived and he had a beer. End of story.'

'Did you leave together?'

'No, dammit. I drove myself there and so did he. It was pure chance. Where he went when he left, I have no idea.'

'That's enough, Stroud,' Tony said. 'Why don't you save your questions for your son? Now, if you don't mind, we're visiting with friends.'

The gray, bristling mustache over the man's lip worked as if he were eating words he'd like to use. The irritated nerve by his eye rhythmically contracted part of his cheek. But he turned away.

'Perhaps you should have suggested he ask his wife,' Harriet said, demurely looking at her hands in her lap. 'Don't forget how she followed Jay to the tea rooms. She's a strange one.'

An ache started over Alex's brows, and a slight buzzing. She didn't dare glance to see Tony's reaction.

'Look at this boy,' Mary said in a loud voice, pulling a zipped bag with wheels and a handle close beside her and leaning it back. 'He told me Oliver takes over the fireplace and won't talk to him when we're gone. So I got this handy thing so he can come about with us.'

Maxwell Aloysius Brady pressed his battle-worn orange face to a mesh window in the bag and looked at them with his one bright eye. He had curled himself into the bottom of the carrier and appeared more than content.

'You don't mind him being here, do you?' Mary asked, not sounding as self-assured as usual.

'Of course not. This was his first home, remember. Even if it was for a very short time.' The dogs flanked the carrier and kept up a sniffing competition. Maxwell ignored them. 'Tony, I do think I'll get home now. This has been a long day.'

He downed his brandy. 'Ready when you are.'

'Just a minute,' Harriet said. 'We wanted to let you know Radhika comes to us tomorrow. We talked to her on the phone. That Detective Sergeant Lamb had been in to try to change her mind about staying with us but she's going to anyway. Mary and I made sure of that. Lamb suggested she come here, but – and I say this as a woman who loves all the fuss and bother – that girl needs peace and quiet. She told us so. She'll have that with us. You don't hear the people downstairs in the tea rooms, not that they're noisy.'

'Is she coming by ambulance?' Tony asked.

Mary cleared her throat. 'Yes. And a police escort. She's got to be watched is what Lamb says and we're all right with that. But we thought you might like to know she'll be there before lunch.'

'She does need peace,' Alex said thoughtfully. 'I wonder what else she needs.'

Carrying a chair, Vivian Seabrook arrived at the table. 'Is it OK if I join you?' she asked, balancing the chair on its front legs. When they chorused that she was welcome, the rest of the chair hit the floor, Vivian slid to sit and scooted closer to the table. 'Thanks. I haven't been in since the night Pamela died. I want to be alone, but then I think I'll go mad if I don't talk to someone.'

'How are you doing?' Harriet asked superfluously. 'Don't be on your own. There's always a pot of tea at our place, or coffee. And I know Alex would welcome you here.'

'Indeed,' Alex said. She didn't know Vivian well. The woman was reserved but she always gave a pleasant impression and was well known for being a wonderful horsewoman and riding teacher. 'This is a bad experience for everyone. We should stick together.'

'Thank you.' Her dark blond hair shone in its shoulder length bob. The much darker, arched brows were striking. 'Did I hear Radhika's getting better?'

'Yes,' Mary said at once. 'She's coming to stay with us tomorrow morning. We've got a pretty room for her. She needs rest and no worries.'

'Can I get you a drink?' Tony said.

She thought about it before saying, 'Half of lager would be fantastic. Thank you, Tony. Are you coming up to look at the new little pony tomorrow. I think she's going to make a good children's ride.'

'I'll be up there.' He stood and went to make little cheeping noises at Maxwell before going to the bar.

'Damn good vet,' Vivian said. 'We're lucky to have him.'

'I was trying to remember how long ago you came to Folly,' Alex said. 'I think you've become a fixture at the Derwinters. Heather brags about you being a wonder. You've got quite an admiration society going up there.'

Vivian accepted her lager from Tony. 'Thanks. Nice to hear a compliment or two. I've been here less than two years. I was another of Pamela Gibbon's recruits. When the last boss at the stable left, she contacted me and put me in touch with the Derwinters. Thank goodness she did. Those people are terrific employers . . . and they've become friends. They've tried to step in and cheer me up over the last few days but I don't like to impose. They're such busy people.'

They all fell into a thoughtful silence.

Just as Tony started to say something about cows, Doc James walked in. He saw them and waved but went directly to the bar.

Close behind came O'Reilly and Lamb. Lamb remained hovering in the archway to the restaurant, or in their case, the inn, but O'Reilly walked straight to the sisters' table.

He bowed over Alex and Tony. 'We have to talk as soon as possible. By morning at the latest. Call me. In the meantime, if some big-ears tries to say Jay Gibbon was murdered, say you know nothing. And stick to that.'

THIRTY-SEVEN

Once Alex had seated herself on her favorite couch in Tony's breakfast room and swung her legs up, he pulled a striped armchair close. The moment the front door opened, the dogs had taken off and thundered upstairs.

'First question,' he said. 'Where the hell is Harry Stroud? When and where will he pop up and is he a killer? That seems to cover our immediate issues.'

'And I can't answer any of that,' Alex said. 'But we have to know why he was fired. Does that make sense to you? He was fired. Not a soul knew, or if they did they kept quiet. But he's never short of funds as far as I know.'

'Bet Venetia knew, you can bet on that. She probably keeps him in the ready.'

'I didn't know what you'd think when I didn't immediately tell you about Pamela's will. Radhika's scared, terrified of something. If she's not, her behavior makes no sense. I was hoping she might open up to me – since she's appointed me her confidante.'

'Let's hope for that,' Tony said, not commenting on the way she'd guarded information. 'She's going to be watched by the police and our budding lady detectives, so I think she's as safe as possible.'

'I was thinking,' Alex said.

'Wish you wouldn't, at least for tonight.'

She plucked the afghan from the back of the couch and spread it over her legs. 'Do you think you could pass for someone in Harry's business, or something similar?'

Tony's eyebrows rose in the middle – the picture of confusion.

'If I find out where all the sharp young movers in the world of wealth management hang out after work, could you go in there – after the booze has flowed a bit – and see if some pretty lady feels like talking about him.'

'I can't just—'

'No,' she said, leaning to thread their fingers together. 'You can't *just* but if I call Lark Major in the morning and pretend I'm a breathless young thing looking to meet up with a guy from the firm who invited me for a drink, I could get lucky. 'Y'see, I can't remember the name of the place we were supposed to meet and I don't want to make a fool of myself by calling him up to ask.' They may or may not give me a name, or even a name or two of local drinking holes. Who knows, if I say I used to go out with Harry Stroud, she might feel like sharing some dirt.'

'Good grief, Alex. Don't you ever slow down? You do know you'd have to use a burner phone in case someone ever tries to trace you.'

She smirked. 'Listen to you. Yes, I intend to get a one-time use phone and toss it. You could wear a suit in the good of the cause, couldn't you?'

He didn't quite hide a smile.

'I'd like to see that. Sounds sexy.'

'In that case I'll go up and put one on right now.' His blue eyes glittered with mock lasciviousness. At least, she thought it must be mock given how tired they were.

'I'd like to duck out on talking to O'Reilly until we've given this idea a try.' She pulled on his hand just a little, but he immediately slid to his knees beside the couch. 'If I make the call early and we can get up to London and stake out any leads I find, we might have some interesting answers.'

'Or we might have nothing but an angry chief inspector.' He sat back on his heels and regarded her through narrowed eyes.

'I do have a theory,' she told him, looking at the ceiling where sounds of racing dog feet beat a tattoo. 'And I want to know if he was advising Pamela Gibbon on what to do with her wealth.'

Tony said, 'We should look into that later.'

THIRTY-EIGHT

Air from an open window slipped across his bare skin. Tony opened his eyes to the sound of Alex's voice. She'd gone to the next bedroom, the dogs' room, as they called it, and was in animated conversation on the phone.

He checked his watch and swung his legs out of bed. Well after nine. He never overslept. His breathing slowed again, his eyes closed and he fell back among the tangle of sheets. For a wounded woman, Alex had showed no signs of handicap last night. Her body bent to his and the lady had a wonderful, wild side.

Her voice continued in the next room. With both hands, Tony pushed his hair back from his forehead. What was she thinking about them? She never mentioned the sadness he knew she felt over the loss of an almost full-term baby girl, or the former husband who had been in bed with another woman while people looked for him and his wife went through the worst moments of her life.

The past months since he and Alex had become close had been a helter-skelter. With her he had known happiness and confusion – even fear. Fear of losing Alex.

His own marriage had ended in deep waters off Australia when Penny went scuba diving alone and didn't return. Her body was never found and she was presumed dead. They hadn't been happy for a long time but still he wanted closure and it didn't look as if that was likely.

Galloping paws approached and the two dogs burst in. They jumped on the bed with enough force to bounce the mattress and went to work on his face with their tongues. He wrestled with them, but wouldn't allow them to stay.

'Good morning!' Alex appeared in the doorway. 'Those two have been outside. Are you ready for coffee? We've got places to go and people to see, or I think we will have. I talked to Harriet but I want to make sure Radhika's settled safely, too.' She still held her mobile. Her black curls were mussed, her face flushed – he suspected from beard burn. The old T-shirt she wore, one of his, clung to the most interesting parts of her body and started another reaction he couldn't afford to indulge immediately.

'O'Reilly expects to see us, and I think we'd better mull over your very good idea from last night because it could get us way out of our depth.'

She held up a hand and limped to the bed where she climbed awkwardly onto the mattress and propped herself against a pillow. 'I'm going to make another call. They should be in at Lark Major by now. Don't make a sound, please.'

'You said you'd get a burner phone.'

'I've decided it doesn't matter,' Alex told him. 'I'm not doing anything illegal.'

He turned up his palms and slid back down in the bed. A sharp crack on the window startled them both. A cuckoo's long beak had connected with the glass. The bird wobbled its blue and red body for an instant, recovered and flapped away.

'Hello,' Alex said into her mobile. 'I hope you can help me. I feel really silly but I met someone from your firm and arranged to meet him after work for a drink. But I don't remember the name of the pub, if you can believe that. Can you give me the names of your favorite locals? Favorites with the firm, I mean?'

Tony closed his eyes. As perky as she sounded, he couldn't imagine anyone falling for her line, and the slightly cockney accent she put on shouldn't fool anyone.

'This is so embarrassing,' she said. 'We've walked together on our way to work but we've never exchanged names, like. He seems nice and I really want a chance to see him – when we can actually talk, I mean. If you think there's someone else I should talk to . . .'

A pen hovered over a small notepad on Alex's knee. Tony took in her serious face and shut his eyes again. He should be on his way to some of the outlying farms and there was the mare and a pony at the Derwinters' place.

'That's good of you, Angela. I love that name. Anyway, what can it hurt? Even if I don't know his name I can take a look around and hope I see him. I must sound like a clot . . . Oh, thank you. You're a gem. Hey, want to get together for lunch one day? Or a drink?'

With difficulty, Tony stopped himself from shaking his head, no, at her.

'Half a mo', The Globe? 'Course, I do. Who doesn't? London Wall, right? I thought that was all wrinklies nowadays. Yeah, yeah. What's that? Bust? No, I haven't been there. Right off Fleet Street. A club?' She laughed. 'What sort of club?' Alex rolled her eyes.

'You're the best, Angela. Why is it . . . I get it. Their new local.

Really, thank you.' She switched off the mobile. 'We can find that. The in-group – that's what she called them – the in-group goes to a club called Bust on Bride Lane. I think she was trying to say, without actually saying, that it's a bit raunchy.'

Tony grunted. This sounded like the longest shot he'd ever heard of.

He got out of bed and looked through the windows at a day unsure of how it felt. There might be sun, there might be hours of the great gray.

'I'm going to this club later today,' Alex said behind him. 'When people leave their offices.'

If he told her it was a lousy idea she was inventive enough to get herself there alone. 'Am I invited?'

Vivian breezed into Leaves of Comfort while Alex was accepting a bag of sandwiches from Harriet who insisted she take them for her 'little outing' with Tony. With help, the sisters had got the impression that Tony was taking Alex for a drive because she needed a change of scenery.

'Grapes for the invalid,' Vivian said, holding a beribboned basket aloft. 'And oranges and apples and some sweeties. She can afford to eat what she likes with that figure.'

Radhika was slender but the saris she wore left almost everything to the imagination.

'She'll love those,' Harriet said. 'Go on up and see her. Give a coo-wee to let Mary know you're coming.'

'Will do,' Vivian said. 'You're looking pretty spry, Alex – and pretty spiffy. How are the injuries doing?'

'Better. But I don't want to fall down any stairs in future.'

'I don't think I've ever seen you in a dress before,' Vivian continued. 'Red suits you. Very sexy.'

Alex felt uncomfortable. 'Thanks.'

'Horrible news about Jay Gibbon.' Vivian winced. 'Sounds unfeeling but I can't help hoping it really was suicide. I wish the police would get a move on.'

The whole village must be discussing Jay's death by now. 'I wish they would, too.'

Vivian nodded and took the stairs two at a time, calling, 'Coo-wee, Mary,' as she got to the top and went into the flat.

'Horsey,' Harriet said, wrinkling her nose. 'She smells of wet tweed.'

Alex laughed aloud. 'You're awful, Harriet. And she's a good-looking woman. I should have asked how her bum's doing since that mare knocked her down.'

The next one through the door sent Alex's stomach into her boots. Bill Lamb smiled at her and she felt even more wobbly. 'Good afternoon, ladies. Just checking up on your charge. You won't forget there's an unmarked car across the way, will you? They're keeping an eye on you.'

'Very comforting.' Harriet's narrow nostrils flattened for an instant. Vivian could tell that Lamb was another one who didn't meet with Harriet's approval. 'Radhika's doing well. She says she's getting up before long. Can't bear being in bed any longer. She's got company at the moment but I'll tell her you checked on her.'

Lamb's expression didn't change. 'I'll go up anyway if it's all the same to you.' His eyes strayed to the loaded pastry case but Harriet didn't make any offers. 'It would be best if Radhika didn't go outside just yet, but I'll mention that to her. Alex, the chief inspector still wants to talk to you and Tony, remember? He couldn't get to it this morning, but he'll call you later.'

'I never forget the good stuff,' she told him. 'Radhika really is healing quickly. She's still a bit of a mess, but the swelling's going down.'

'Very gentle woman,' Lamb said. 'But she's got courage even though she's not the pushy sort.'

It could have been her imagination but Alex thought there was something meaningful in the sergeant's glance. She wasn't imagining that Radhika had made a significant impression on him.

'Any new breaks in the case?' Alex asked. He already thought she was pushy. What did she have to lose?

'I'm sure we'll have an announcement to make soon.' Nothing in the tone of his voice made her believe him but it was a nice idea.

'Can I give you a lift somewhere when I'm finished here?' Lamb said. 'I didn't see your car and you won't want to be walking far.'

'How nice of you.' Tony had dropped her off and was coming back. She saw his Land Rover through the bay window. He slid in to park outside the fence. 'My ride just got here, but I'll take you up on that another time.'

She made it to the door and outside even faster than she had hoped. Tony got out and opened the passenger door for her. When she was belted in she ducked to see the tea rooms. Bill Lamb stood in the window watching them.

THIRTY-NINE

C lose to Fleet Street, Club Bust was a surprise. Tucked away on the third floor of a plain building in Bride Lane, home to the City of London's gin distillery, rather than neon and strobe lights, loud music and a miniscule dance floor crammed with sweating bodies, it was an exotic wood-paneled place with supple green leather-covered banquets curved into half-moons.

No bar was in evidence but waitresses in black tuxedoes circled ceaselessly, serving patrons while classical music played softly. The formal black ties were worn around bare necks with no shirts under the jackets. Alex saw what had prompted the club's name.

Alex and Tony got their drinks as if by boomerang. A tall brunette took their order and returned with glasses of white wine in minutes.

'They call it in,' Tony said when the woman left on her four-inch jewel-encrusted heels. 'They've got lapel microphones.'

Alex saw what he meant. 'That's different. It's hard to be different anymore.'

'So, we're here, now what? Do we start asking who works at Lark Major?'

'Very funny. We're going to buy Angela a drink.'

He looked around the busy room. 'We are? The Angela you spoke to on the phone, you mean?'

'Yes. Just listen. You're the man I was looking for.'

'But—'

'Let me get my story out. I made a mistake when I thought you worked for Lark Major. We just met up, by the way, so you've only just found out I got the wrong end of the stick. You're with a firm of chartered accountants.'

'Over my dead body.'

'But I'm going to recognize Angela. I called her back and she's coming on her own to break the ice between me and the man I thought she worked with. A couple of drinks, some of those luscious-looking oysters, and leave the rest to me. I don't see how she can smell a rat, but if she does, we'll be nice, but we'll leave.'

'You do have it all worked out. I need to know how you'll approach what you want to find out.'

'Better if you don't know. You'll be more natural.'

'What if she's only been with Lark Major a few months and never heard of Harry Stroud.'

'You're not supposed to guess at my strategy, Tony.'

He groaned. 'Why did I agree to bring you here?'

Alex sipped her wine. 'Because you trust my judgment.'

'Then I shouldn't have this sickening feeling about the approach of doom.'

'No faith. So sad. You have to work on that.'

He started to speak, pressed his lips together and smiled.

'What?' Alex frowned and leaned toward him.

'I love that dress and I love you in it.'

'Is that why you're looking down my front for my belly button? Wow, I think this is her. Calm down, and don't look too familiar with me.'

Unless she had a clone, Angela had long, lustrous black hair and huge eyes to go with a gorgeous figure encased in a white suit, gray platform shoes and most eyes were trained in her direction. She'd been right when she said she resembled the model Misha Wilhelm.

Alex waited for the woman to look in her direction and waved. The red dress hastened Angela's confident walk in their direction.

Tony shot to his feet and held out a hand to be wrapped in yards of elegant fingers and long-painted nails, but Alex said, 'Sorry, I've done my foot in so I'll just smile and say you're incredibly beautiful.'

'Don't,' Angela said, waving a hand in front of her face. 'You'll make me go all shy.'

Alex doubted that. 'Sit down and tell me what you want to drink. Tony and I are ordering oysters . . . This is Tony. I found him right off and he's an accountant who doesn't work for Lark Major.' She giggled. 'I got that one muddled up, didn't I?'

'I'll have an Appletini, please,' Angela said, sitting on a chair opposite and crossing legs that ought to be illegal. 'And I love oysters. How did you get it wrong about Tony working for us?'

Alex spun her tale and Tony made sure the Appletini appeared almost at once. He ordered oysters, lots of them, and made yeoman's work of keeping his eyes mostly on Alex.

Angela drank her martinis like a pro. After three she was still very coherent and slid oysters down her throat as only a woman with lots of practice could do.

Tony ordered a bottle of the wine he and Alex were drinking and an extra glass. '*Just in case.*'

The many groups of well-dressed men grabbed a good deal of Angela's attention, as she did theirs.

'I didn't tell you how I came up with Lark Major,' Alex said, pausing to slip an oyster into her own mouth. 'An old friend of mine works there. I haven't seen him for ages and I can't think how I got so mixed up, except I do that a lot when I'm excited.' She cast Tony a little smile.

'What's your friend's name?'

'Harry Stroud. Good-looking bloke.'

'Stroud?' Angela's huge oval eyes took on a startled expression. 'He's not with the firm anymore. Hasn't been for, ooh, a couple of years, I think. Although he's still talked about when none of the partners are around.'

'Everyone thinks he's still with Lark Major,' Alex said with an attempt to match Angela's wide eyes. 'That's just like him. He always was a fibber. I don't actually . . . Well, I only know what other people tell me about him. I should have said we used to be friends, if you know what I mean.'

Angela poured herself a glass of wine and drank half of it swiftly. 'This is good. If he hadn't worked for a firm that can't afford to sully its reputation, he'd probably be in jail. Not that I know all the details of what he did. Some of us are still ticked off that he got away with it.'

'*No,*' Alex said in hushed tones. 'What did he do?'

'I shouldn't talk about this but my job's secure and plenty of people say he's a creep.' Angela looked around and lowered her voice. 'Supposedly he took some poor old man with dementia to the cleaners. A poor old rich man. Or at least a very well-heeled one. But you didn't hear that from me.

'Stroud got him up to his ears in South American mining futures only there were never any actual mines. Harry was always trying to run with the biggest guys so he kept getting more money out of this man and getting deeper in. That's how the inside talk goes, anyway. He got away with it, mostly because the client died. But the old man was gaga and there wasn't an easy way to try prosecuting

Stroud – not without casting a great big shadow on Money Bags.'

'Who?' Alex leaned closer.

'That's what we call Lark Major. Between ourselves, of course.'

'And this happened about two years ago?' Alex was getting a lot more than she'd expected, only she didn't see how it made any difference to what was happening in Folly.

'I don't suppose you know who the old man was. Gosh, that's horrible. If I see Harry I'll be thinking we were always right about him. But I'm never saying a word. I don't like getting involved in things.'

Angela drank more wine. She'd become thoughtful and a little distant. 'Neither do I,' she said at last. 'I bet Walter Lovelace wished he hadn't got involved with Harry Stroud. Not that it matters with Lovelace dead.'

'Lovelace of Lovelace Construction,' Tony asked ingenuously and despite Alex's frown.

'Not them. This was Lovelace Meats or something, only Walter had sold off most of his interests in favor of opportunities too good to pass up.'

'Following directions from his wealth manager, was he?' said Alex.

'I've already said too much,' Angela said. 'I've thought a thousand times about trying to do something about it. But whistleblowers finish last and now it's too late. I'm not proud of that.'

FORTY

'The short straw.' That's what Alex had told Tony. She had drawn the short straw and was in Folly, supposedly working normally while he researched Walter Lovelace's story.

They had agreed that they shouldn't be seen looking as if they were on a joint mission, and driving around together two days in a row.

Walter Lovelace had existed, that had been easily corroborated on Tony's computer. And they found a lot of minor facts about the now defunct Lovelace Meats, but details of what had led to the company's failure had been scanty so far and tied to the death of the owner and founder. He had a minority partner who sold out to Lovelace suspiciously close to the company's demise but that partner was now also dead.

Lovelace Meats had operated for three decades as a successful purveyor of high-quality meats to specialty stores, then slipped away in a matter of months.

Those who worked in the plant had apparently been in great demand by outfits anxious to take over Lovelace's spot.

Alex walked slowly and without her crutch, using a protective shoe, wearing her sling and holding Bogie's leash. He was ecstatic and behaved as if his mistress had abandoned him for so long that a lone walk with her was an almost forgotten joy.

He carried an overly long and crooked stick in his mouth and each time he swung his head to look at her she feared he would whack her legs, but she didn't want to spoil the bliss in his black eyes.

Sun struggled to compete with a bank of dark cloud and the wind that had plagued them lately had picked up again. Still Alex smiled at the fresh air on her face and the waving fronds of goldenrod as she got closer to Leaves of Comfort.

Noon approached but after coping with the morning crowd, she hadn't felt like fending off questions from the lunch crowd at the Dog, and a call from Harriet Burke urged her to visit Radhika who had been agitated and asking when Alex might come.

Tony, he of the long straw, was closeted away with the computer in his offices while the answering service fielded routine calls. So far the computer search hadn't turned up the most important details they wanted and Tony had an old school friend with a mysterious government job helping him open up the dead ends. Tony and Stephen Hansen didn't make contact often but Tony's respect for the other man was evident.

Mist hung on the hillsides, the sun disappeared and a darkening sky promised rain and soon. Alex passed the unmarked police car without glancing at its driver and followed Bogie, who turned in at the gate to Leaves of Comfort as if on remote control and pulled to get to the front door and the promise of treats.

She went into the fragrant tea rooms and found Harriet going through piles of newly acquired second-hand books. 'Anything?' Alex asked, unable to control the urge to search for her beloved children's books.

'Hmm, one or two possible. I'll put them aside for you, don't worry.' Harriet smiled, but quickly became serious. 'I didn't like taking you away from your work but Radhika is upset, I'm certain she is. You know how she tries not to be any trouble, which she couldn't be, but I heard her crying this morning, very softly. And she sits in a chair in the corner of her room where I'm sure she's keeping an eye on the door and the window. She's jumpy, Alex. It's not normal even for someone recovering from a shock, not when she's being closely watched. I don't think so anyway. She hardly eats a crumb and we can only get her out into the sitting room in the evening when the shop's closed and everything's locked up. She checks to make sure the police car is across the way.'

'And she actually asked to speak to me?' Radhika's trust felt like a heavy responsibility.

Harriet nodded, yes, and Alex returned the nod. She took off Bogie's leash and went upstairs.

Mary sat with Maxwell on her lap casting Oliver smug blinks. His purr sounded like a small chainsaw in need of oil. 'Hello, Alex. I think your little friend will be very glad to see you.' Mary smiled and indicated for Alex to go into Radhika's room.

As Harriet had described, the small woman sat in a corner of the old-fashioned room, farthest from the window and the door, where she apparently kept watch. Dressed in green and gold, exotic despite her bruises, Radhika's drawn expression shocked Alex who

shut the door behind her and went directly to take her hands. She
drew back when the bandages and splints reminded her of the
woman's injuries.

'You must sit,' Radhika said. 'Sit now. On the bed. I should not
have troubled you but I'm glad to see you.'

Roses in a china bowl scented the air. It all, the room, the
fragrance, Radhika herself, seemed unreal.

'We're all a little scared,' Alex said. She perched on the white-
painted metal bed close to Radhika's chair and Bogie put his head
on the woman's knee. 'It's serious. They say . . . the police say
they're getting close but until they have whoever has done these
things, we're going to stay scared.'

'I don't know how to say it,' Radhika murmured. 'What you say
is true, but . . . there are other things. Alex, do you think I have
been concussed? Was I unconscious? I think perhaps I was.'

Alex frowned at her.

'I can't remember what time I walked with dear Katie that night.'
She stroked the dog's head. 'I think it was very late, but it was
morning when they found me, wasn't it?'

'Yes, early morning. I'm not sure how early the reverend got
there.'

'Could I think of things in little pieces . . . not in complete
memories? I know how it felt when he hit my head. It was the back
of my neck, I think. I was too shocked to think of what was happening
or what might happen next.'

The window rattled. Alex looked around to see tree limbs waving.
The wind was picking up in earnest. 'Have you talked to Doc James
about this? He would know the answers to your questions.'

'No!' She put a hand to her mouth. 'I am not happy talking to
men about such things. The doctor is so kind. Perhaps I can ask his
advice soon but not yet. There is too much else to consider. I think
I am in great danger, Alex. If . . . I am found by people who think
they should . . . it is so hard to explain. They think I have dishonored
them and that I should be punished.' She finished with her eyes
downcast and her hands still in her lap. The bruises, fading to green
and yellow, were an insult on her smooth skin.

'I don't understand things like that,' Alex said honestly. 'I know
what you're talking about, I think, but not enough to deal with it.
We have to have help from people who do know it all.' She hadn't
expected this.

'A man from my family thinks he must do this thing. I have been warned that I'm not safe anywhere. And now I have been warned again . . . in a different way, I think.'

Alex wanted to be receptive; she didn't want Radhika to stop talking because she decided Alex was shutting out what she said. 'Why now? You mean, you've heard from this man?' Where was he? Until now she'd only read of these issues and heard snippets on the news.

'I don't know.' Radhika closed her eyes and bowed her head. 'I think I was told again. I left Cornwall because I heard from my brother that I had been found wanting because I would not marry the man my family agreed to. He said I could still go to the man – but I could not. I left, ran away, and was lucky to come here to Pamela. She understood what I told her and had me stay with her. We knew each other from the clinic where I worked before. And she was the kindest person I have ever met.'

'But you've heard from your brother again?'

'I don't know. In my head, I hear it. Perhaps I am not well – really not well, in my mind.'

'You've had a horrible experience,' Alex said. 'It's too soon to be over what happened to you.'

'I think I should go away again and hide but it's hard until I am really well. Everyone would look at me like this. How should I make sure I am not noticed?'

'Look at me,' Alex said, and waited until Radhika raised her face. 'You must not go anywhere. We have to find out if what's happening . . . no, what's happening in Folly is nothing to do with you. I'm going to help. Please let me help you. If you run, you put yourself in danger. You shouldn't be alone and we can keep you safe here.'

She didn't know how much of Radhika's story she believed. It was possible the thump on the head and the shock she'd sustained had caused a subconscious issue, but how would anyone but an expert know?

'I would trust Tony,' Radhika said softly. 'Perhaps you might ask him what he thinks. When I close my eyes I think I am losing my mind.'

Three light taps on the door startled both of them.

'Who is it?' Radhika asked, her voice surprisingly steady.

'Sergeant Lamb,' the man said as he opened the door. 'The ladies said you were visiting Radhika, Alex. I need you to listen to something and tell me if it means anything to you. You, too, Ms Radhika, if you would.'

Lamb's smile at Radhika made a different man of him. Charm and interest glowed in his light-blue eyes. Now here, Alex thought, was a cause lost before it began.

'Of course,' Radhika said with a shy smile that almost made Alex groan.

Lamb closed the door. 'Thanks. It'll only take a few seconds. He took out his mobile and pressed a button. Music played, slightly tinny, only a few bars then it stopped.

Alex swallowed. Her skin prickled.

'Ah, yes,' Radhika said, touching first one, then the other suddenly damp eye. 'It is the music someone left for Pamela quite often. On her answering machine. She called it a message to make her happy, and she would laugh.'

'What is it?' Lamb said a few minutes later when Alex followed him hurriedly from Radhika's room. 'What's on your mind?'

There was no helping Mary's presence in the sitting room. 'I've heard that music, too, but not on Pamela's phone,' Alex said. 'It was on a small recording device on Harry Stroud's kitchen counter.'

His narrowed eyes and full attention were to be expected. 'Stroud's?'

'I will tell you all of it later but it's too long now. I was there. He wasn't at the time. I did something foolish and got stuck in his flat. I was looking for a mobile.' She shook her head emphatically to stop his next question. 'Let me finish. I think something's going to happen and you have to find Harry. Why would he have the same little snatch of "Greensleeves" on a recorder as you found on Pamela's phone?'

'They were friends,' he said slowly. 'Good friends. Could have been a joke between them.'

'Yes. Or it could have been their signal to get together. What if on the night Pamela went to Ebring Manor – which must have been where they usually met – that message was left to let her know he expected her?'

FORTY-ONE

Tony's friend Stephen Hansen found his way around the cyber world with the kind of ease that mystified Tony but he was grateful to have his help. If Stephen came through with the photos he was sure he could get, they would force O'Reilly to take Tony and Alex absolutely seriously. With the obscure details already printed out and ready to go, it would be impossible for the police not to go into action.

Tony waited with Katie at his feet. A cat recovering from minor surgery cried in the next room and a recently spayed dachshund grumbled in her sleep.

Ducks swam by on the tiny river trickling by outside his windows. The near silence didn't bring him any peace. He watched his screen and felt ready to leap from the chair.

Even if he got what he expected, there was more work to do. But he'd proved there could be supposedly small things hidden from the all-seeing eye of the great electronic watchdog – the Web. How suitable a name that was. Almost everything got captured in its sticky tendrils.

Nothing was likely to change fast, not until all the players were gathered in, but he wanted to be where he needed to be when the pieces started falling into place; with Alex.

His service rang in. They had a personal call for him and he had it put through. 'Harrison here.'

'Son,' his dad's strong voice said. 'I ran into that nice Dr Molly Lewis. She'd have my guts for garters if she knew I was passing this on, but Jay Gibbon was already paralytic when the exhaust got to him. By the levels that showed up in toxicology, if the alcohol hadn't poisoned him regardless of the fumes, we'd all be surprised.'

'But he still put the line from the exhaust into the car and shut himself in,' Tony said.

'Not in that condition, he didn't. Left alone, he would probably have died anyway. The window dressing was almost just that, although it probably speeded things up. He wasn't a suicide.'

FORTY-TWO

Mary Burke wasn't smiling. The pinched, apprehensive expression on her fine-skinned face showed Alex how anxious the old lady was and it only intensified her own tension.

They had looked at each other while Bill Lamb ran downstairs and the bell over the front door jangled as he left.

'Will you say what that was all about?' Mary asked, her eyes darting behind very thick glasses. 'Should we be taking extra care with Radhika? We won't let anyone hurt her, y'know. I shouldn't say this, but Harriet and I have a way to look after ourselves and that young woman – and you – if necessary.'

Alex didn't pursue that. 'It's all right. We can trust the police.' She must not reveal anything else.

Mary didn't ask for more information.

'I should go down now,' Alex said. 'I have to find out what Tony's up to and check in at the Dog.' She didn't say that she kept expecting O'Reilly to descend on her with his promised questions.

'You go,' Mary said. 'We'll be here looking after Radhika.'

Harriet waited below, still shuffling books back and forth although she didn't appear to have shortened the piles. 'What did he want?' she asked. 'Lamb, I mean. Not my business, I suppose.'

'I think we all have a stake in this,' Alex told her.

Her mobile rang and she checked but didn't recognize the caller's number. 'Excuse me,' she said, wishing it had been Tony.

At first all she heard was sobbing and garbled words.

Alex held still, steadying the phone with both hands. Bogie had followed her down and bumped against her knee for attention.

The caller was incoherent.

Harriet stepped toward her, alarm tightening her features. The sound from the phone would be easy to hear. Alex shook her head and put a finger to her mouth.

'Alex?' At last a clear word, loaded with tears and hiccups and rasping breath. 'Is that you?'

'Yes,' she said, as steadily as she could. 'Who is this?'

'Vivian,' the voice shrieked. 'I'm terrified. I don't know what to do next. The police will come for me and they won't believe me. He's planned it all and now . . . I don't know what to do. Have you seen him? I can't find him but he's around, I know him. He's here and waiting to finish what he started.'

The last person Alex expected to hear sobbing into her mobile was Vivian Seabrook. 'Shush, Vivian. What's happened?'

'H-Harry. He planned this. I'm going to be blamed for everything. It isn't right. It isn't fair. All I did was love her.'

Alex's mind blanked.

'I loved Pamela. She was my best friend and the only one who ever cared what happened to me. But it was more than that and he couldn't stand it. He had to poison everything. I don't know what happened but he's made sure I'll get the blame, I tell you. It's that bag the police asked about.'

'What—'

'You'll help me, won't you?' Vivian said, her voice grating but no longer broken by sobs. 'I want you to see this. You'll understand. You'll believe me.'

Her mind spun but reason didn't fly away. 'The police will understand. If there's something Harry's done, they'll deal with it.'

Vivian hung up.

Staring at the phone, Alex marshaled her thoughts, ugly, confused thoughts. She redialed the number and it rang six times before Vivian answered with a whispered, 'Yes?'

'Meet me,' Alex said. 'Let me help you.'

More tears, volumes of tears followed. Vivian finally gasped out, 'Thank you.'

'Where are you?'

'At the stables.' Her voice broke into a high wail. 'With my horses.'

'I'll come to you. Just stay put. Is anyone else there?'

'They left when they heard me,' Vivian sobbed. 'Must have sh–shocked them. I want to be in here with my mare. Pamela gave her to me.'

'OK,' Alex said gently. 'I'll come. Just hang on. We can talk, then I want you to go to the police with me and let them help.'

'Noooo,' Vivian keened. 'They won't believe me. There's a letter from her. Poor, Pamela.'

'I'm coming, Vivian.' She frowned at Bogie but Harriet took hold of his collar and waved her outside.

At least the Fiesta was familiar and light enough to handle. Not big enough to please her, but something she didn't have to think about. Lily hadn't been amused, although Alex's insistence that she was only going up the hill helped. She hadn't told her mother exactly where on the hill.

The Derwinter stables were reached by a road branching away from the main long drive to the big house. Alex took this and drove the wide sweep around one of several grassy mounds topped with copses of trees before setting off on the uphill drive to famous Derwinter Stables and Riding School.

Draped in blankets because of the threatening rain, horses nibbled grass in nearby fields. The stables, with riding rings behind them, stretched in a long line. No horses poked their heads from the open upper halves of their stall doors and a wide entrance was open at one end of the building.

It looked as if Vivian was right and she'd managed to scare off staff and anyone else in earshot.

Alex parked and scrambled out as fast as her gammy foot allowed. She had grabbed a cane left in the umbrella stand at the Black Dog and moved much faster than she could with a crutch.

Lily had sewn a long zip into the leg of Alex's jeans and she was grateful to be a little more comfortable again. She wished she'd brought a jacket but the long-sleeved blue T-shirt would do.

'Vivian!' she called, entering the stables. Horse, hay, and cleanup work yet to be done congregated into their own scent. 'Vivian, where are you?'

In one of her uniform tweed jackets, breeches and boots, Vivian appeared at the end of the hay-strewn walkway between stalls. 'Down here,' she said. 'It's here.'

Alex tried to hurry. The uneven floorboards made walking more difficult.

Vivian was in a corner area with a stall on either side of her and open doors at the back. Feed bins, tack strung from hooks and shelves lined with supplies almost filled the space. Gracie, the mare Pamela Gibbon had left Vivian, grazed outside with reins tossed over a post.

'We've got to keep our voices down just in case,' Vivian said.

Her normally rosy complexion resembled tear-streaked putty. 'I found it in there.' She pointed to an open feed bin. 'He knew I would. That's Gracie's and I'm the only one who feeds her. He knew I'd see the bag before I refilled the bin.' She pressed a fist to her mouth and closed her eyes.

Leaning over the bin in the dingy corner, Alex saw the same heavy green canvas bag she and Tony had found at the top of the tower at Ebring Manor on the night they discovered Pamela's body. 'You said you knew what was in it,' Alex said. 'But you left it in there.'

'I put it back to show you where it was.' Vivian hooked the end of a pointed shovel through the bag handles and hauled it out. She held the spade toward Alex until she took off the bag.

She thought about that night. An officer had . . . a figure had left the tower during the search as they secured the scene. It didn't have to have been a policeman.

Inside she found the box of glacé chestnuts and the Zeiss binoculars.

Vivian cried, and sniffled out, 'Look at the bottom of the bag. Under everything.'

What Alex found was a long, stiff envelope with a card inside. On the front, a giraffe with an impossibly long neck said he'd never been so happy.

'Read it,' Vivian said. 'She's dead now so I don't have to guard her privacy.'

A single folded sheet of paper slid from inside the card and Alex started to read:

Hello, my hero, I should have come to you about this as soon as I knew but I've never been good at trusting. I was wrong to wait. We have something more than the great sex. I love you. Now I've said it. And I'm going to have our baby.

Of course it's a shock, but it makes us act. You need out from Venetia's thumb and all that rubbish with your parents and I need you. You'll never have to worry about money again and you can go into business for yourself – if that's what you still want.

We have to talk. This wasn't something we ever thought about but it's happened and I want the baby. I'm asking you to marry me – something I never thought I'd do. I won't cramp

your style, we won't cramp your style, only give you more of
the freedom you love.

I'm giving you this because I want to watch your face. I'm
hoping you smile. I'm hoping for all kinds of things. We can't
change what is, Harry, so let's make a damn great success
of it.

Pamela

Staring down at the page, sadness flooded Alex, and amazement
at the woman's clumsy approach to something guaranteed to change
the man's life without telling him the facts first and seeing where
that took them.

'He had to have her,' Vivian said behind her. 'But he didn't want
more than a fling.'

'We can't be sure of that.'

'He spoiled everything, leaving his mark on her like that. I told
her to get rid of it but she wouldn't listen. I even said I'd bring up
the baby with her if that's what she wanted. She laughed at me.
Look what she made me do.'

A stabbing jab, like an attack by a poisonous insect, a huge
poisonous insect, assaulted her ribcage and intense burning flowered
in the side of her body. Alex caught herself on the feed bin as her
knees would have given out.

She turned to stare at Vivian. The other woman held an empty
syringe. 'What have you done? Oh . . . oh . . . Vivian, help!'

Vivian didn't say a word. She watched Alex's legs give out and
the loose, heavy impact of her body against the wooden floor. When
she tried to speak, her tongue lolled to the side in her mouth.

'If you and Tony had left it all alone I wouldn't have to do
this,' Vivian said. Her face swelled and shrank before Alex's eyes.
'I know you're looking for things that should never be brought
into the light again. I can't let you do that. I've suffered enough
already. He took the only one I ever wanted away, and she let
him. I need to pay him back and I've only got one more chance.
I have to have it.'

Alex tried to get up but it was as if she had no arms or legs and
she didn't think she moved at all.

She started to laugh, the sound like a snorting animal. *Tony
will come, and the police,* she wanted to shout. Softly colored
flowers floated past her eyes, their petals moving like bee wings.

Nausea flooded her, knocking out her breath. She couldn't breathe anyway.

Turning her, rolling her this way and that on the floor, Vivian handled Alex's heavy arms and legs. She was tying her up. As if . . . as if she could move. The flowers faded into flashes. There were misshapen crows, their wings luminous.

No part of her body would do as she told it. This was Vivian's plan, her reason to get Alex up here, so she could paralyze her and then kill her slowly.

She was to watch her own death.

'I expect your Tony will be here soon.' Vivian's voice came from a distance. She took a big red can from behind the bins, unscrewed the cap and put it close to Alex's head.

Alex tried to speak but her tongue filled her mouth.

'Might as well kill two birds with one stone.' It was Vivian who laughed this time.

FORTY-THREE

Too late, damn it. He'd called Alex too late to stop her leaving and she wasn't answering her mobile.

'. . . gone to the stables at Derwinters'. Vivian . . .'

That was as much as he registered of what Harriet said when he reached Leaves of Comfort and before he raced back to his vehicle, dragging out his mobile as he went.

O'Reilly picked up on the first ring and Tony didn't wait for greetings. 'I'm on my way to the Derwinter place. Where are you?'

'Leaving Bourton-on-the-Water. On my way to Folly.'

'Do you know where Harry Stroud is?'

'In custody. We picked him up a couple of hours ago. He still swears he didn't have anything to do—'

'He didn't. Not directly. I don't know it all but I will. Alex went to meet Vivian Seabrook about an hour ago. I think we'll find out – Vivian only wants one thing. That's to see Harry spend the rest of his life in jail for murders he didn't commit. Including Alex's.'

O'Reilly was silent for moments. Then he said, 'I'm coming. Bill's with me. I'll call for backup.'

'Don't come in like the bloody cavalry, Dan. I don't know what I'm going to find—'

'I want you to stay put just where you are and let our people go in.'

Tony pulled his lips back from his teeth. 'You've got to be kidding. Follow me and come quietly. Alex didn't know what she was walking into. Does the name Lenore Seabrook ring a bell? The pianist.'

'A bit. Famous, isn't she?'

'Wasn't she? Yes. She had a long affair with Walter Lovelace of Lovelace Meats. Lovelace was Harry Stroud's last client for Lark Major. Lovelace had advancing Alzheimer's and Stroud frittered away the man's fortune on useless investments. Vivian is Lovelace's daughter by Lenore Seabrook. The kid was never spoken of because her mother wanted it that way. But mum was ill a long time in the end and went through all the money Vivian should have inherited. But Vivian didn't think all was lost since she intended to squeeze her daddy, only that had already been done.'

'How do you know all this?'

'Later Dan. This is simple revenge – if it's ever simple. I've got a picture of Vivian on horseback with her mother and another of Lovelace with Lenore, same date. There were whispers about who the girl's father might be, but they kept it mostly quiet. Vivian's lost it. I've got to get there.' He threw his mobile on the seat beside him, on top of the photographs.

He had a fleeting vision of O'Reilly and Lamb fuming over interference, but driving like escaping convicts just the same.

The drive to the Derwinters felt longer than it ever had. Tony set his jaw and almost yelled aloud when he drove onto the estate. He knew the way to the stables – he ought to.

His first off-kilter impression was that there were too many horses in the fields. But rain pelted in a continuous sheet and Vivian valued the expensive stable too much to risk its health.

The Land Rover was too loud and too obvious to get very close. Tony parked the vehicle by a lower paddock and ran, doubled over, using anything he could to cover his progress.

Before the final rise to the stables, he fell on his belly and crawled until he had a clear view of the building.

Nothing moved.

No horses appeared at the doors to their stalls. Not surprising when they must all be in the fields. Tony wiped his sopping hair from his eyes. Mud beneath him didn't feel good but it helped him slide without raising his head often.

To the left, Lily's Fiesta had been parked.

Tony put his forehead on his muddy hands. His last hope had been that Alex had decided against coming here but he should know better.

There was no way to guess where the two women were or what was transpiring. With a lot of luck he'd walk in on nothing more than a heated conversation.

He gave up on crawling and walked rapidly to the open doors into the stable. Once inside, he edged forward to the passage between empty stalls and took a look toward the far end. Nothing.

A faint rustling came and went. Tony thought it must be an animal moving around.

He walked the length of the building, searching left and right but seeing no movement.

'Hello, Tony.' Vivian's voice jolted him.

'Good morning,' he said. 'Or should I say good afternoon. I'm looking for Alex.'

'She's right here.'

'Right here' was trussed in a heap in front of more open doors at the back entrance. He made to go to Alex but Vivian held up a hand. 'Stay where you are until I say otherwise.'

'Alex,' he said urgently, ignoring Vivian.

Only desperation in Alex's eyes showed she was alive. She didn't move a muscle. 'Why isn't she moving?' he snapped at the other woman.

'She's just tired. I need your help with something.'

'I'm getting Alex out of here and you'd better pray I don't find you've done something to her.' Not far from Alex's head stood a red petrol can. There was no nozzle but the cap was off. 'That petrol's open – get it away from Alex.'

Vivian swayed from her back to her front foot, to her back and forward again. She kept up the rhythmic movement. 'It's where I want it. If you don't want me to spread the contents all over your girlfriend, do as you're told.'

An arrival by the cavalry couldn't do any harm.

Pamela Gibbon's mare moved restlessly outside. The animal was saddled. 'Planning to ride off into the sunset?' Tony said and hoped he sounded more flippant than he felt.

'How did you guess? Take this.' She raised her right hand to show him a full syringe. 'Just hold it. For now. Drop or throw it and the petrol gets kicked over.' In her left hand she held a lighter.

Tony made himself smile at Vivian even though her eyes haunted him.

He took the syringe. 'Let me guess. Now I inject myself with this and we wait for me to react. What is it? Ace and special K?'

'You taught me how, Dr Harrison. Acepromazine and ketamine. And you're right. That dose is for you. Take it like a man and when I know you're both down, I'll get on my horse and ride.' She gave a nervous, spiraling laugh. 'Out of Dodge, right?'

Tony didn't laugh, and he didn't point out that giving himself the shot would only prove he was a fool. Why should he think she wouldn't go ahead with her pyromaniac plan?

'I can see what you're thinking,' Vivian said. The tears that welled in her eyes seemed bizarre until she choked out, 'I've lost everything I cared about but Harry Stroud will take the fall for it. Do it, Tony. Do it now.'

He did.

He jabbed the needle through his heavy Barbour coat and released the entire contents of the syringe.

And he stared straight at Vivian when he dropped the syringe and clasped a hand over his side.

Vivian all but danced now. 'They found out Jay didn't kill himself. But, didn't they think he was the murderer suffering from guilt? Just for a while? They weren't supposed to find out someone killed him for much longer than it took them to figure it out. They're too damn clever now, but it doesn't matter. It was a good diversion and Pamela hated that piece of slime. Anyway, Harry will be blamed for that, too.

'Radhika was unfortunate. She lived. She was supposed to die. But she swallowed the story that her creepy brother had found her. She'll keep quiet – definitely after I work on her some more. She was the only one who knew Pamela meant the world to me, and that I hated Harry Stroud's guts. She's too much of an innocent to understand the kind of love I had for Pamela, or what drove it away. I wanted us to be together – the baby too if it had to be that way – but Pamela didn't understand. Oh, my God, I . . . it was him, he blinded her to what we could have had.' Vivian's eyes had lost focus. 'For now I'll help Radhika run away. Far, far away.'

Tony kept looking at her.

'I told Harry to suggest Jay should stay at Cedric Chase and he fell for it. Everyone knew he wouldn't really want Jay in that house.

'Pamela and Harry had a signal, silly bit of music, but I knew all about that and I used it to make sure she came to me up at the manor that night. I thought everything was going wrong when the torch fell back into the shaft but it was on a piece of line and I managed to pull it up. She . . . Pamela was screaming.' Vivian's mouth hung open in a dead white face.

She stooped sideways to pick up the green bag he and Alex had seen in the tower at Ebring Manor. 'It was just luck I remembered this and went for it the night I heard all the fuss was going on at the manor. Scratched myself to pieces getting up the tower with no light.' She slid the handles up her right arm and over her shoulder.

Tony fell heavily to his knees, taking himself closer to Alex, and blinked several times.

'Now you know how the poor horses feel,' Vivian said. 'I should go now. Poor Harry. I don't think he'll like it in prison.'

When, Tony wondered, had love turned to hate. When had the
burden of it all become too heavy for her. Didn't she expect him
to think all the animals being removed from the barn was a sign
she was taking them away from the fire she intended to start? He
toppled forward and his head settled almost on one of Vivian's
boots.

In a single move, snaking an arm around Alex's waist, he lunged
at Vivian's legs.

And he almost made it.

The toe of her left boot connected with the petrol can a second
too soon, at the same time as Tony saw an arc of lighter flame spin
into the hay. But he had Alex. Carrying her trussed body, first under
his arm, then over his shoulder, he heaved them both through the
stable doors as he felt an explosion of heat hit his back.

Vivian was ahead of them and leaping into the mare's saddle.

He kept running . . . until he heard the scream. It went on and
on and he swung around.

Gracie, Pamela's beloved mare, instead of running away with Vivian,
had bolted toward a wall of fire engulfing the side of the stables. 'Get
back! Get back,' she cried at the horse, then, 'I'll still get you two.
You're finished.' After that all he heard was the roar of fire.

'You're fine,' he yelled at Alex. 'I hear sirens.' And he slid her to
the ground and ran, raced and scrambled toward the rearing animal.

The long scream came again. Gracie balked, drove her hoofs into
the wet earth, and Vivian hurtled from the saddle, over the horse's
head and into the inferno.

Tony caught the animal's reins and hung on with all his weight.

On the ground lay the green canvas bag.

At least the hospital had individual ER rooms.

Stretching first one hand, then the other, Alex watched her muscles
react.

She had never been so captivated by, or so grateful for, the simple
movements of her body.

This was how 'lost, alone and dependent' felt. She had been left
to wait for the drugs Vivian had injected to wear off. No amount
of trying to signal with her eyes that she didn't want to come here
had made any difference.

While she'd been in the ambulance at the Derwinters' place,
she'd heard how Vivian had been dragged, alive but badly burned,

from the stable. Alex didn't want to think of what that meant. But she also couldn't concentrate on the level of hatred – and avarice – that had led a woman to go mad, first over a lost inheritance, then because Pamela had spurned her. Alex could understand what the depth of despair must have been, but not the way Vivian had turned once more to her desperate grab for revenge against Harry, so desperate she could kill, violently, the one person she might have cared for deeply.

What now? What did it take to have the strength to come back from near death as she and Tony had? She knew Tony had managed to empty his own syringe into the thick layers of his coat, but the slightest mistake and they would both have burned to death, aware of everything around them but unable to move.

The police didn't want anyone near her yet. She groaned at the thought of the streams of questions to come. An officer stood guard outside the door and she saw only nurses and an occasional doctor who all smiled at her as if she were either an interesting lab specimen, or a not very bright child.

What did she want? How did she make up her mind what to do with her tomorrows? There was a hole inside her where understanding belonged.

The door opened and Tony walked in, smiling at her with his mouth but with dark concern in his eyes. 'Hey,' he said, almost inaudibly.

Alex pushed higher in the narrow bed. She wasn't sure what to say.

Then reality came flooding in, complete clarity. The only one she wanted to see was Tony, and he was here. She didn't need to think about tomorrow or next week, only now. The wounds caused by Vivian Seabrook wouldn't heal immediately, not for anyone in Folly.

But this was right.

Disheveled and with mud smeared down the front of his coat and jeans, he carried a duffel bag. There were bandages on his left hand and scrapes on his face, but he came to the bed and set the bag on a chair beside it.

She gave him a half-hearted grin.

Tony rested a hand on top of her head and stared at her. His hand moved carefully to the side of her face. Then he pulled fresh clothes, her clothes, out of the bag and spread them on the bed.

He would take her home.